HOUSE of HEARTS

ALSO BY SKYLA ARNDT

Together We Rot

HOUSE of HEARTS

Skyla Arndt

VIKING

VIKING
An imprint of Penguin Random House LLC
1745 Broadway, New York, New York 10019

First published in the United States of America by Viking,
an imprint of Penguin Random House LLC, 2025

Copyright © 2025 by Skyla Arndt

Penguin Random House values and supports copyright. Copyright fuels creativity,
encourages diverse voices, promotes free speech, and creates a vibrant culture.
Thank you for buying an authorized edition of this book and for complying with
copyright laws by not reproducing, scanning, or distributing any part of it in any form
without permission. You are supporting writers and allowing Penguin Random House
to continue to publish books for every reader. Please note that no part of this book may
be used or reproduced in any manner for the purpose of training artificial
intelligence technologies or systems.

Viking & colophon are registered trademarks of Penguin Random House LLC.
The Penguin colophon is a registered trademark of Penguin Books Limited.

Visit us online at PenguinRandomHouse.com.

Library of Congress Cataloging-in-Publication Data is available.

ISBN 9780593693193
1st Printing

Printed in the United States of America

1st Printing

Edited by Maggie Rosenthal
Design by Lucia Baez | Text set in Arno Pro

This book is a work of fiction. Any references to historical events, real people,
or real places are used fictitiously. Other names, characters, places, and events are
products of the author's imagination, and any resemblance to actual events or
places or persons, living or dead, is entirely coincidental.

The publisher does not have any control over and does not assume any responsibility
for author or third-party websites or their content.

The authorized representative in the EU for product safety and compliance is
Penguin Random House Ireland, Morrison Chambers, 32 Nassau Street,
Dublin D02 YH68, Ireland, https://eu-contact.penguin.ie.

To my darling boy, Pyro, for teaching me that the harder you love someone, the larger the scar. You are so, so loved, and you always will be. 🐾

There once was a girl
whose heart was much too big,
much too broken,
so she dug within the garden of her ribs
and ripped it right out

1

I didn't come to Hart Academy for a $40,000 high school diploma, but something tells me "cold-blooded revenge" would've looked bad on my admissions essay. At the very least, I'm sure they wouldn't have sent me the brochure if they knew I'd cross the headmistress's eyes out in black Sharpie.

I slap on the smile I practiced in the mirror and bury my vendetta six feet deep. I'll unearth it later, but for now I need to look like any other perfectly adjusted, super-excited senior. I could at least pretend to be happy, right? I'm standing at the gates of the crème de la crème of boarding schools: a wealthy academy in Upstate New York where old-money families off-load their children each fall. Anyone in my shoes would be ecstatic to be here—well, almost anyone. My mother's wearing an identical pair of sneakers, and all she's doing is sniffling into a tissue.

"I promised myself I wouldn't cry," she says, crying.

She's been doing that all morning. It started after her tenth snoozed alarm, and it continued the entire three-hour drive in the car—Google Maps couldn't get a word in without my mother blubbering into the steering wheel.

I hand her the last Kleenex in the pack. We've gone through several. "I'll call every night."

She accepts my offering with a final blow of her nose. "You better! Oh, Violet, I'm so worried about you. You packed your pepper spray, right?" she whispers entirely too loudly. "You know I don't trust rich kids—their parents have good lawyers. They could get away with anything."

God, don't I know it.

I stretch that fake smile further for my mother's sake. It's starting to chafe. "Yes, Mom. It's in the front pocket of my duffel bag."

"And your little whistle?" she presses.

"Yes, Mom. It's on my key chain."

"What about—?"

"Mom, trust me, I've got it all. Do I have to show you my laminated checklist?" I swivel around to pull it out once again. My packing list (however small) has been highlighted and checked off several times over. If it were up to Mom, she would've packed a mismatched pair of socks, an old blanket I had when I was five, and then nothing else because she would've been too busy bawling.

"Oh, Violet, when did you get so grown up?"

Probably at age eight when Mom's deadbeat ex smashed a beer bottle against the wall and I spent the rest of the night in my room staging our elaborate escape. "I'm pretty sure I was born this way."

She harrumphs but doesn't argue with me there.

"Quit worrying so much. C'mon, isn't it breathtaking? It looks just like the website."

This time I'm not lying. It *is* breathtaking, but I'm also completely and utterly out of my element. Our trailer-park home is a far cry from the Gothic gray stone library; our Ford Fiesta sticks out like a sore thumb against the lot of sleek armored cars. "Did you know this school was featured in *Architectural Digest*?"

I gesture to the building beside us. The Great Hall lies in the quadrangle like a sleeping beast, its enormous body embellished with sandstone and its oriel eye focused on the courtyard ahead. Students mill through its arched ribs, their bags slung across their backs and their phones poised at the ready. I don't blame them; every inch of this place is begging to be immortalized on canvas. It's beautiful. It's perfect. It's the site of an open murder investigation. Or at least it should be.

"C'mon!" I urge, tugging Mom deeper into the crime scene.

It hardly looks like one anymore. Instead of police tape and chalk lines, we've got cotton candy and balloon animals, WELCOME BACK, STUDENTS! strung high from dogwood trees. It's a lesson in extravagance, a nightmare of confetti and rose topiaries and Golden Goose sneakers.

Nothing about it screams "a girl died here a year ago"—no funeral attire or memorial imagery scattered among the fairgrounds. My best friend's death has been scrubbed away in time for orientation. Headmistress Lockwell and her family saw to that.

"Ooh, can we see that?" Mom's voice rips me back to the present. She cuts off an exhausted custodian before he can toss a crumpled map into the trash. Smoothing out the wrinkled folds, she jabs at the center. "God, Vi, all right, I'll give you one thing: This place *is* fancy. There's a regulation tennis court and an Olympic-size swimming pool and—"

I cut her off gently. "We don't have time to look at the pool, Ma. We need to get to the new-student orientation. We're all the way over here, and we have five minutes to get there."

"Here" is sandwiched between the Great Hall and Fitzpatrick-Wallace Library. "There" shines like a beacon in the distance, a journey beyond a sprawling family of green hills.

She huffs like a lectured child but doesn't press the issue. Instead, she follows my lead as I push our way through the crowd. What we lack in money, I more than make up for in false confidence. My power walk is honed from years of customer service—shoulders back, chin up, arms crossed. It's all about making the world believe you're stronger than you really are so they don't chew you up and spit you out.

Though, to be perfectly honest, I do feel like a used wad of bubble gum right now. But that's less confidence-based and more due to the fact that the sun is stuck on the broiler setting.

Mom pauses to wipe a bead of sweat from her brow. Above our heads, a trellis reads THE LITTLE GARDEN. The space around us is a bleeding canvas of color: bright yellow marigolds, stalks of purple-bellied aconite and pink valerian, patches of poppies and beds of wormwood. All of which are tucked away inside carefully placed shrubbery.

"Aww, Violet, let's stop for a second. I want a cute photo of you in front of the violets," she says, like it's an ingenious, novel idea and not something we've been doing since the day I was born. "Here, take this, I have to look for my phone."

She passes me the wrinkled trash-pamphlet, and I squint through the creases as she looks. " 'Funded by an alumnus's generous donation, the Little Garden is a curated collection of Shakespearean variety. A campus favorite, it is not uncommon to find students and staff alike basking in the beauty of—' "

I stop reading as red splatters the page.

HOUSE OF HEARTS

... Blood?

The very thought has my lungs seizing and my mind hurtling sixty miles per hour back to the gruesome past. Back when my friend's body was found broken at the bottom of the school clock tower, a dark puddle beneath her soaking deep into the roots.

Her body wasn't even cold when the press statement was released. Headmistress Lockwell issued what can only be described as a tragedy Mad Libs, with "Emoree Hale" slotted conveniently into the blanks. I learned that day that anyone can rewrite history for the right price. A "tragic fall" became an "intentional jump," and one by one, everyone came to the consensus that Em had meant to die that day.

Everyone but me. Because I know she didn't jump. She was pushed. And as for the murderer? It was none other than the headmistress's eldest son, Percy Lockwell.

I growl at the memory and drag a sticky finger up the page. Just as I think I might pass out, I catch a whiff of cherry filling. Not blood but dripping jam.

"My bad!" Some girl squeezes past us with a half-assed apology, a jelly-filled donut poorly balanced in her hands. The stranger is as disorienting as this world around her—her outfit an eclectic hodgepodge of fabrics that pulls me out of my haze. I can't help but tally the cost—it's the type of mismatched attire that you can only pull off with an ungodly amount of self-assurance and money. The floral pattern of her mesh top has no relation to her striped skirt; the skirt has no link to the random tie slung loosely on her throat. Then there's the studded glasses and the knifepoint of her earrings. None of it blends, and yet, on her, it's seamless.

She gives me a once-over, and I'm suddenly conscious of the

stain on my sleeve. Maybe I can pretend it's avant-garde.

"Oh my God! Wait, are you Violet Harper?" she asks, mid-bite.

Mom looks between us in a not-so-subtle attempt to suss out a connection. Meanwhile, Donut Girl is fumbling around with her belongings. Her messenger bag lifts open to reveal a camera that's worth more than several of my vital organs, but she pushes it aside to grab at her equally expensive phone. With a series of clicks, she's pulling up the student portal and flashing my photo. I've got that "sun-starved Victorian factory child" thing going on in my picture. The perfect casting call for a horror-movie extra: wispy, bone-pale hair, twiggy limbs, and dark shadows. A true ghost of a girl.

"We're roommates this year. I'm Birdie, remember? Birdie Pennington."

I swallow my nerves and take her manicured hand in mine.

Nothing about my roommate assignment was random. No one asked me if I was a morning bird or a night owl. Messy or organized. If I liked long walks on the beach or late nights hunched over my computer screen reading over the obituary of my best friend, wondering how everything broke apart in a single, horrifying instant—

No. Birdie was matched with me because the last roommate she had hit the pavement and broke every bone in her body. Now I'm here to fill a vacancy.

I chew the insides of my cheek, and my molars trace over the familiar scarred skin. *Don't think about that, and most importantly, don't cry.* Crying doesn't bring the dead back, and it certainly won't help me get my revenge. I don't know yet what that revenge will look like, but I do know one thing:

I'm going to haunt the Lockwells until the bitter end.

"Are you on your way to the new-student orientation?" Birdie

HOUSE OF HEARTS

asks, unaware that her new roommate is plotting out someone's demise in her head.

"Yeah, it's part of crashing in here my senior year. I've got to play freshman today."

"You and me both," she says with a wave of her camera. "I'm on yearbook duty, so I've got to take pictures. In fact, I think I've got you beat—I've been 'playing freshman' all four years."

She snaps a couple photos on the way down to prove her point, the shutter flashing twice as we enter the Greek Theater. Stone slabs cut into a hill, giving the whole area the appearance of a naturally occurring formation. We take our seats in what could be an eighth world wonder, and Mom recycles the school pamphlet into a makeshift fan. More students have started to fill in around us, and understandably, they're all fresh-faced fourteen-year-olds with their parents.

The headmistress positions herself before the podium at long last. She might be exorbitantly rich, but her appearance is elegantly understated. No flashing designer labels or fancy blowout waves. She has a sheath of gray hair resting above her shoulders and a set of pale green eyes creased in the corners. The longer I look at her, the more I wonder whether wealth is skin-deep or if it's buried in her bones.

"Welcome, welcome," she speaks into the crinkle of a microphone. "My name is Meredith Lockwell, and I am the headmistress here at Hart Academy. As an alumnus myself, I understand the mix of emotions on your faces today. Looking out at the crowd, do you want to know what I see? Excitement. Hope. Fear. For many of you, this is the first moment you fully embark from your parents' homes and begin a new chapter in your lives. Everyone standing before me today has made a great stride toward their academic futures—"

That's where I stop listening. The speech is a nauseating ordeal that has me grinding my teeth and digging divots into my palms. It's complete with long monologues about the weight of a Hart diploma, grand declarations that Ivy League colleges will duel to the death for us, and smug sidebars about all the famous alumni who have sat on these very steps. That last part has students swiveling like there might be an autograph under their seat.

Their palpable excitement has me thinking about Emoree. How did she feel about all this? Was she nervous? Hopeful? Did she feel like the world was finally flinging its doors open for her?

"You remember Percy's club, right?" she whispered to me a year ago now, her voice whizzing through miles of telephone wires.

Percy Lockwell gave me premature scowl lines. She'd met the guy only a few days into her first semester, and he'd become a glorified conversation poltergeist in no time. He'd pop into every discussion as unwelcome as a plague pustule, and I'd spend the rest of the call waiting for it to burst into a Percy Lockwell crush-fest. He was her Prince Charming, the knight in shining armor to whisk her further and further away from her old life.

Until the day he ended her life altogether.

"Yeah, yeah, I remember. The Illuminati, right? Or was it the Free-masons? Skull and Bones? One of the three." I eyed a new stain on my work uniform.

She groaned into the receiver. "Hysterical, *V*. Very funny. No, it's nothing like that. I know I'm not in it yet, but there's no way they're holding Illuminati board meetings at a high school. *Anyway*, they have a pledge night coming up soon, and I want to join. I'd kind of do anything to get in, actually."

"A secret society of rich kids. That doesn't sound like the Illuminati at all." I picked at my nails. "Are you doing this for Percy?"

HOUSE OF HEARTS

"Would that be such a bad thing if I was?" she asked after a quiet moment, and I could just envision her in her dorm room, kicking her feet at the thought of wedding bells and white picket fences in Nantucket. "I really like him."

"That's great, Em," I said, injecting as much fake enthusiasm into it as I could. I'd come to learn that it was a finite resource of mine.

"I think he might like me, too," she continued to prattle on, emboldened now. "I found an old half-heart locket shoved in my bag the other day. I have no idea who put it there, but I think it was him."

As she was my best friend in the whole world, I should've been happy for her. Instead, I was sick and tired of her "fairy tales" and feeling like the dragon in her old castle.

I return to reality at the sound of Headmistress Lockwell clearing her throat and ushering in a small choir behind her. "Students, if you will, please give your full attention to our choir as they perform our school anthem."

It doesn't take a genius to figure out which chorister is the headmistress's daughter. Sadie Lockwell is the spitting image of her mother, minus the fact that she hasn't gone gray yet. Instead, her hair is dyed stark black against her skin, falling down the planes of her back like an oil spill.

The rest of the students scatter behind her, not a single one of them daring to strip away her spotlight as she approaches the mic. All except one. He branches away from the group and takes a seat behind a piano that was shrouded in white cloth moments earlier.

His fingers glide effortlessly across the keys as they begin to sing. It's hypnotizing to watch him work, from the slight furrow in his brows to the dart of his tongue wetting his lips. Piano Boy's no stranger, though. I recognize him from my late-night dates with Google.

9

Calvin Lockwell, aka Sadie's twin and the Lockwell Most Likely to Have an Enormous Digital Footprint. I'd know because I spent at least two business days scouring through his Instagram and I still didn't reach the end. There were thousands of photos of him: selfies on the hood of a Bugatti, the leather keys dangling from his grip; reels of him popping champagne, fizz erupting in the air to a chorus of laughter and cheers. His entire feed was backlit by purple strobe lights, his lips kiss-bruised and his eyes like spent cigarettes—stubborn flecks of amber engulfed in ash.

Beautiful in excess.

The song ends, and not long after, the applause dies with it. We're all hushed as Headmistress Lockwell personally welcomes us to Hart, one graduating class at a time. It's the welcome-day equivalent to "get up and tell the class five fun facts about yourself"; it might not be *quite* as mortifying, but close.

The freshmen flood the stands in a tidal wave of camera clicks and shuffling feet. Parents beam from their sidelines as the clapping drones on for several minutes. There are a handful of transfer sophomores next, and when junior year is called and not a single soul stands up, I know I'm in trouble. When new seniors are invited to stand at long last, I'm the only student on my feet.

It's every bit as awkward as you'd expect, only probably worse, actually, because my mom's decided now is a great time to cry again.

The applause trickles in slowly with my mother at the helm. She's sniffling, swatting messily at her cheeks with a mascara-blackened sleeve but still managing to clap because God forbid her baby is the only one who *doesn't* get clapped for. My new roommate is tilting the lens of her camera up to get me and my sobbing mother together in frame. There's a low whispered current of gossip sifting through the crowd—"Who transfers their senior year?"

And Calvin is looking at me.

It's not like everyone else's casual pitying glance. No, he's full-on staring, completely slack-jawed at the sight of me. Brows furrowed in a silent sort of horror. I can't help but notice his teeth. They're overbright, very Wolf that Ate Grandma. I'm struck by the idea of him opening his mouth wide, those pretty, perfect pearly whites snapping my head clean off. Weirder yet, I'm struck by the thought that I'd let him. It's that magnetic charm, whatever's swimming in the Lockwell blood to make them all Venus flytraps.

And maybe that's all the rest of us are. *Flies.*

"Is it okay if I borrow my daughter for a second?" Mom asks after the presentation tapers to an end and she's made a mess of her makeup. "I promise I'll bring her back, just want to get my sappy Mom goodbyes out. It was lovely meeting you, Birdie. You actually remind me of"—she grimaces, catching herself too late—"an old friend of Violet's."

Birdie grins at that and scampers off. She doesn't see the heat flooding my cheeks, my teeth grinding together, the heavy rush of grief, ever-present.

"Em," I whisper when we're alone, and it's not a question but a horrifying revelation. "She reminds you of Em."

"I shouldn't have said that."

I hiss in a breath. Count to ten. And then I blow it out. I can be objective about this without bursting into fat wet tears. "Why? It's not like you're wrong."

Birdie and Em aren't exactly the same, I can tell that already, but there's familiarity in the way Birdie's eyes light up when she speaks. Not an Eeyore like me but a ray of sunshine stitched into the shape of a girl.

"Violet," Mom tries again, and her tone makes me wince. "I don't know about all this." She waves vaguely at that last part, gesturing to the world around us: the sprawling campus grounds and ivy-strewn buildings and families who look like they wouldn't survive another French Revolution.

I ball my fists on my lap. "This school will look great on a résumé. We talked about this. It'll help me get into a good college—"

"I don't care about college. I care about you. Are you sure you're okay?"

I stiffen to my very bones. "I'm fine."

Mom shifts her attention to a loose seam in her skirt. She's fixed that spot once before, but no matter how many repairs she makes, it always seems destined to unravel. "You're strong, Violet. You've always been strong. But there's a difference between being strong and being . . . whatever you are right now."

I don't say anything. My nails dig into the meat of my palms.

"You didn't cry at the funeral," she whispers. "And you went right back to school the next week. I thought you were in shock, but then . . . The point is, you didn't talk to me. Not once. Not when it happened. Not at the vigil. Not when you applied. Not now."

"Then take the hint already." We both wince at my tone, and I want to blurt out a sorry, but my stubborn tongue holds all the apologies in. "I'm okay."

I've always been okay because I've always had to be okay. I'm the stronghold for Mom, built to weather every storm. For the longest time,

I became that for Em, too. I was a rock for those always adrift. Now I'm the one lost at sea.

"I don't want you to worry about me."

She lowers her hand, and I hate the way I tremble beneath it. Hate the way I draw in a breath and avoid crying because that's exactly what she wants from me.

"I'm your mother. What else should I do?"

"Be proud of me."

Mom smears at her already-wet cheeks. "I am proud of you. You studied hard to get in and wrote a stellar admissions essay. You even got a heck of a nice scholarship to cover this place. You've done so much to be proud of, but, Violet, you're not happy. That's the problem."

I force a smile. I know it's as frayed as her skirt. "I am happy," I say, the words almost comical as my voice wavers. "I'm so happy right now."

Last time I lied this hard to myself, I was staring down at a closed casket. *Not dead, not dead, not dead.*

Mom opens her mouth to fight me further but doesn't get the chance. A familiar buzz shears through the tension, the gas station manager's name flashing across her phone screen. She grimaces down at the text:

the new guy's a no show . . . need you to work

a double shift tonight ASAP

"What does he mean 'tonight'?" I ask, my voice too small in my throat. "You've got a hotel. You're here for the night."

She averts her eyes and studies a speck of dirt on her sneakers. "About that, Violet . . ."

"You never booked a room, did you?" I ask.

"I wanted to, but the hotels were all out of budget. And the cost of gas to get here and back alone—"

"It's okay, Mom. Really. I get it." I grip her hand and muster up another worn smile for her sake. "You should go. Birdie's waiting for me anyway."

"You sure? Promise you'll call?" she asks, and we both know how hard it will be with her schedule. Two full-time jobs, bleary mornings and late nights. It breaks my heart to hear her voice like that.

"Promise."

She pulls me in for a crushing, consuming hug. At this moment, I'm a kid in too-big shoes, drowning under the weight of fears twice my size. Back in the sandbox with cardboard armor and a play sword, pretending I could see the monsters in Em's make-believe world, but I could only ever see the real ones.

"I love you."

I mumble an "I love you" of my own into her hair and wave as she walks away, her silhouette growing tinier in the distance. It's only after she's gone that I readjust the chain slung across my throat. Just one more secret to pile high atop the rest of them.

The half-heart locket Percy gave to Em before she died. The one I found in my mailbox a week later, a single plea scrawled in our secret code:

If something happens to me, find Percy.

She said she was prepared to do anything to get into Percy's club, but I wonder if she was prepared to die.

2

Birdie decides to live up to her namesake and cluck at me like a mother hen when I get back. She loops an arm over my shoulders, and I'm trapped in a one-sided conversation as she titters on about homesickness and how sweet it was that my mom cried and how it's okay if I want to cry andandand—

And it's exhausting, but I do my best to smile and nod when prompted. Thankfully, Birdie is so focused on parading us around that she fails to notice when my grin falters and my eyes skirt back to the stage. Calvin's gone, but the imprint of him is seared in my mind.

Ahead of us, greenery spreads as far as the eye can see. It's even on the lake across from us in the form of big, fat lily pads; the water beneath a stunning blue, the last traces of light reflecting clearly off the surface. I turn away from it to see two strangers sitting in front of me.

"Violet, meet the newspaper team behind the *Hart Herald*. The workaholic in front of you is Oliver Walton. He's . . ." She scrabbles for the right word before deciding to be mercilessly blunt. "A total asshole most days, but he means well, so don't let him scare you. I swear he's a big softie when he's not lecturing people about em dash usage."

"I seem to recall winning that argument," the boy—Oliver—remarks before snapping his journal shut. From our fleeting, split-second eye contact, I can say he's rather good-looking. Warm black skin and lashes so long they tickle his cheeks.

"And the girl who likes him despite his grammatical tyranny is Amber Yamada." She nods toward the girl sitting beside him. Her dark hair is gelled into a twist bun, and her skin is glowing beneath an embroidered Miu Miu dress.

Before I can say hello to either of them, Birdie's gaze shoots down to the papers splayed on the ground. "Do I even want to know what you're doing?"

"*It's not a hit list,*" Amber says, involuntarily incriminating herself. She points down at what most definitely looks like a hit list. That or a satanic ritual. It's complete with a pentagram of ripped-out yearbook pages, HART ACADEMY in the middle. Red ink bleeds onto the page beneath her, and she scratches a circle over her next target. "It's a hit-*on* list for you, Bird. Because you're painfully single and it's depressing to all of us."

Birdie's face beats a hot, telling red. "God, it must be hard being so delusional, but you make it look easy."

"I'm serious!" Amber squawks. "It's not a joke."

"For starters, I'm not '*painfully single,*'" Birdie returns, peppering the last two words with air quotes. "Secondly, shouldn't you be focused on your article about move-in day? I'm over here snapping photos at the welcome ceremony, and you're drafting the next season of *The Bachelorette*. And thirdly, most importantly here, can either of you at least attempt to say hi to my new roommate?"

I shimmy in place. "No one needs to say hi to me. It's fine."

"No, it's *not fine*. Amber, quit meddling and say hello. Oliver, pretend to care . . . and for the love of God, don't try to indoctrinate her into your anti–em dash agenda."

He swivels to me instantly. "Em dashes should be used sparingly, if at all, or you risk muddying the clarity of your article and minimizing the overall impact."

"I'll *minimize* your *impact.*"

"That doesn't even make sense." He rolls his eyes at Birdie, but I don't miss the playful smirk lifting his cheeks. They jab at each other, but it's obvious that this trio is stitched together by some tender thread, and it almost hurts to stand here, thinking of my own friendship unraveled.

"Oh, hi, Violet." Amber's voice rips me out of my own mind by the scruff. "From the ten seconds you've known Birdie, do you agree she's hopelessly single?"

I don't know what to say to that, but it turns out I don't have to because Amber thrusts a yearbook page into my hands to read. I squint at the rows of faces. Last year's date is printed across the page, but that's not what ages this. There's a face circled, but I'm distracted by the girl I see in the corner. It's Emoree's photo, all five billion of her freckles and the gap-toothed grin she used to press her tongue to when she was lost in thought. The starlight of her eyes when she smiled, radiant and alive to the world.

My gaze cuts briefly to the clock tower looming ahead. I shudder at the hour hand, the diligent beat of time that stops for no one.

I'm suddenly conscious of Birdie peering over my shoulder at the page. "I'm sorry, is that Calvin Lockwell you circled?"

I'm used to his social-media smiles, the smug gleam in his eyes, and the lipstick stains on the collar. This Calvin isn't champagne-sprayed. He stares soberly at the camera, his expression more in line with a kenneled dog.

Amber shakes her head and points at the little scribble she made on the page. "Christ, no, sorry, that was a mistake. I'd never dream of setting someone up with Calvin. Total heartbreaker." She taps the face beside him. "Sadie, on the other hand . . ."

I didn't think anyone on this earth could make Birdie speechless, but I guess I was wrong. It takes her a solid ten seconds to regain her voice, and when she does, she's bright crimson.

"Not so loud!" She swivels around to make sure no one is listening, as if she suspects someone paddling across the lake might run and tell Sadie that Birdie has a big, fat, embarrassing crush on her.

"Seconded," Oliver groans, waving his notebook in the air at the three of us. "Some of us actually want to work here."

"School hasn't even started. The school paper can wait. Relax a little, Olly." Amber blows him a kiss, and he grumpily accepts it. "I'm only trying to help you out. I know you've liked her for ages. Plus, maybe if you two date, she'll help get you into the Cards." She cuts a scathing look at her boyfriend. "Lord knows Oliver's no help with that. He won't tell me anything."

The Cards, huh? Those words bring up memories of late-night calls with Em. I guess that beats calling it "Percy's Illuminati Club." I have to bite my tongue to keep from blurting out anything too obvious, but I immediately straighten my spine and direct my full attention to the conversation. "What are the Cards?"

"Well," Amber taunts, her grin positively Cheshire, "why don't you tell her?"

"You know I'm not supposed to talk about it," Oliver retorts, doing

HOUSE OF HEARTS

his best to sound nonchalant but failing horribly as his voice notches up an octave. "I take my vows seriously. Isn't that an admirable trait in a partner?"

"Not when it comes to keeping secrets from *me*," Amber huffs, blowing her cheeks out like a puffer fish.

He deflates her pout with a poke to the face. "Need I remind you that you're a gossip columnist?"

"A gossip columnist that you *love*," she amends quickly.

Oliver's ears flush pink. "I'm not debating that, but—I say this with all the love in the world—you can't keep a secret. I already know my birthday and Christmas gifts, and it's only September, so no, my lips are sealed. Sorry."

She groans but eventually tips her head back in defeat.

"It's a . . . student organization here at Hart," Birdie fills me in. "They have a private clubhouse and all sorts of special privileges, but since no one knows what it is that they do, well . . . you know how it is. Shroud anything in enough secrecy and it will take on a life of its own. Everyone has a theory. Everyone wants in."

I toy with the straps of my duffel bag, playing with the frayed edges. "What sort of privileges do they have?"

"You'll see, trust me," Amber says. "Oliver only takes advantage of the boring perks—like having an after-hours library pass—but I swear they can get away with *anything*."

I imagine a roomful of alibis and murder accomplices. Based on the five seconds I've known Oliver, he doesn't seem like he'd care to get involved in any of that, but . . .

I take my vows seriously.

"To be fair, we know the basics about the Cards, like how everyone starts their four years off with a Joker." Amber fishes through a Chloé bracelet bag to show me a worn-out playing card. The jester on the front is creased and smudged from a cocktail of pen ink and concealer, a true testament to the three years it's spent living in her $4,000 purse. "It's supposedly your ticket in, but once you submit it, you can never try out again. You've got one shot to prove yourself to the Cards, and if you blow it at Joker Night, you're done."

I swallow down the bulk of my questions. "What's Joker Night?"

"That's what everyone wants to know. All we know is that they pick new pledges that night. We're told the date and dress code each year, and that's it. Not what they're looking for or what they want—none of that. You show up at HOH—the House of Hearts—and hope to God they choose you . . . And for reasons unknown, they picked Oliver."

"House of Hearts" summons an image in my mind—a memory of the school map printed across my frontal lobe. I remember the house as a Gothic nightmare splayed out across the lawns, an enormous two-story building carved out of a different, bleaker era. I'm tempted to pull out the school map and trace a pathway to it with my finger when I hear a voice shout out in the distance.

"Don't walk away when someone's having a conversation with you, Calvin!" Sadie storms into my peripheral, and the smiling face she wore on the school stage is long gone. She's traded it for a sneer as she chases after her brother, but no matter how fast she power walks, he stays two steps ahead of her.

Amber's eyes light up, and she swats excitedly at Birdie's arm. "This is like divine intervention," she whispers, pointing rapidly between Real Sadie and Circled Yearbook Sadie. "Now's your chance! Go up there! Drag her up to the lookout!"

I squint at the Juliet-style balcony a quarter of the way up the clock tower.

The look Birdie gives me is pitying, one that says I've got a ton of catching up to do around here. "I forget you're brand new here. Basically, it's a well-known makeout spot, but aside from that"—her cheeks burn red—"there's the belief that if you go up there with your crush, you'll be together forever. It's a silly superstition."

"Nothing says true love like an ancient, musty clock tower." Oliver snickers before getting jabbed in the ribs by his girlfriend.

"Don't forget that you kissed me up there, too."

He stammers and buries his face back in his book.

"Now, c'mon! Don't lose this chance!" Amber gives Birdie one final send-off push, and I catch my new roommate's eye as she throws me a pleading glance. I can't save her from this, but I've got my own reasons for hooking my arm through hers and tagging along.

"I don't mind coming with you."

"Ugh, you were supposed to be my savior!" she whines, already caving by the expression on her face. "Fine, fine. I'll go. What is it that you want me to even do?"

Amber's grin grows. "Flirt! It's not rocket science! Go up there, say hi, and ask if she'd like to go up with you. Easy."

Nothing is easy about walking up to the tower where my best friend died, but I've already made up my mind. Birdie is chittering nervously in my ears, though I've stopped tuning in. I'm busy calculating the fall from the top of the tower, where the clock hand strikes, to the unforgiving earth below. The grass is dry now, but I know a year ago it was bloodstained. The lookout itself isn't even halfway up, and it's still giving me hives. The thought of Em scaling even higher . . .

Fear bobs in my throat, surging forward with every miserable step. By the time the two of us make it to the entrance, I've gone as cold as a body on an autopsy table. Beyond us, the sign on the wall reads:

IMPORTANT SAFETY REGULATION: PLEASE PROCEED TWO AT A TIME FOR THE LOOKOUT.

I force my legs to move, my gaze cutting back up to the balcony. Heights were never an issue, not until last year. Now the only thought in my head is how easily humans are unmade.

Sadie doesn't notice us approaching. She's too busy furiously tapping her foot against the grass. Meanwhile, Calvin's a wild animal caught in a trap, ten seconds away from gnawing off its own leg. His eyes dart to and fro with a slightly rabid look as he searches for a way out.

"We need to talk about this," Sadie hisses, her voice lowering to a whisper. "If it means what I think it means—"

She stiffens at our approach and whips around, her gaze positively lethal. "Can we help you?" she snarls. I don't think that was part of Cupid's plan.

Birdie flushes hot, going about as red as the school crest. "I, um, was going to ask you if . . . uh . . . wanted to go up in the . . . uh . . . never mind . . ." With supreme secondhand embarrassment, I watch as she ditches my hand and trips over herself in her quest to make it back to the group. I think this is the moment where I'm supposed to chase after her with my tail between my legs.

But I'm not the type to back down, so I lift my chin higher and get ready to ask the real questions.

Maybe it's thanks to Birdie's mortifying, rambling invitation, but something gleams in Calvin's eyes. I can see the half-baked idea take shape before he even opens his mouth and strides toward me. Suddenly

HOUSE OF HEARTS

his arm falls across my shoulders as he pulls the two of us into the open doorway of the tower.

"Sorry, Sadie. Looks like I'm busy after all," he remarks. "What kind of Hart student would I be if I didn't personally welcome the new girl?" He turns to me, and his eyes gloss down to my student-ID lanyard. "Violet, right?"

I hate the traitorous flip in my stomach at the way his fingers tighten on my shoulder. He hurries to shut the door behind us, but Sadie wedges her fingers in the gap.

"Oh, yeah, classic Calvin," she spits into the crevice, her glacial eyes rolling from him to me. "Not even the first day of school and you're going to go make out with some random girl in lieu of having any important discussions. This isn't over."

He pries her fingers off one by one, his expression sickly sweet. "Really? Because it seems incredibly over. Now, if you'll excuse me, we're going to need some privacy. Thirty minutes should do."

With the last finger ripped off, he pushes his weight into the door, and his smug expression smears right off. He groans and massages what can only be a brewing migraine.

I'm in the clock tower with Calvin Lockwell.

But all I can think about is the room growing tighter. Panic blackens the corners of my vision, constricting my view until it feels like the world has me in a choke hold. *Em was here.* Those three words spiral viciously in my skull, a nasty reminder of what happened and a taunt of all the things I still don't know. One thing is for certain: She climbed these very steps to the top, stood on the ledge, and was pushed off.

I fan myself to get my shit together. I'm sure my cheeks are turning a scalding, awful red, and my hair has gone sweaty on my scalp.

23

Calvin glances up from his headache. His amber eyes sweep over my skin, and he recoils at the very sight of me.

"Don't act so nervous," he whispers, pushing past me for the staircase. He doesn't bother stopping to glance back at me. He carries on like he's seen more than enough. "I'd never dream of kissing you."

3

I've got to hand it to Calvin—his ego is so enormous that I momentarily forget why I was nervous in the first place. My anxiety takes a back seat to rage.

"Who said I want to kiss you?" I ask as I climb after him, and yes, okay, I'm secretly thrilled I got the question out without stammering.

He rolls his shoulders—shaking free all the imaginary daggers I lodged into his back—and throws a cursory glance in my direction. "You wouldn't be the first."

Ha. *Ha*. The man is Narcissus in the flesh: beautiful but too aware of the fact. If he wasn't spoiled and rich, I'm sure I'd be another lovestruck fool clamoring in his wake, but I know better. Falling for a boy like Calvin is the same as losing your footing on a ledge, a dizzying free fall and a crushing blow you can't come back from.

The way he looks at me, you'd think I was the scum beneath his shoes. That has me balling my fists and cataloging all the things wrong with him.

For starters, he bites his nails. I can see jagged crescents where his teeth ripped them off. There's a particularly angry wound on his pinkie where I'm guessing it bled earlier.

His nose is also upturned—as stuck up as the rest of him.

Oh yeah, and I think his brother murdered my friend.

"I can feel you staring at me." He freezes with his hand on the banister and forces me to stop in my tracks. "You're not subtle."

I avert my eyes and try to hold my tongue. It doesn't work. "I'd assumed subtle was off the table when you said we needed thirty minutes of alone time."

"Touché." His voice echoes, the sound rippling like water. The tower around us might not be massive, but it certainly feels like an eternal climb upward.

I search for the scuff of Emoree's shoes on each step, something that would mark the memory of her forever. The way Paleolithic humans have come and gone, but their lives are still spelled out in chalk lines on cave walls.

There's nothing to see here. Her memory has rinsed right off.

"Well, this is it," Calvin says with an exaggerated flourish at the lookout. The landing is a welcome reprieve after all that climbing. An arched cathedral-style window sits to the left of me, the glass fogged from time but transparent enough to showcase the full scope of the school. It's predictably breathtaking, but it's not what I'm looking at. I'm gazing up at the next level of stairs, hypnotized by the spiral railing ascending into the shadows.

"What's up there?"

Calvin hesitates. His jaw clenches ever so slightly as he follows my gaze. "More stairs."

"Where do the stairs lead?"

He toys with his collar and loosens his tie at the throat. "The pearly gates. It's amazing, really. It goes on forever into the sky, and baby cherubs wait for you on the final floor. I've been told they play the harp."

"Okay, fine, I get it. You're not going to tell me." I'm trying not to lose my cool again.

There's a pregnant pause before he asks, quieter, "Why do you want to know?"

"Curiosity."

"Bad trait to have," he mutters to himself. He taps a steady rhythm against his cheek, the phantom strokes of some song only he knows. "Or so I'm told."

I turn to face him fully, but he slides down the wall and ignores me for a hangnail on his ring finger. If I thought conversation with Calvin was a stilted, horrible affair, silence is worse. I shift to stare out the window—risking anxiety over whatever this is.

As much as I hate this place, I can't deny that it's beautiful. The campus is an otherworldly green. The color spreads up the throats of academic buildings, thick tangles of ivy like branching arteries. And if those are the arteries, there's no denying what the heart is.

A hedge maze sprawls as far as the eye can see, a never-ending labyrinth locked away by an ornate metal gate. Wind slices through it, breathing life into the shrubbery and making it pulse in tandem with my own heart. This high up, the world feels particularly violent outside. I shudder and imagine what it'd be like standing at the top, feeling the sharp air against my cheek.

I rip my gaze from the window. Calvin's a cat curling in on himself, his head propped against his shoulder as he splays on the ground. He's gotten ready for the long haul.

"Comfy?"

He flutters an eye open. "I'd be comfier with a down feather pillow and the sound of the ocean spraying through Bose speakers . . . but otherwise, yeah. This will do. If you need me, which I hope you won't, I'll be taking a nap."

I cross my arms to keep my hands from trembling at my sides. "And I'm supposed to believe this is the best napping spot on campus?"

He winces, and I know he's been caught. "The stone floor is comfier than you think."

I level him with a look until he finally huffs in defeat. "I thought it was fairly obvious. I need a break from my sister."

"What does she want?" I conjure the image of her red face and glaring eyes snapping between us. Glaring at me like I was a gnat that flew too close.

Calvin wets his lips. He looks every inch a Grecian tragedy on the floor. Splaying out like an art class might arrive with charcoals and canvas to capture his melodramatic anguish.

"What doesn't she want?" he answers finally. "A conversation? A lecture opportunity? Maybe Mom got tired of telling me I'm a disappointment directly, so she decided to have Sadie play messenger."

"So, you'd rather hang out in a dusty old tower than talk to her?"

Calvin stands up, and I feel the heat rolling off his skin as he peers out the window behind me. I stiffen as he approaches, his body so large it eclipses mine. We're not touching, but if I were to lean back, I'd fall right onto his broad chest. The closeness has me holding my breath.

"I'd lather myself in honey and jump into a grizzly's cage if that's what it took. What, you think I came up here for the view?"

"It's . . ." I'm about to say "pretty," but the word doesn't come. I've made the mistake of looking straight down. Vertigo has me by the throat, and I'm suddenly Emoree. Zeroing in on a patch of grass before the world rushes past me. An impact. And then darkness.

At least it was quick. I remember someone whispering that at the funeral. *Painless.*

The wind knocks out of my lungs, and no matter what I do, I can't tear my gaze away from the lawn. My grief is a hole only I can see, ruptured through the thicket of green, green grass. It's black and never-ending, and I've tumbled down it before. You fall and fall and fall, and when you think it couldn't possibly go any further, you're wrong.

I swallow down bile. She's gone, I know that, but now I feel like I'm falling, too. The world sways, and my knees buckle, and now I really am falling, and . . .

Arms. I'm halfway to the floor when I feel the heat of someone pressed against my back. Gentle hands lowering me to the cool stone floor. A rushed, worried breath sticky against my skin. And then Calvin's face is way too close to mine.

He brushes the back of his hand to my forehead. It's refreshingly cool against my flushed skin. "Jesus, are you okay?"

Less than twenty-four hours here, and I've already lost it twice. I wave his concern away—or I try to. My arms are as weak as the rest of me. "I'm fine."

I really need to stop saying that.

"Sure about that one? Because from my viewpoint it looks like you nearly blacked out and I'm the only thing that kept you from cracking your head open on the floor."

I squeeze my eyes shut at that. The casket was closed at the funeral, but my mind is strong enough to fill in the gaps.

"I'm okay," I repeat, woozy. "I'm . . . scared of heights."

Calvin makes a show of swiveling around us. "I hate to break it to you, New Girl, but you're in the tallest building on campus. I'm not sure if you noticed that coming in."

Is it possible for my cheeks to burn any hotter? "I didn't, actually. I was far too busy being dragged in here against my will." I leave out the part where I thought I could handle it up here. I thought I could handle a lot of things.

He blanches like he hadn't considered that. "You could've told me you had a phobia."

"Told you? I don't even know you," I jab, even though that's also not entirely true.

I know enough. Though his world existed on a cracked phone screen to me. I know his favorite spot to vacation is Greece. I know that he's got an endless parade of girls who adore him. I know that his last post was a year ago, a golden-hour selfie with the caption LIFE IS GOOD.

"For what it's worth, I wouldn't have dragged you up here if I knew." He has the gall to look sincere. I don't believe him for a second, but I let him hold on to the scraps of his morality.

"Whatever."

"So, what now? Do I need to carry you down?"

No way in hell. "I can walk on my own. Just . . . give me a second to distract myself." I make the wretched mistake of dropping my eyes, and for a horrible moment, I'm staring at his mouth.

"A distraction, huh?" He snorts, wetting his lips again.

I've never whipped away faster. I struggle to keep my tone even. I worry there's a slight gallop in my words as I answer: "Not that. Just talk to me. Anything. Five minutes."

"You're the new one here. What do you want to know about Hart

HOUSE OF HEARTS

Academy?" he asks before monotonously reciting everything off the school's FAQ page. "Our Ivy League acceptance rate? Our college-readiness program? Our—"

"The hedge maze," I blurt out, and I could slap myself for it. There are a million more important questions to ask, but I'm over here asking him to tell me about a glorified garden.

He cocks a brow. "What about it?"

I guess there's no turning back now. "Why is it locked up?"

Calvin groans like this is a story he's heard before and one he doesn't want to hear again. "Because it's also a private cemetery."

A chill sweeps over me. "Who chooses to be buried in a hedge maze?"

"I'd tell you to ask them, but seeing as how they're all dead and buried, I imagine that would be difficult," he drawls. His damnably long legs stretch out by my side, and I bristle when they brush against mine. "There's four standing mausoleums in the center, but the only one people seem to care about is Anastasia Hart's."

Recognition flares at the name. I've stalked the Lockwells long enough to know they're direct descendants of the original Hart family. They own the school because their forefathers built it. "One of the founder's daughters?"

"Bingo. Want a prize?" he deadpans. "My dearly departed great-great-great-ancestor is something of a bogeyman at this school. Truthfully, the maze is only locked to keep people away from *her* grave in particular."

"I'm . . ." I hesitate to say I'm sorry because no one in his family deserves an apology after Emoree's death. "Why would anyone want to break in, anyway?"

31

His lip quirks into a devilish smile. "You're a smart girl. What do you think?"

I'm sure that velvet voice has conned a fair number of girls in his life.

"Glad you could deduce my intelligence from our stilted thirty-minute conversation. I'm flattered."

"You got in on the Whitlock academic scholarship. Believe me, they don't hand those out like candy. You're the only recipient this year."

I roll my eyes, but I'm starting to feel better. The lightheadedness has tapered off, and my thoughts have veered away from girls falling. Once again, Calvin has proved himself usefully irritating. "Fine, let me guess. Students here are so bored with their pampered lives that they're willing to risk expulsion or a slap on the wrist in order to break into private property?"

He grins wider like this is all a fun little game to him. "That and . . ." The humor drains gradually off his face. "People want to see her ghost."

Funny how a single word can spring you back in time. "Ghost" has me crisscross applesauce in Em's room on Halloween night in eighth grade. We were cutting holes into two old bedsheets and slipping the makeshift costumes over our heads.

"Guess how I died," Em sang with a twirl. She spun like a macabre ballerina, and her outfit billowed in dramatic flair.

"Peacefully in your sleep?" I ventured with my eyes still glued to my own work. Unlike Em, who sheared through her gown with reckless abandon, I was drawing my eye holes with a bottle cap.

She groaned. "Boring. Try again."

"Heart failure?"

"Bo-ring!"

"How is that boring?" I huffed. "They say high blood pressure is a silent killer."

"Ghosts don't appear for no reason! Something really bad has to happen to bring them back."

I bury the memory where it belongs. "You don't honestly believe in ghosts, do you?"

He shoots me a glare, and I can tell he's scowling harder to make up for his flushed cheeks. "And if I do?"

"Believe what you want."

"Thank you for your blessing. I don't know how I'd ever live without it."

We sit in silence for an agonizingly long second before I attempt to breach the gap between us. I don't know why I'm even offering an olive branch in the first place, but I blame the awkward tension. "Why do you believe in them?"

A contemplative look washes over him, and his eyes lift to the stairs above us. "For my sanity."

"I don't think seeing a ghost would have a lot of people feeling sane," I say. He squints at me, and I wave away his expression. "I'm not calling you crazy. I'm only saying a lot of people would lose their mind if they saw one."

He takes a breath and doesn't look at me. "I'd rather be haunted by someone I lost than be haunted by silence. Nothing is worse than the quiet. It's . . ." He abandons the thought with a sigh. "You don't even realize how much space someone took up in your life until they're not there to fill it. So yeah, I believe in ghosts because I'd rather there be something left behind than nothing at all."

My fists clench at my sides. I don't trust this guy as far as I could throw him, but he's spoken like someone who's seen grief of his own. "I know what that feels like"—I swallow—"to lose someone close to you."

I'll never forget the day. I remember wanting to rip off my own skin and run away from my body. Instead I found myself retching into a toilet, hands on white porcelain, purging out the pain. I wouldn't be surprised if my own heart went spinning with the flush.

He studies a spot on the floor. "What's your reason for not believing in ghosts?"

The question sizzles beneath my skin. It reminds me of the church sermon before the funeral—a weathered Bible, a geriatric priest, a promise of forever in a Hallmark heaven. There's a reason for everything, one we don't understand yet, the priest had said, like it was that easy.

"I believe in what I can feel and touch and see," I say, hugging my knees to my chest. I shouldn't be telling him all this. Especially not when his own brother is the one who stole everything from me, when I'm only here in the first place to drag him and his family down, and yet the words find their way out all on their own. "People die every single day. If ghosts really exist, don't you think they'd be everywhere? Besides, I don't need to be haunted by a poltergeist. I'm already haunted by the past—everything I should have done differently. How I could have stopped someone from dying if I had only tried harder."

He looks away like he doesn't want to stare my grief in the face. I don't blame him—it's tough for me to look head-on, too. When I found out Emoree died at midnight, it made perfect sense. The clock kept ticking, but my world stopped.

We sit in silence for a moment before Calvin finally stands up. He dusts off his already-clean pants, brushing his vulnerability away like specks of dirt.

HOUSE OF HEARTS

"Are you feeling better? Your panic, I mean." He hoists me up.

I'm not lying this time when I say, "I'm okay."

Surprisingly, the conversation did its job. I've managed to cram all the bad emotions into a ball and banish them to the far corners of my mind. I'll revisit them later, but for now I can at least make it down the stairs. Which is when he grabs my hand.

"Don't leave yet."

I spin on my heel. "Why not?"

He actually looks a bit shy. "We've spent all this time up here. Alone. Listen, I'm known for a lot of things, but I don't want to be known as the guy who sat up in a dusty old tower talking about ghosts with an absolute stranger. For everyone's sake here, can we pretend that we were up here making out or something?"

I blink at him. "I thought that idea was repulsive to you?"

He blanches but doesn't deny it. "I wouldn't actually kiss you. I'd pretend. It'd be a win-win for us both."

"I don't see how on earth I'd be winning here."

He lowers a hand into his pocket and offers me a playing card. I accept it with trembling fingers and trace the court jester's painted face. A juggling fool stares back at me, hollows for eyes and a cartoonishly wide smile.

The Joker.

"You're new here, but in case you didn't know, I'm kind of a big deal. You usually only get these if you're a freshman, but an exception can be made since you're a transfer." He rubs the back of his neck. "This will get you into the party at HOH Saturday night."

I tuck that information away neatly into my brain. Joker Night is this week already, huh?

I'd rather die than have Calvin think I was champing at the bit for clout. I'd love nothing more than to storm off and tell him I don't need this, but I'd be a damn liar.

Swallowing down my reservations, I gingerly accept the card and bury it in my pocket. "Whatever, fine, I don't care."

He leans forward to bridge the gap between us. He's so close I can count every eyelash. "First, you need to look the part."

I brace myself for a lot of things: for him to kiss me and for me to stiffen like a possum playing dead. I don't brace myself for the brush of his thumb across my lower lip. He pushes in, applying enough pressure to get the blood rushing to my mouth. Anything to make my lips look swollen. Then he messes up his own hair before shaking a hand through my straight locks. "There. Now you look like you've spent time with me."

I stumble back to the staircase railing, and I've suddenly grown wobbly-kneed. "G-got it."

"And, Violet?" He winks. "Make sure to tell everyone how good of a kisser I am."

4

"Absolute worst kiss I've ever had in my life."

"Get out," Amber gasps, the shrill pitch of her voice competing with the thud of her tray hitting the dining room table. She momentarily abandons her ridiculous school-crest-branded waffles to gawk at me, her bulging eyes darting between me and the narcissistic blond on the opposite end of the cafeteria. "Really? He kissed *you* in the tower? *And you hated it?*"

If the hedge maze is the beating heart of this school, Sutherland Dining Hall is its bloated belly. Hammer-beam ribs arch above our heads, and walnut walls press inward, giving this room the impression of being swallowed whole. The darkness is only broken by a series of leaded-glass windows and an assortment of low-hanging chandeliers. Golden light spills from lit candles and gathers across a gallery of grim portraits.

"Uh-huh . . ." I trail off, unsure what to say. It's not like I haven't kissed anyone before, but the problem is I can count the number on one hand and still have most of my fingers up. "It was too much everything, really. Just gross. But at least I got a Joker card out of it."

I'll feel a little guilty if this gossip gets back to him, but if the only rumor spread about that man is that he's subpar in the kissing department, then Calvin will live.

"Only you would find a kiss from Calvin Lockwell gross," Amber insists. "I can't believe he really kissed you. I mean, *I can*, it's Calvin we're talking about. Huge player, so I don't recommend going out with him. It must have been good for Calvin to give you a card—at least on his end."

"Believe me, I have no intention of dating him," I say cheerily. And then, solely to be petty, I tack on, "*In fact, I'd never dream of it.*"

"Are you hearing this?" Amber squawks to Birdie as she drops down beside me. Birdie's got a heaping serving of those branded waffles, smothered in syrup.

"Are you still pestering her about yesterday?" Birdie asks with a snort. Yesterday's fashion has been pushed aside for the school's uniform. There's not much you can do about a starched white polo, a red-plaid skirt, and a matching burgundy blazer, but Birdie does her best. She's littered the side of her skirt with safety pins and accessorized with a large Gothic cross dangling around her neck.

"You act like I'm interrogating her," Amber huffs, which is a perfect description of what she did the moment I set foot outside the tower yesterday.

I probably would've caved a lot sooner if the panic hadn't found me again when Calvin left. He'd somehow kept the brunt of it away, but the very second he stormed off, it returned with a vengeance.

"Sorry, I have a migraine," I'd lied, dodging Amber's persistent questions and letting Birdie usher me back into our dorm room. I'd immediately collapsed onto the mattress and covered my head with the duvet to block out the light.

She'd left me there to fake a nap, and somehow that fake nap turned

HOUSE OF HEARTS

into a real nap, and that real nap turned into me conking out entirely. I woke up only a couple of times in the night, mainly to the soft snores rumbling from my roommate and the steady thumping of students running along the halls.

"It's okay, I don't mind the questions," I say into the rim of my coffee mug now.

"Birdie, I swear, you have the wildest luck when it comes to roommates and Lockwells," Amber says, swirling a spoon in her own morning tea. "Here you are with a crush on Sadie, and now your new roommate kisses Calvin on day one ... and then there was that whole business with your old roommate ..."

"Em." The name slips out of my mouth before I can think better of it. It's enough to summon Birdie's full attention, and I stiffen under her gaze. I could tell her everything right now. I could let them know that Emoree isn't some unmentionable tragedy. That I know about that awful night and that I need as much help as I can get to make it right.

But then Oliver takes his seat at the table and I remember his vow of secrecy and Amber's penchant for gossip and how I cannot—will not—ruin my chance for revenge this quickly.

"*Erm*," I recover quickly, widening my eyes in an effort to play dumb. "What do you mean by that? I thought the Lockwells were twins. Do they have another brother or something?"

Birdie and Amber look between each other uneasily, and I do my best not to let on what I know or how much I care. There's a reason therapists act like a blank slate, a psychological tactic in being no one that makes people want to spill *everything*.

"Percy Lockwell, but he graduated already," Oliver informs me idly, his gaze caught between the veggie omelet on his plate and the Advanced Latin textbook splayed out beside him.

Birdie shrugs off his answer and taps her cheek. "If you believe that . . ."

I quirk a brow, but I don't have to bother asking what she meant by that. Amber feeds on my confusion and carries the rumor where my roommate left off. "The whole thing was weird as hell. He disappeared before spring semester. Poof. *Gone.*"

"I'm fairly certain he left for Le Rosey in Switzerland," Oliver clarifies, his tone a tad tart but his expression betraying nothing. He lets the book fall shut beside him and stuffs it into his Patagonia bag. "I doubt he was abducted by aliens."

Amber's cheeks bloom a telling red. "Did I say I thought he was abducted by aliens?"

"No, but I'm sure you were thinking it. Not everything is some big conspiracy or piece of gossip. Sometimes things just happen."

"Switzerland?" I demand, trying not to sound outwardly rattled while *inwardly* rattled. Should I have applied to Le Rosey instead? How the hell was I supposed to know he was in Switzerland of all places? Why did Emoree tell me to *find Percy* but leave out the little fact that he's already fled the country?

"So I've heard," Oliver says, dabbing at his lips with the end of a cloth napkin. "Which, as far as rumors go, is far more believable than him vanishing into thin air."

It's just a rumor, I remind myself with a measured breath. I force down another bite of my breakfast and do my best to wipe the concern from my face. I don't need to freak out. Even if he's halfway across the world by now, his siblings aren't, and I'd bet anything that Calvin and

HOUSE OF HEARTS

Sadie know exactly what happened that night, and they for sure know where their brother is hiding. I made the right decision in applying to come here. The place that's still 100 percent in the Lockwell family's control.

Clearly, this rumor has been debated among the trio a million times. Birdie stabs at her own waffles, and I wince as the metal teeth of her fork scrape the ceramic. "You can't deny the timing of it."

"The timing is why it makes sense, though," he says, but any hint of nonchalance in his tone is gone. In its place is a tight hitch in his throat and a flash of something in his eyes I can't quite pin down. "His girlfriend died in a tragic accident. I don't blame him for leaving."

"God, I'll never forget that day," Amber laments, her voice taking on a sullen tone. "It was horrible. A huge production. Police. Yellow tape. Reporters. A twenty-four-seven crisis center for students. Headmistress Lockwell was frazzled every time I saw her."

Birdie slumps in her seat, her breakfast long forgotten. "It really was awful. Her death weighed on me for a long time."

I want to tell her I know exactly how that feels, that I still feel it now—that inescapable, horrible burn in my chest—but I settle on a soft nod. We sit in silence, none of us knowing how to recover after such a heavy topic and no one wanting to be the one to try.

Our reverie is interrupted by obnoxiously loud laughing and jeering. Calvin's table, of course.

"*Look at the state of you, bruv!*" one of his friends jeers, slapping Calvin a little too hard on the back. He's got a cut-glass accent and a way of making even slang sound posh while shrieking. "My God, Cal. You lose weight over the holiday? You should've summered with me in Buckinghamshire. I swear, did you leave your room even once?"

41

I recognize the posh stranger as one of the crossed-out faces on Amber's hit list. Ash Rajput, a British Indian transfer student with a gold hoop through his ear and a chiseled jaw. ("I only crossed him out because he's dating Mallory Hunt. Enough said.")

Calvin's not laughing. He's too busy twirling his fork on his plate, his gaze locked vacantly ahead. It's only as I lift my head that our eyes meet and he stares at me like a man suspended in a strange waking dream. He squints as if trying to decide whether I'm real or a desert mirage.

Breaking away, I settle on one of the portraits hanging behind him. The man in the frame is the very first Lockwell to grace these hallowed halls. OLEANDER LOCKWELL scripted in elegant serif lettering. He is depicted in his prime, handsomely distinguished and distinguished by a streak of gray in his otherwise-brown hair. His glasses are perfectly perched across the slope of his nose, and his mouth is set in clear disdain for the viewer.

As much as I don't believe in spirits, I can't help wondering if everyone else sees his scowl or if it's reserved purely for me.

If I thought the cafeteria was bad, the main academic hall is ten times worse. The decor in this building needs to go to couples counseling. The past and present refuse to marry, and all they're doing is yelling over each other.

There are wall sconces and overhead fluorescent lighting, whimsical grotesques and state-of-the-art sprinkler systems, sleek metal railings and aged mahogany. I allow Birdie to lead me through it all, her arm dutifully locked with mine.

HOUSE OF HEARTS

"Looks like you're stuck with me for a bit longer," she says with my printed schedule clutched in her free hand.

Ovid's *Metamorphoses* stares back at us in bold black lettering. I didn't have much of a choice when it came to picking out courses for the semester. I wanted to follow Emoree's footsteps as best as I could—which meant taking whatever elective screamed out her name.

The only class I can't follow her in is choir. I might be academically gifted enough to weasel my way into this school, but I don't have a musical bone in my body. Em was two bad test scores away from flunking math, but she had the voice of an angel.

"You're in Ovid, too?"

She nods. "Hopefully you're not sick of me by the end of this."

"No, it's nice to have a—" I cut myself off. "Friend" lodges in my throat, and I taste the betrayal of the word on my tongue. "It's nice to have someone I know in class."

I follow Birdie as she ushers us both into an auditorium-style classroom. It has a certain Old English feel to it: a coffered walnut ceiling and paneled walls, lofty balcony seating lifted above rows of wooden benches. Sitting in the top gallery, I imagine this is what it'd be like in an opera house, forced to squint down at the stage through a pair of binoculars.

Our teacher strides up to the podium in front and pushes a pair of glasses up the bridge of his nose. He looks like a cadaver dragged out of the crypt to teach our class.

"My name is Dr. Sampson. 'Doctor' is an earned title. There will be no 'Frederic' or 'Mr. Sampson.' Do I make myself clear?"

There's a murmured hum of agreement that spreads across the room. He acknowledges us by clearing phlegm from his throat.

"We will be moving at an accelerated rate in this course. As you know, I assigned reading prior to class. They will do the same in college, especially at the Ivies, so it's important you adapt quickly. Now, if you open your books to page fifty—*Late on the first day, are we?*" His speech ends abruptly at the sound of the door squealing open.

A red-faced boy stands panting in the doorway. It's obvious from the sheen of sweat that he ran here when the bell rang, his white shirt splotched in the pits and his bangs plastered to his greasy scalp. He fiddles with his tie and mutters some excuse under his breath.

"Detention sounds appropriate. You can use it to reflect on your poor time-management skills."

The boy's shoulders slump, but he accepts his punishment without a fight. Not a second after he's collapsed in his seat, two more shadows stain the doorway: Calvin and a guy I recognize from my Instagram sleuthing, Theodore "Tripp" Griswold.

"Lockwell. Griswold," Dr. Sampson mutters beneath his breath. I wait for a lengthy reprimand, but it never comes. Tripp flashes a red Queen of Hearts card in the air, and although he might not have a crown perched on his head, the symbol acts as his royal scepter. It's a Get Out of Jail Free card if I've ever seen one.

Our teacher sneers, but it's obvious in the way he grips the podium that there's nothing he can do. Even he bends the knee.

"See what I mean?" Birdie whispers beside me. "The Cards get all the special privileges. Even the teachers have nothing on them."

Calvin waltzes in first, his mouth set stubbornly. His uniform might be perfectly tailored to him, but he still manages to wear it with reckless abandon. A loose tie hangs from his throat, and the tail of his button-up slips out from his pants. All he's missing is bed head and a lip-

HOUSE OF HEARTS

stick kiss to his collar. Beside him, Tripp looks like an NFL linebacker. Hair buzzed to his scalp, big and bulky, with a cocky smirk and a white scar slashed through his left brow.

A muscle leaps in Dr. Sampson's jaw as Calvin and Tripp sprawl out in the back row. I'm surprised he doesn't develop a nervous twitch as Tripp kicks back in his chair and plants his dirty shoes up on the desk. I'll give Calvin one thing—at least he's sitting upright, even if he's openly ignoring the lesson and staring at his phone.

"'Of bodies chang'd to various forms, I sing,'" our teacher starts finally, his voice weathered with restraint. "This didactic epic poem by Ovid centers on the very fiber of human nature—shown through physical metamorphosis. We see the wrath of slighted gods, the power grapple between humanity and the natural world, and the calamitous, often tragic aftermath of passion: how heartbreak can drive us into violence."

He swivels to write the lesson plan on the chalkboard, and Calvin is still swiping on his screen. Tripp, on the other hand, has pressured the girl beside him to copy a second page of notes for him. God, it's frustrating how little of a shit they give. Their futures are basically promised. I'm sure they'll slack off all four years and then get into whatever college they want anyway.

My own pencil pierces a hole through the page as I write down the title on the board:

BK VIII: The Minotaur, Theseus, and Ariadne.

The period at the end of "Ariadne" slashes downward, the tail end cutting off with the abrupt snap of chalk. Dr. Sampson curses beneath his breath and scrambles for a replacement stub, only to find his drawers noticeably empty. "One moment, class. I trust you all to behave as I grab a new box."

Famous last words. The moment he's out of earshot, all hell breaks loose.

"Think that dead lady in the maze is a Minotaur or something?" a student in the front row blurts out to his friend. I can tell by the shit-eating grin on his face that he's been thinking of this joke for ten minutes now and waiting for an opening. "I swear, man, a hundred dollars if you hop the gate to go look."

It doesn't earn him the cheap laugh he thought it would. All it gets him is a sneer from Tripp as he abruptly slams his feet back down on the floor. "Oh, there's something in the maze, all right, fresh."

The guy is probably scared shitless to have Tripp's eyes on him—I can tell by the slight hitch in his breath and the bulge of his eyes—but the hubris of a teen boy can't be beat, especially when his friends are beside him. "I'm not a freshman."

Tripp snorts and flashes his teeth. "Oh yeah, what are you, then?"

The boy's own teeth chatter, and I see that he's got a mouthful of neon blue braces. "A s-sophomore."

"Same fucking difference. Maybe you didn't learn much your first year, but you should know the maze is Cards property. Any asshole who tries to break in on their own is going to regret it. And that 'dead lady' you're talking about—Anastasia Hart—I guarantee you'd piss your pants if you saw her. Hell, you look like you already have."

The boy gulps. "She's not real, though."

"Oh, isn't she?" Tripp's grin is borderline sadistic. "There's nothing she likes better than stupid underclassmen. She'd love you. Isn't that right, Cal?"

"Yeah, sure, whatever." Calvin hums. All his attention is trained on his pencil—an instrument he's deemed worthless for note writing and perfect for spinning between his fingers.

HOUSE OF HEARTS

Tripp visibly deflates at that, his mood souring at the same moment I rip off a piece of paper and silently slip it to Birdie.

What do they mean about Anastasia?

It takes Birdie a second to flip the page over and write out her response. My heart hammers in my chest as she slides it back my way.

It's just a ghost story. The cards LOVE freaking kids out about it lol.
Anastasia is their Bloody Mary. She supposedly ripped her own heart out
in the maze when her fiancé cheated on her with her sister.
Now if you invoke her wrath, she'll rip out yours, too

Right on cue, I'm interrupted by a deafening *riiiiiip* from the floor below us. The room watches in horror as Tripp tears the boy's Joker card in two, shredding it apart until it's reduced to a shower of red and white confetti.

"You really should've learned your first year not to talk back to upperclassmen," Tripp taunts as he reclaims his seat. "This should teach you some respect. Consider yourself blacklisted from Joker Night." His gaze slides over to Calvin again for approval, but Lockwell's own grin is reserved for the successful tornado spin he just pulled off.

I hardly have a moment to process what happened because Dr. Sampson finally arrives back and the room goes deafeningly silent. Completely oblivious to the turmoil of the last five minutes, our teacher pauses to clean his glasses before returning to the board. The rest of the class proceeds without incident before he finally wraps up his seminar with "We're running short on time, so I'll end the lesson with a quote from renowned late author Jorge Luis Borges. 'It only takes two facing mirrors to build a labyrinth.' I'll let you dwell on that for today. Class dismissed."

The bell rings not a second later, and students clamber from their seats to grab their belongings and scamper off to the next class.

Birdie swivels my way with a knowing smile. "Welcome to Hart."

5

Helen Hall has no business looking like it was plucked out of a Shakespearean tragedy, but that's the impression the dormitory gives off with its infestation of ivy, dreary granite walls, and antiquated parapets. I've been here for nearly a week now, and I still feel like I should be holding a random jester's skull and reciting soliloquies about death.

Instead I'm picking out my nail polish for tomorrow night.

"Once in a Blue Moon or Meet Me at Midnight?" Birdie asks, thrusting two identical shades of navy at me like a manicure morality test. I pick the first choice, and she nods sagely like I've made a wise decision.

"Knock, knock—can I come in?" Amber asks in our doorway, not bothering to knock or wait as she waltzes right in. By the time the question is out of her mouth, she's already sitting next to me on the bed and dumping a suitcase's worth of clothes on my mattress.

My mattress. Huh. Nothing in this school feels like *my* anything, but it's weird how quickly our brains can adjust to new environments. Less than a week has flown by, and this room has become a paradox: It's a sanctuary when the lights are off and the covers are draped over my head, but a prison when it's the three of us—Birdie, me, and the dead girl we don't speak about.

I turn my attention back to Amber and immediately notice the matching set of black bags beneath her eyes. She's usually so well put together, but right now it looks like she's pulled two consecutive all-nighters and still found the time to participate in the Boston Marathon. Exhaustion sours her features, making her dewy skin sallow and her sparkling eyes shadowed.

"Hey, Amber, you look . . ." I struggle to finish that thought, but luckily I don't have to.

She groans and collapses on top of the mountain of satin and chiffon she dragged in with her. There's a boutique's worth of dresses and skirts and corset tops, all haphazardly spilling across my plain blue Walmart duvet.

"Like shit?" she guesses with a telling twitch. "Yeah, I know. I feel like it, too. I had two hours of homework to get done before I came over here. Who assigns homework the first week of school—especially before Joker Night?"

With Amber here, Birdie scrambles to turn the fairy lights on to complete the "sleepover ambience" we've got going on. The outside of this building might be borderline medieval, but the lights illuminate all the ways this school has been gutted for the current century: The old fireplace in the corner is entombed in white plaster, the scratches in the furniture have been buffed out, and the walls are slathered in a fresh layer of paint like a corpse dressed for a wake. Not quite alive but pretending to be.

"I'm only here right now because I'm running on two cans of contraband Celsius," Amber drones on. "It's basically off-brand cocaine. Here, can you feel my pulse and tell me if I'm dying?"

She throws her wrist in my face, and I dutifully press three fingers to her expanded artery. "The good news is you're not dying," I say with a smirk. "The bad news is that you're probably going to be jittery until it works its way out of your system."

She groans but accepts her fate with a dramatic flourish of her hand. "Well, that's fine, because we're going to be up all night figuring out what the hell we're going to wear. I don't know about you guys, but I still have no clue."

It's Birdie's turn to balk at the sight of all the outfits crumpled behind Amber's back. "You might have more clothes than I do, and that's saying something."

"I raided my wardrobe before I left home." Amber sifts through her assortment of gowns and pulls a sequined piece to her chest before scrunching her nose and tossing it aside. "Birdie and I waited all three years so that we could go out with a bang our senior year. I was not about to be caught off guard by the Joker Night theme. You don't show up underdressed to a masquerade ball."

I toy absentmindedly with the hem of my pajama top. "I was going to wear my uniform."

"Like hell you were," Amber says with jumpy adrenaline. "No ifs, ands, or buts. You're taking something. Unless Birdie or I get super into layering in the next twenty-four hours, there's no way either of us could wear *all* these clothes at once."

Speaking of Birdie, she's busy squawking over my smudged my nail polish. She snags my hand back to reapply a coat of Once in a Blue Moon to my pinky while Amber gestures again to the national landmark she's made of couture. Birdie relinquishes my hand, and I carefully hover my navy blue nails in the air.

"I couldn't possibly—"

"Yes, *you could possibly*," Amber says, throwing my own words back at me before peering over my shoulder at my roommate. Birdie's since wandered over to her own wild pile of clothes on the floor.

Before today, Birdie's closet was enviably organized—she might be a mess when it comes to cleaning up her makeup vanity or making her bed, but she's meticulous when it comes to color coding her wardrobe. It's a blend of school-uniform staples and weekend fits, bold accessories and colorful coats. Tonight, it's become a scattered collection of *maybe*s and *no*s and *why did I even pack this in the first place*s.

"No seriously why *did* I pack this?" Birdie asks us, brandishing what appears to be a zebra-print vest with peekaboo side cutouts.

Amber squints at it and crosses one silk pajama leg over the other. "I see the vision."

Birdie looks back at it with renewed hope. "Would you wear it?"

"Oh no, I wouldn't be caught dead in that." Amber snorts, and that has Birdie chucking the hideous vest at her head.

"You're the worst, you know that?"

She blows a kiss in return. "And yet you invite me everywhere."

It's true that their styles couldn't be any more opposite. Amber is all old-school prep, and Birdie is an eclectic hodgepodge of vintage bomber jackets and yellowed Dad-Star sneakers. I've never had enough money to care about fashion, but even I can't help the silly surge of excitement.

The dorm hall comes alive on a Friday night. There's a low thrum of chatter bleeding through the walls and the ever-present thumping of feet on the second floor; beyond that is a combination of music drifting through ancient vents and the quiet tone of Birdie's TV playing in the background.

Birdie—who I've learned is unable to be left alone with the sound of her own thoughts—has always got something playing. Today it's the remastered version of *Sleeping Beauty*. I look up in time to see Aurora get cursed. Maleficent storms in with a ragged gust of wind, damning Aurora for the petty hell of it all. By the time we make it through the first thirty minutes of the film, we've eliminated a third of the clothes on the floor from the running.

"Oh my God, I forgot I had this. Thoughts?" Birdie asks from her spot on the floor. She's got a leather skirt with a fire-breathing chain-mail dragon up one side hanging in her hands like a prize fish.

She gets a thumbs-up from Amber with her free hand. Her other hand is busy painting her toenails a bright, bloody red, the perfect shade match for her dress choice. She's "settled" on a Mirror Palais number; a crimson minidress that sweeps romantically off her shoulders, the bodice cinching tight at the waist.

"Here, Violet. Try this on. I think it'll be a good match for your skin tone," Amber tells me as she caps her nail polish and tosses a dress for me to try on. With foam separators between her toes, she carefully bends over and scoops up a handful of rejected gowns. "Bird, help me, please. We're drowning over here, so let's drag this back to my room while Violet tries that on."

Oh thank God.

It's not like Birdie and Amber aren't nice. They're way nicer than they ought to be, but there's nothing quite like being alone. Letting the mask slip and feeling the tension flee my body.

I swap my smile for a horrified grimace as I check the price. I can hardly afford to *look* at this thing, let alone wear it, but while I'm looking anyway, I can't deny that it's beautiful. The bodice is a stitched depiction of the Ionian Sea, a deep, resplendent blue with a tidal wave of embroidered mermaids. At the waist, the skirt extends in an exaggerated flapper silhouette of bright blue ostrich feathers. I fiddle with the back zipper, and I'm this close to shedding my pajamas and trying it on, but I don't get the chance.

My phone beeps, and my mother's face flashes next to her text.

Doing anything fun this weekend? Miss you lots, it reads, complete with a hyphen-nosed smile. :-)

I consider sending a selfie because it seems like the kind of thing you do when you're playing dress-up and your mom texts you. Except I've been on the receiving end of those kinds of texts. I remember the blue halo of my phone in the break room. Fluorescent light flickering and my thumb brushing against Emoree's rags-to-riches life. Wanting her to be happy but also looking around miserably at my own life.

I drag my phone to the window instead, snap a photo of the sunset in the courtyard, and type a quick not much <3 just having a night in with some friends before abandoning my phone on the bed.

"*Violet*," a girl's voice calls on the other side of the door. "Violet . . . Violet . . . Violet!"

I make a playful show of grunting and padding my feet noisily against the carpet. "All right, jeez," I sing, playing up the theatrics. "I'm on my way, you guys. Please tell me that you didn't come back with even *more* clothes."

I can already envision it in my head: Birdie and Amber will throw me sheepish grins and pass me a bundle of dresses, and Amber will mutter something about forgetting she had a fifth suitcase packed under the bed. Already rolling my eyes, I grip the door handle and swing it open. Except when I look out into the hallway, I don't see anything. Not a second avalanche of outfits and certainly not a pair of students knocking to be let in.

Despite the earlier chaos of girls running all over the place, the hallway is now completely empty. From one long stretch to the other, I see nothing but outdated carpeting and shadowed walls. I did hear my name, right? Not once or twice but *four* distinct times on the other side of the door.

It's only after another dumbfounded minute of me standing there that Amber and Birdie finally make their appearance. Birdie is empty-handed, oblivious, and chatting to Amber like nothing is wrong and her roommate isn't actively hearing things.

She meets my eyes and lifts a brow before I can even blurt out my question. "Were you guys calling for me?" I ask, cracking my knuckles one handed as I shift in place.

She exchanges an uneasy look with Amber before shaking her head. "Uh, no? You might've heard bickering, but that's it. Amber here was second-guessing her entire outfit and wanted to try things on again."

I shift my weight back and forth and swallow down my paranoia. "Yeah, you're probably right." Aside from them playing a dorm version of ding-dong ditch with me, there's really no logical explanation otherwise, right?

Amber's eyes cut to my pajamas instantly, and she groans as we make it back into the room. "Don't tell me you already changed out of it!" she sputters, glancing between me and the dress still bundled in my hands. "I wanted to see!"

I offer them both an apologetic smile and mumble a quick sorry, not wanting to fuss with a fashion show. It's not like it matters all that much what I wear tomorrow. Anything is an improvement from the clothes I brought. Plus, if it looks this good in my hands, I'm fairly certain there's no way it could look bad on me.

There's more complaining, but thankfully they don't push me. Instead, they take the dress and hang it next to their outfits on the rack.

who is that?

Huh? I squint at my mother's message and return to the hastily snapped photo I sent. I'd meant to capture a pretty, if boring, image of the courtyard at sunset, but a lone figure stands on the hill. It's Calvin, caught mid-step on an obvious path to the girls' dorms, his blond hair windswept.

I snicker to myself at the very thought of him red-faced in the hallway. *You told everyone our fake kiss was* that *bad?* If the voice at the door hadn't been a world away from his own, I might've assumed it was him after all. He was probably just here to hook up with someone. I have no problem imagining him slinking into the dormitory and a girl beckoning him quietly into her room. What a player.

No one, I text back like the liar I am. Not only is he a very irritating *someone*, but my entire plan hinges on him. I need to weasel my way into the Cards' lair and dig up as much dirt as possible on his brother. Joker Night is quite literally my one and only chance here.

"This is my favorite part," Birdie says, and it takes me a second as I set my phone down to realize she's talking about the movie. Amber snickers about her being a Disney Adult, and her quip is met with a playful jab to the ribs.

The scene plays out like a medieval tapestry. Aurora spellbound in Maleficent green, her bright figure creating a chiaroscuro against the blackened staircase. She scales the spire in measured, dreamlike steps, up and up until she's fully engulfed in the curse. One tiny prick of the spindle is all it takes for her to be cast in perpetual twilight.

Stuck in a beautiful limbo between life and death.

6

Joker Night blows in with a late-summer storm Saturday night.

Thunderheads sap the last of the heat, and a fierce wind slashes through all Birdie's hard work. The hour and a half before was filled with primping, curling, spraying, teasing, back-combing, and a million eye-shadow swatches on my wrist. Now I feel like a drowned rat thanks to this torrential rain, but Amber's more optimistic.

"I knew the waterproof setting spray was a good call. Your makeup still looks amazing," she shouts over the storm. For as rich as she and Birdie are, we're all still sharing one flimsy umbrella, our heels held in cheap plastic bags. "Is that narcissistic of me to say since I'm the one who did it? Oh well, who cares, it's true. I did a great job."

I shiver and rub the goose bumps on my arms. My dress is ill-equipped for the chill snaking through the air, but I'm sure the party will fix that.

"Does it even matter how I look if they're handing out masks?" I ask.

Birdie presses in tighter to the left of Amber. Her hair is darkened by a mix of gel and rain. "The masks are the perfect accessory! Plus, even if we don't get into the Cards and we have to rip off our masks and go home, at least we look good for some post-party selfies."

Somehow I don't see that as a great consolation prize. I brush Emoree's pendant under my collar. The chain is slick and cold against my throat. "How does this work again?"

"We'll have to find that one out together." Birdie smirks. "We've never been before."

All around us, the storm has made a mess of the school's landscaping. The ground has become one big mudslide. Each step forward dredges us deeper, the way a stone drowns on its last skip.

Birdie's teeth chatter, and she clutches the umbrella handle tighter. "All in favor of running the rest of the way there?"

"Yes, please."

"Then let's run, girls!"

I shouldn't laugh at the way Amber squeals in the rain. I shouldn't clutch Birdie's hand and giggle as we dash out onto the lawn. There's something electrifying in this moment, though. The ridiculous dress Amber gave me that feels like I'm playing dress-up, the pelt of cold rain spraying against my exposed skin, the roller-coaster flip in my stomach as we get closer.

"You know what they say about fairy tales?" Em's singsong voice flutters through my thoughts. *"Everything comes in threes."*

That might ring true tonight, but I know better than to believe in perfect storybook endings. Even the real fairy tales never ended in happily ever after. The Little Mermaid hacked off her tongue for the Sea Witch, and the prince didn't want her in the end, so she turned to seafoam. If anything, I'm not a fairy tale but a lesson for the Lockwells.

The House of Hearts is monstrous at night.

An awning separates us from the storm, and we take turns shaking off the rain like a pack of wild dogs. Dozens of students mill around us, all of them in various states of disarray. Girls who've managed to make an immaculate red-carpet appearance and ones with mascara running down their cheeks. Guys shucking off their white button-ups and wringing rainwater out onto the ground.

"Thank God we're mainly unscathed," Birdie mutters as she checks her reflection in a compact.

I can't even think about what I look like at the moment because I'm too busy staring at the world around me. Lamplight illuminates the windows above us, a wash of orange burning onto the shadowed lawn where we stand. There's a frieze of martyred saints directly above our heads. Strange but fittingly morbid for the night. I make eye contact with an imp-faced gargoyle overhead, its mouth slashed in an eternal scream.

Birdie chuckles and jabs me with her elbow. "I was like that the first time I saw this place, too. Isn't it something? I can't wait to see the inside for the first time."

Unfortunately, the first thing we see inside is a bold printed sign.

PLAY YOUR CARD. WIN A MASK.

The man holding the sign is silent behind a Venetian mask. Its face is split into an exaggerated smile with painted gold lips, and it has haunting mesh eyes. Even the cheeks are bloodied with a gory red heart on the left and a black diamond on the other.

"Sick mask, dude," a freckled guy in the front of the line says. "Where'd you get it?"

I recognize the boy as one of the incoming freshmen who stood for the ceremony. According to Birdie and Amber, wasting your Joker card as a freshman is the worst possible move to make. In their words: *"Why ruin the next four years for yourself if you don't get in? You'll forever be blacklisted from future Joker Nights and you'll spend your whole Hart experience knowing you wasted your shot. High risk, high reward."*

The jester says nothing in response, just taps the demand on the poster.

Freckles offers up his card with a fumbling hand and a sheepish wince.

The masked man examines it, holding the Joker to the light like a cashier examining a counterfeit bill. After a long moment of consideration, it's finally deemed legitimate, and the boy is spared his misery and sent ahead to the table of masks. With a snap of nylon strings, he dons the moon-faced gaze of a barn owl, his freckles concealed by a faceful of snowy-white feathers.

If the next girl is nervous, she refuses to show it. She presents her card with all the haughty arrogance of someone who has never been told no in their life and has no intention of hearing it now. Her confidence might be impressive, but it dies brutally at the hands of the doorman as he rips her card in two.

"Wh-what the hell are you doing?" she sputters, whipping around like someone might come to her aid. "You can't do that!"

The masked jester speaks his first word of the night, loud and clear for the world to hear: "Fake."

Bright splotches of color stain her cheeks, and her tone scales higher in her throat. "Please! This isn't fair! I—I deserve to get in. I'll get it next time. Let me keep playing! I—*don't touch me, damn it!*"

A current of gossip swims downstream, the whisper traveling the length of the line and ending in a mocking peal of laughter: "How embarrassing!" "Oh my God, I'd die if that was me." "Who is it? Do you recognize her?"

She might not have a mask, but the girl conceals her burning face

HOUSE OF HEARTS

as she shrugs off the jester's arm and storms out on her own. Her tulle cape slashes past me in her retreat, and just like the boy who disappeared into the shadowed mouth of the manor, her silhouette is swept away by the storm.

The jester turns our way next, and although I know my card is legit, I'm suddenly worried I hallucinated the whole experience with Calvin. I can't shake the visual of a kid in a liquor store, sliding a false ID across the counter and hoping I'm not exposed as three kids stacked in a trench coat.

Birdie goes first.

Then Amber.

And then I'm sweating as I hand over my clammy card and the jester looks at me through the slits of his mask. It only takes ten seconds for him to examine my card, but it's long enough for me to count each breath and feel my eyes dry out as I forget to blink.

I wait for the rip of paper. He'll tear mine up next, shout out something about me being a good-for-nothing fake, everyone will laugh, and Birdie and Amber will tut apologetically before disappearing into the night.

None of that happens. Instead I'm escorted to the masquerade table, and I join Amber and Birdie in rummaging through the masks, relief washing over me. The night is far from over, but the first test is aced. Birdie has not only swapped her galoshes for heels, but she's also swapped her face for the delicate snout of a deer.

"All we have to do is play their game," Amber tells us from behind the feathered face of a peacock. Her new skin shimmers blue, and her dark hair is adorned with a fan of colorful feathers. "Before you can be a player, you have to be a pawn."

The ballroom is ripped out of a storybook.

Silver slants across the checkered dance floor as the moon winks at us behind a shawl of black clouds. The night sky pierces through the domed ceiling; the storm is on full display beyond the glass. I shiver with each jagged streak of lightning and the distant roar of thunder.

All around me, beautiful gowns glimmer like fallen stars. The chaos from before has washed away, and I've been plucked from my everyday life and thrown back into a medieval court.

Among all the finery, there's a singular portrait hanging over us on the far wall. The first thing I notice about the subject is her hair. Similar to Emoree's, it's a riot of red against swan-pale skin. It swims down her scalp and grazes her oval cheeks in loose waves. There's a Pre-Raphaelite softness to her jaw and a lost quality in her gaze, her eyes wandering all the way off the canvas and onto me.

ANASTASIA HART, the plaque reads.

I turn and meet my own eyes in the wall-length mirror ahead. I might not be able to see my face, but I stop to admire the dress on me for the first time. Amber had promised it was no big deal to borrow, but it feels like one tonight.

It hugs me just right, the fabric bluer than a bruise, the same shade as the sky before the sun comes out. Despite it all, I feel like a wine stain, out of place and needing to be scrubbed out of the gown.

"We look like the start of a bad joke." Birdie snickers, brushing a curious finger along her mask. "A peacock, a deer, and a rabbit walk into a ballroom."

I'm the rabbit in this equation. My mask transforms me into a whiskered creature, prowling across the dance floor. Neither a girl nor a beast but something else entirely.

"That's fine as long as I'm not the punch line." Amber snorts in response, twisting and turning so that her dress twirls alongside her. "Come on! Let's at least have fun before the madness starts."

She drags us out to the dance floor and giggles at my yelp. I don't know about the rest of them, but my only frame of reference for a school party is my homecoming ball sophomore year. Em begged me to attend, and we spent the entire semester trying to scrounge up the money for the tickets. It was fun because Em had a way of making everything feel festive, but it didn't prepare me for this.

This is a far cry from a school gym with a Kool-Aid punch bowl and party streamers and the PE teacher playing chaperone in the corner. There's a massive gilded cage in the center of the room with a goddamn aerialist hanging from a lyra hoop. She's angled to tell the time like a human clock counting down to midnight.

"This has to cost more than my tuition," I mutter, and Birdie giggles at that.

"More like all of our tuitions combined," she adds over the elegant hum of a violin.

A server spins through the crowd, her metal hoopskirt fashioned to hold dozens of glass bottles. She interrupts our conversation to offer drinks, and just like the man's at the door, her face is a painted Venetian smile. The liquid sloshing in each bottle is a curious storm blue. They're all corked and labeled with an identically scrawled note. Two words in a delicate cursive script: DRINK ME.

Before I can think too hard about it, I knock back one of the bottles. There's a hint of blueberry, bubbling and sweet, but I can't say for sure what it is. It's . . . good.

Birdie and Amber clink their own cups with a shared "santé" before the attendant moves on to the next unassuming victim. With that, we're off, the three of us swept up in the revelry of the dance.

I feel like I'm in one of Emoree's fairy balls. Emoree was always frolicking around in the woods, hoping for some fae prince to sweep her off her feet and whisk her away to a far-off land. She must have felt like all her dreams finally came true here. Was this how she met Percy? Was this how he lured her into a world of lies?

The walls spit my reflection back in every direction, the illusion making the party go on for an eternity. Amber and Birdie each take one of my hands, and we're spinning like girls singing gruesome nursery rhymes. *Ashes, ashes, we all fall down.*

The crash of percussion is the only marker of one song ending and another beginning. It's alarmingly easy to lose yourself to the thrall, the music demanding all of you at once. A particularly bright streak of lightning flashes overhead, with a loud clap of thunder not long after.

Amber gasps at the sound of it, her shoulders hunched like she's the rabbit among us.

"Is the storm freaking you out?" Birdie teases, and I'd bet there's a smirk behind her snout.

"I'm easily spooked, that's all," Amber huffs, throwing her shoulders back and shrugging off the sensation. "It's nothing."

I surprise myself by spinning her, a playful pirouette to lighten the mood. "The scariest thing in this room is my two left feet."

Amber giggles. "You could really do some damage in those heels."

"The night's early. I still have time to break someone's foot."

Suddenly we're all laughing and dancing and . . . and it's nice. Dare I say "fun," as guilty as that makes me feel inside. I've carried around my sorrow for so long that I've forgotten what it feels like to not have it slung across my back.

We carry on together for a song or two more before the music

HOUSE OF HEARTS

shifts into a coupled waltz. I'm lost to the crowd, and like with everything else in my life, I find myself completely and utterly alone in the end. My smile slips off my face the instant I realize I'm by myself.

I'm this close to finding a good corner to hide in when a stranger appears. The tide of the crowd sends a fox drifting over to me. His mask is handcrafted from pheasant feathers like all the others, but his suit is unique to him. It's the same shade as crushed berries and split lips. He extends a gloved hand, and somehow it feels twice as dangerous as the bottle I drained.

"Care to dance?" he whispers, his voice hauntingly familiar but lost to the blur of the night.

I don't know what compels me to take his hand, but I do. Pressing my body to his side, I can't fight the shiver at his touch.

"You should know I'm ridiculously clumsy," I warn.

"I think I can handle you." His words strike a match inside me, and our sudden proximity only fans the flames. His movements are as graceful as the aerialist in the gilded cage. "Follow me. Step forward as I step back."

I shiver with the sensation of his hand on my back, and I pray to any god listening that, whoever he is, he doesn't feel the hitch of my breath, sticky and hot against his skin. Our chests are pressed flush together, my heart knocking on his ribs and begging to be let in.

"There, not so bad, is it?" he whispers. His eyes shine through his mask. They're firefly bright, the same shade as mulled cider on a cold autumn night.

Our reflections molt in the mirror as we dance. We become someone else in the glass, no longer two strangers but Em and Percy. Their image feels suspended in time, their dance immortalized forever. They're figures spun by clockwork, a music box left open so long the gears have rusted over and the song has grown distorted and strange.

Did they dance like this? Is this how Emoree felt when Percy looked at her—like the whole world was ready to rip apart at the seams?

"Now for the dip." I'm only vaguely aware as I'm lowered to the floor. His hand rests scandalously low on my back, and suddenly I'm falling in his arms. Just like Em and Percy, we're trapped together in this moment as his eyes chart a course down the length of my throat. If this was Emoree's monstrous, magical world, his lips would part and his canines would carve into my throat.

All at once, the lights cut out.

The room shrouds us in near-total darkness, and even the moon has retreated into the passing thunderclouds. We're left with nothing but the hazy imprints of the dancers before us and the all-consuming night. There's a flurry of panic in the room and the shuffle of feet and then, finally, the glimmer of candlelit sconces casting an amber glow upon Anastasia's portrait.

She begins to weep in the dark, her portrait leaking tears like a blessed Mary Magdalene. Blood drips from the center of the canvas and blotches her chest a crimson red. There's a horrified gasp, and while some of the students attempt to laugh it off, I notice the barn owl freshman stumbling his way out of the room.

What follows is a heavy hammering in the walls, pounding like my heart. Phantom fists slam all around us, loud and turbulent like a woman trapped within the wood and begging to be let out. *Thump, thump, thump.* It's enough to drive a man mad, pulsating like another round of thunder. The dreary words of Edgar Allan Poe cross my mind, and I remember his "Tell-Tale Heart" well: *tear up the planks!—here, here!—it is the beating of his hideous heart!*

More students stumble over themselves to leave, but I keep my eyes trained on the portrait. This can't be real; there has to be a sensor of some sort, a vial of prop blood breaking open behind the canvas and bleeding through the portrait. Hidden speakers. Something. *Anything.*

I recall the Venetian jester's voice, loud and echoing through the corridor. *Fake.*

The masked fox lifts me back to my feet and continues our dance like nothing has gone wrong. At least someone else knows it must all be for show, I praise inwardly, letting the young man carry me through the motions. Our dance continues in the midst of the chaos surrounding us. We're lost in each other's company until the moment I see something move above his shoulder.

The stranger's gown is shapeless and white, the fabric fluttering with every spin like a cloud of fog. She's built like a ballerina, all long limbs and lithe grace, wispy auburn hair, and moonlit skin. It's only when she brushes past me that I see the constellation of freckles on her arm, the ones I used to connect with Sharpie back in grade school.

She isn't wearing a mask, but it wouldn't matter if she was. I'd know her anywhere.

Even beyond the grave.

7

Emoree.
Emoree!

Her name jolts me back to life. Every little hair lifts on my body. She's here. She's really, really here.

I tear myself from the fox boy without a word. Maybe I'm shell shocked or maybe I've lost my mind, but either way I don't stop to ponder the horrific impossibilities of it all. Science be damned, it almost feels normal for her to be here. This is where she's meant to be, alive and dancing and not rotting six feet deep.

She's perfectly intact now. Remade and glowing, and I am calling—no, I'm yelling—but she won't hear me. Why won't she hear me? Her body floats against the dance floor, bobbing like a buoy in the waves. I wait for someone else to notice her, to gasp or scream or call her name, but the world pays her no mind. Beyond me, she ceases to exist.

I weave gracelessly through the crowd, my shoulders knocking into dancers' backs and my elbows meeting their ribs. I'm met with huffs and groans and *watch where you're going*s, but I don't care. None of this matters. She's all I see, and I chase after her like a girl possessed.

I let Emoree lead me farther away from the ballroom and the music that was once beautiful but has since grown shrill.

She's a stray gust of wind down the corridor, her body so paper thin that she breezes forward without the slightest sound. I'm hypnotized by the arch of her heels and the sway of her tiptoes inches off the floor.

We enter a deserted parlor room, and the candles flicker upon our arrival. Velvet curtains billow down from the ceiling and sensuously frame a matching set of oxblood leather armchairs.

Beyond them, a fireplace sits untouched, the logs blackened behind an iron grate. Oleander Lockwell hangs like an omnipresent god above the mantel. In this painting, the gray strands from Sutherland Hall have won the battle; they dominate his hair and the fringes of his beard. He's stern-faced and harsh in the low lighting, painted in the violent strokes of a hurried artist who couldn't get away fast enough.

Emoree doesn't spare the man a glance. Her attention is reserved for an object on an end table, her finger tracing a careful pattern in the air as she studies it. She breaks away the moment I get close, and I can't help it, my curiosity gets the best of me. I pick up what turns out to be a wooden labyrinth, a perfect miniature of the hedge maze outside. I brush my thumb across the careful ridges and chart the same path she did, from the clearing in the center to the exit, but I feel no residual warmth in her wake.

I don't feel any warmth at all.

The body heat in the ballroom is a distant memory. What I'm left with is an icy pocket of strange gust of frigid wind. My breath clouds the late-summer air, and I marvel at the ghost of it leaving my lips. It shouldn't be this cold in here, but then again, Emoree shouldn't be here.

Instead of leading me to a cursed spindle, the room gives way to a balcony behind a set of French doors. Her body drifts straight through the glass, rippling like the tail of a flame cutting out.

I welcome the storm as I follow her out into the night. It's a sobering feeling, the rain pelting me out of a dream and back into the harshness of reality. The first thing I notice is the quiet. Rain striking the ground without a sound, thunder tapering off in the distance, and wind softening to a gentle lull.

The second thing I notice—finally, really notice—is Emoree.

Those pretty locks of hers mat with blood, red seeping from the cracked corners of her skull. She transforms before my very eyes, a grim Cinderella decomposing at midnight. Her ivory skin sallows, and she opens her mouth, the black hollow of her lips like a burial plot in the earth.

"Emoree Hale sat on a wall,
Emoree Hale had a great fall.
All the king's horses and all the king's men
Couldn't put Emoree together again!"

That morbid nursery rhyme is the last thing to leave her lips before she tips over the railing's edge. I'm aware I'm screaming, scrambling over the side to catch her, but there's no point.

She dies in front of me, a splatter of bones against the pavement.

No.

No.

No, she didn't—she couldn't—none of this could possibly—

Hands. There are hands gripping my waist, fingers digging into my skin. Someone looming over me, their hot breath against the back of my neck. Terror seizes me in a way I've never known. I watched Em

HOUSE OF HEARTS

die, and now I'm next. Someone is going to throw me over and have my body join hers on the unforgiving earth. *They're going to kill me just like Emoree. They—*

"Stop struggling! Damn it, you're going to make us both fall!"

We *do* fall, but not to our deaths. I tumble over the stranger, our bodies splaying out against the balcony floor. Muscles pulse under mine, and I feel the steady thrum of a stranger's heartbeat traveling through their skin.

I watch, captivated, as the fox mask slips off the boy's face.

Calvin Lockwell.

I don't know how I didn't sense it before. I feel like the hairs on the back of my neck should've tingled or I should've caught a whiff of his signature cologne, a spiced floral blend of ginger and lavender.

He's drenched from the storm. My eyes rake down his body, the wet shirt clinging to his chest, the rain tracing a lover's path from his temple down his cheek before dripping off his jaw.

All at once, the world comes back to full sounds. The torrential pour of rain slapping against the hard ground, the roar of the wind, the labored sound of Calvin's ragged breathing as we lie there, staring at each other.

"This is becoming a bad habit," he muses when he rediscovers his voice. It's pitched higher in his throat. "How many times are we going to keep falling for each other?"

I don't have it in me to summon a clever retort to that. "You don't understand," I insist instead, and maybe I don't understand either. None of what happened is possible, and yet reason and logic don't seem to matter.

"You're right. I don't," he echoes tersely. His voice is wound taut in his throat, and his attention narrows to my collarbone—on the pendant swinging between us. Recognition flares hot. "But I think I'm starting to."

He pulls me closer with a hook of his finger and a tug of the chain. We're a whisper apart, but his focus is solely on the cool metal in his fingertips. If anyone saw us like this, they might think it romantic. The two of us, rain drenched and pressed into each other on a hidden balcony, our breath clouded together in a shared fog, his lashes tickling my cheeks.

But there's no misreading this situation. Especially not when his glare cuts sharply back up my face. "This doesn't belong to you."

"Doesn't it?" I counter, ripping myself from his embrace and staggering to my feet. "It's on my neck, isn't it? Wouldn't that constitute some form of ownership?"

He squints at me for a minute, his expression difficult to read, before he finally turns and grabs one of the kitten heels on the ground. He toys with my shoe in his hand, brushing a thumb against the sequins before holding the shoe out of reach.

"Give me my shoe, Lockwell." I utter his surname like the curse it is and extend an impatient hand his way.

His gaze slants downward, his expression smug beneath the blond sweep of his lashes. "It's in my hand, isn't it? Wouldn't that constitute some form of ownership?"

You've got to be kidding me.

"Hysterical." I've got him against the French doors, my one hand holding a fistful of his tie and the other grappling while I'm on my tiptoes to reach. "I'm not playing this game with you. Give it back."

"That's what this night is about," he reminds me. Rainwater sluices down the arch of his brow, and I watch a droplet disappear between his parted lips. "Or have you forgotten?"

HOUSE OF HEARTS

I flex my toes against the cold tile, and I don't miss how surreal this situation is. The horrors I witnessed minutes ago are eclipsed by this irritating human in front of me. "Whatever, keep my shoe. Maybe it'll fit you."

He scoffs down at me. "Games are only fun when two people are playing."

I lift my chin to meet his eyes. "Have you considered I don't want to play a game with you?"

Calvin swallows, his throat bobbing with the action. "You've been playing one from the very start," he corrects. "I'll give it back if you answer my question. Who gave you that necklace?"

I toy with the silver chain, looping it anxiously around my finger. "Why do you want to know?"

"Because I know it doesn't belong to you."

I grapple for the right answer to give him—whatever half truth I can offer that doesn't get me immediately kicked out of this manor and expelled from Hart. "Emoree, when she insinuated your brother killed her" won't get my shoe back.

"It was a gift."

"From who?" he presses, but instead of answering him, I slip out of my left shoe and offer it up to him as a matching set.

"The same girl I followed out here," I say, injecting the truth with enough syrupy sweetness that it rolls off smoother than any lie. "Or didn't you see her? I swear she was just here. Weird, maybe she disappeared."

He studies my expression, his brows set in a harsh line. "Has anyone told you how aggravating you are?"

"Once or twice," I retort with a defiant jut of my chin. "Though they typically haven't also chased me onto deserted balconies."

His ears tickle a flustered shade of pink. "You're lucky I did."

"You still followed me."

"I was curious," he admits, masking his emotions behind a careful shrug. "I wanted to see if you were scared away by the game."

It's my turn to flush, and I'm thankful for the darkness as I twist my head into the shadows. "You knew it was me this whole time?"

"You're hard to miss, Violet," he answers, surrendering my heels to the floor. "I'll see you inside."

He abandons me without another word, giving me space to finally do the one thing I'm dreading. Alone in the rain, I peer over the balcony, expecting to see Em's body. I imagine a whole host of horrible things— blood blackening the grass, bones set at all the wrong angles, the milky whites of her eyes aimed lifelessly upward—but she isn't there. And I have a horrible feeling that she never was in the first place.

8

I'm a little afraid of the dark.

I blame it on my ancestors. Something about cavemen and night predators and shared DNA. It's hardwired in human nature to be afraid of what we can't see, and right now the sky is pitch-black, the path to the hedge maze shrouded in darkness.

The last hour and a half is a blur, but I trace it from the beginning: the ballroom descending to chaos; the sight of Emoree drifting down the hallway—hard as it is to believe; the mass exodus of students scrambling over one another to leave the dance floor ("Where's Amber?" "Her last words were 'screw this haunted-house bullshit, I'm out'"); the Cards standing in the center of the room and telling the remaining club hopefuls that we might've passed their first test, but they have something much worse waiting for us outside in the hedge maze.

It hardly feels worth celebrating, but with the way Birdie keeps giving giddy grins to me in the dark, I can't help the excited bubble in my chest. It's currently fighting for dominance against the other overwhelming emotion of the night: fear. I throw a look to my right as we approach the hedge maze, if only to remind my Neanderthal brain that there aren't any saber-toothed tigers or woolly mammoths waiting for me. No ghosts, either . . . though I doubt anything could be much worse than what I saw on the balcony.

The remaining pledges follow the Cards through the gentling storm. The rain has tapered to an on-again, off-again shower, and the wind has ceased screaming. It wails instead like a distant banshee, and I shiver as a gust racks against my damp shoulders. My dress remains plastered to my back, and my bun is slick against my scalp. The only thing that warms me up even remotely is the knowledge that Calvin is suffering, too.

He's managed to find a new blazer, but his tie remains loose around his throat and his white button-up is wrinkled with the contours of his skin.

Everyone is deathly quiet around me—"everyone" being the non-Card members surrounding me. There's Birdie and a couple of kids I recognize from my classes now that they've taken off their masks. The rest are starry-eyed strangers, everyone's emotions a cocktail of excitement and nausea—but mostly nausea.

There are several Card members joining us, but I only recognize a handful of them. There's Oliver, who has only just joined us for the evening. He doesn't look at either of us, too absorbed by the blue screen light on his phone. Then there are the other familiar faces: the Lockwells, Tripp, and that British guy from the cafeteria this morning. Ash is sauntering forward with his arm slung across a girl's shoulders. Her hair hangs in a honey-brown bob, and her lashes flutter above glittered cheeks.

"Isn't it beautiful out here?" the girl croons—Mallory Hunt, presumably, if Birdie's yearbook debacle is to be believed.

No one says a word.

HOUSE OF HEARTS

"She asked you a question. Would it kill you guys to answer? And smile while you're at it," Tripp taunts, demonstrating what he wants us to do with a finger hooked on either corner of his lips. "The entire school would die to be in your shoes. Act like it."

I force a grin on my lips, but I feel more like a feral animal flashing my fangs.

A guy beside me sticks his sweaty palms in his pockets. He gulps at the approaching gate. "If you enjoy mud and rain, sure," he jokes weakly, as if he's expecting a chuckle.

Mallory smiles back at him, her teeth as straight as a military cemetery and her eyes so Fiji Water blue you could sell them at Erewhon. "You're out."

"Wh-what?"

"You heard me," she retorts as she swivels from her partner's side. "We don't need any smart-asses here."

"I'm not . . . I didn't mean—"

Tripp glares at him, the threat clear.

Meanwhile, Calvin examines the crescents of his nails in the moonlight. "Don't take it personally. We're already at capacity for smart-asses."

The boy ducks his head and runs back to his dorm with his tail between his legs, and Sadie not-so-subtly smacks her brother in the arm.

"Mallory's right. It's just a spot of rain. Not the end of the world," Ash insists as he herds us closer to the gate. "The game's easy, besides. All you've got to do is go in, have a look about, find the heart we've hidden, then walk out. Quite simple. We've hidden two of them in the maze, which means most of you won't get in. If you find it before sunrise, you're in. If not . . ." He lingers, his gaze cutting to Sadie.

She stands there with a hip cocked and her cold eyes narrowed. Her lips are a devilish red, like the hourglass on a black widow. It makes sense for her to be a cunning spider. This whole school might as well be a web beneath her. "If not, I'm afraid this is private property. Trespassing the first week won't earn you any points with my mother." She directs her attention my way. "For some of you, it might mean expulsion."

A key swings from Sadie's throat, and she slips it off her neck and turns to the gate. It's a wrought-iron vision in front of us, an enormous fence that surrounds the entire northern perimeter of the campus grounds. There's a heart crafted around the keyhole, formed by a conjoined set of metal S-scrolls. Melded beside it is a tiny plaque:

THE FINAL RESTING PLACE OF ANASTASIA HART

LOVED DEARLY BY HER SISTER

I brush a hand over the railing. Students have littered the gate with heart-shaped love locks. A miniature Parisian Pont des Arts with young lovers leaving behind their initials. Some names are engraved in Edwardian script, while others are simple silver and stamped in permanent marker.

I narrow my eyes at the one beside me. Fairly nondescript despite the two letters carved into the back: *E+P*. It hits me like a blow to the gut. Could be a coincidence, but . . .

Somehow I know it isn't.

"A girl died here over a hundred years ago, you know," Tripp says, clearing his throat as the rest of the Cards line up next to Sadie.

Oh good, we're starting this shit already. We all stand next to one another in the maze's first courtyard. If the earlier map is to be believed, there are dozens of these small clearings littered throughout the maze, the largest of which sits smack-dab in the center.

"She came into this world in . . . uh . . . in 1860 . . ." says Tripp, treating this little ghost story like a failed book report.

"Anastasia Hart came into this world crying in 1860, and that's how she left it," Sadie interjects. "She was the baby of the family. Always in love. Always crying when her love wasn't returned. Her heart was too big, and when she fell for someone, she fell entirely."

"She fell super hard at sixteen," Mallory continues, and her voice has that airy, whisper-tone quality that lends itself well to ghost stories. "And this time felt different. The guy's name was Oleander Lockwell, and—not to be weird, Cal and Sadie, but he was hot."

This has to be scripted, because Oliver suddenly lifts his head up like a marionette pulled to life. He tugs at the collar of his vest and throws a disparaging look at the wet ground before addressing us. "Their meetings were a clandestine affair. They'd hide out in the heart of her family's maze on campus under the shadow of nightfall. Anastasia was the only one who ever spent any time in the maze, so it felt like the one thing that belonged to her. And now she thought Oleander would belong to her, too."

Birdie throws a weak smile his way, but he doesn't return it. He struggles to even look at us and opts instead to stare at the ground.

Calvin picks up the ghost story next, digging his hands into his pockets. "But legend has it his sister was a bitch."

Sadie twists from her spot in the circle to glare at him, and he amends with a groan, "My bad. *Her* sister."

Ash swings an arm over Birdie's shoulder, reeling her in like he might whisper a secret in her ear. "Helen, Helen, Helen," he tuts. "What a nightmare her older sister was. Couldn't let Ana have a bloody thing. Admittedly, Anastasia was pretty, but Helen was prettier. Couldn't even let her get laid, could she, now? Had to be a home-wrecker."

Birdie wiggles out from under his arm with a grimace and shuffles instantly back to my side.

Tripp's grin slashes through the dark. "Shit came to a head when Anastasia caught them together by the lake. Oleander was down on one knee, proposing, and she totally lost it. It absolutely broke her. So, next thing you know, she was running into the maze. But this time she'd never leave."

Mallory takes over and mimics the breaking of a heart with her hands. "Her heart hurt. It burned in her chest. She could feel every crack in it, and she wanted it gone. So she took a knife and dug it right out."

In true performance-art style, someone else has to carry on the last monologue. I bet it's really killing them right now that this isn't around a campfire, no bulky flashlight to point up at their chins.

Sadie finishes the story with a dark gleam in her eyes. "She didn't stay dead. Some say her grave site swelled with a bad storm, and her body was lifted out of the dirt. Others claim that she practiced black magic and cast a curse before she died. Either way, she's lurking in that maze, waiting. Looking for her missing heart, and believe us when we say any heart will do." She lets that last word hang in the air as she stares down each one of us.

All righty, then. I look around to see if anyone's buying this, and sure enough, most of the students look actively freaked out, but two of them are elbowing each other excitedly. It's got "fake urban legend" written all over it. For starters, I doubt she could stay conscious long enough to drag a knife through her rib cage and pull out the very organ keeping her alive. She'd probably die from blood loss before getting very far. It also reads like a bad pun with her last name, so there's that.

HOUSE OF HEARTS

"The time has come for you to pledge your loyalty to the Cards and your hearts to Anastasia."

There's a flurry of movement as each new recruit is matched up with an existing member. Birdie is red-faced and stumbling at Sadie's side, a kid from my econ class is trembling beneath Tripp's hard gaze, and I'm left behind with Calvin.

He bristles as I reluctantly walk toward him, rolling his eyes at me until his sister snaps in the air and the pledge begins. It's all very methodical and well practiced, almost routine, even, as Calvin lifts a whole pomegranate from his pocket. The fruit is a deep, dusky red, the ends unfurled like the jagged points of a crown. He tosses it once in the air before peeling into its tender flesh with a pocketknife. "Eat."

"Excuse me?"

He grins, sly and dark, his fingers bleeding red from the fruit. "Isn't that the first rule of hell?" he whispers, his voice scraping and raw. "You need to eat its fruits to stay forever."

I stomach my hatred and reach for it. I can eat a damn pomegranate.

He yanks it out of reach. "Open wide. Pledge your loyalty to us above all else."

I flush but comply. "I swear it." He leans in, his fingers brushing across my waiting mouth. As he does this, his spare hand steadies the anxious tremble that's sparked to life in my veins.

Calvin pushes a bit of fruit between my lips, his ring finger lingering as it brushes against the sharpened tips of my canines. It feels as if he's silently urging me to bite down and draw blood. The acrid taste of pomegranate trails my tongue and rolls its way down my throat, and just like that, he pulls away.

I try not to look at the fruit in his hands and think of the way I leaned into his touch. It was intimate and terrifying, but I'm not one of his pretty girls. If his type is roses, I'm a ragweed girl. Stubbornly sprouting in the cracks between the pavement, growing into my bristles.

"You want to be one of us so badly?" Sadie projects to the group of us, her voice echoing in the night. "You've pledged yourself to us; now it's time to offer up your heart to Anastasia."

Mallory grins. "Finally, time for the fun part!"

"This hasn't been the fun part?" Calvin counters, and I briefly stop breathing as he brushes his finger on his own lips.

"You'll be blindfolded and brought to a random point in the maze," Sadie instructs, and there's a smug gleam in her eyes as a nervous shiver ripples through the group. "At that point, you'll pledge your heart to Anastasia and be left to find your way out. Find her heart, bring it to us before the sun rises, and you're in."

"Ladies first," Calvin says to her without a chivalrous bone in his body. If I didn't know better, I'd guess he doesn't want to go any farther inside. He's got that stricken look across his face, and he gnaws on his lower lip.

Why is he afraid?

I'm hit with the memory of the one and only time I've been in a maze before. Four years ago, Em and I scrounged up enough money for the county fair and beelined for the corn maze. We rushed in giddily. It'd been fun at first, but we'd taken one too many wrong turns, and as the evening descended into night, the fear of being lost forever went from comical to very real. We'd worked our way out, but the nerves lingered long after.

What must it be like to be trapped here in death? Lost forever? I clench my teeth. It probably feels like nothing. You can't feel anything once you're dead. I try to catch Birdie's eye, but she's focused on the dark path ahead.

"There won't be any working together," Sadie tells us, her voice swallowed by the enormity of the maze. The lights on campus don't make it past the hedges, and we're only able to navigate our way forward by the dull glow of a flashlight. It catches on a forked path, and that's when Sadie twists back to address the group. "Each one of you will go on alone. Got it?"

Even in the dark, I can see the furrow in Calvin's brow as he approaches me.

"Remember," Sadie hisses to her brother, her manicured finger stabbing into his chest. "Play by the rules and take this seriously. No screwing around."

"Got it, boss," he retorts flatly.

She scoffs in frustration and abandons the two of us with a sneer. Calvin waits until she's gone to fumble with the edges of his own burlap bag. "Do you mind slipping this on? I think my sister would have a stroke if you didn't wear it."

I'd rather not, but I don't have any bargaining chips here, so I let him blindfold me. The two of us stumble in the dark with him as my guide. His hands are warm against mine, not a single callous to them as he steers me forward.

"I know who gave you the locket," he whispers when we're deep in the maze, his earlier composure immediately gone. I can't see him, but the words seem to lodge in his throat, and his fingers tighten sharply.

I grit my teeth behind the burlap, and I'm secretly grateful he can't see my face either. He's silent for a second. All I can hear are the sounds of his breath and the shuffle of soil beneath our feet. All I can feel is his skin flush with mine.

"Is that so?" I ask finally. I was supposed to have a plan, but suddenly I don't know what to do. Lie or tell the truth?

When it's obvious I'm not going to fill in the blanks for him, he clears his throat. "Emoree Hale, right? But I guess that's not the real question here. Why would she give it to *you*?"

So much for lying. I gulp and switch tactics. "I'm sure you can figure that one out. You figured the first part out on your own, after all."

He barks out a strange, undignified noise. "Answer the question."

"Because I'm her best friend."

He's silent, and I get the sense that he's waiting for me to elaborate.

"If you're looking to figure out why I'm important, I'm *not*. I don't have a pedigree. I grew up in a small town, just like Em. I'm here on scholarship, but you know that. Unlike Tripp, my dad doesn't own an oil rig out in Texas. In fact, I don't have a dad at all. But none of that matters because Em gifted this to me for the simple reason that I'm her best friend. *Why?* Are you upset that you didn't get rid of all the evidence?"

Grass squelches beneath my steps as we round the corner. "Evidence of what?" he asks.

"Murder," I blurt without thinking. The word momentarily sets both of us aback, and we freeze there in the middle of the path. It takes him a second to find his bearings, and in that second, I know I'm the biggest screwup to have ever lived. One week in and me and my smart mouth ruined it all.

"You think someone murdered Emoree?" he snaps, swiveling around and yanking my blindfold off briefly to look me in the eyes. He's haloed in green ivy, his white teeth clenched together and his focus solely on me. From a cursory glance, I see that we're standing in yet another clearing, this one empty save for a single stone bench in the corner.

There's no turning back now. "I know she wouldn't jump on her own . . . not unless someone pushed her."

"You think my brother killed her," he hisses in my ear, the proximity sending shivers skittering down my spine. It's hardly a question. "Is that why you're here, then? To get revenge?"

I lift my chin defiantly. "So, you admit he did it?"

"I never said that!"

"But you didn't deny it, either, did you? So, tell me, did your brother plan it from the start? Was it some sick, twisted game of the Cards'? Or did she piss him off one day and he decided enough was enough, so he lured her up to the tower and—"

His hand snakes across my wrist, and his fingertips press divots into my skin. "*Percy loved her!*" he yells. His voice splinters apart like cut glass in his throat, all broken syllables and sharp points, and his eyes brim with unspent tears. "No one would ever dream of hurting her, least of all Percy. He loved her more than you could ever fucking imagine, so don't act like you know my brother or the relationship they had. Last I checked, only one of us was here last year, and it wasn't *you*."

His words deeply puncture my chest, and I stagger back on impact. "I knew Emoree better than anyone."

"Clearly you didn't know everything," he counters, his voice wet and sniffly. "Not at the end."

I ball my hands into fists at my sides, and for the second time this week, I feel like crying, but I can't and I won't, not in front of this arrogant prick. "And I suppose you do, huh?"

He's silent, but the answer is obvious from his devastated expression.

"So, if your dear old brother didn't kill her," I say, unsure what to make of his random burst of emotion but unable to fully trust him, "who did?"

"This isn't a good place to talk," he says, thrusting out his hand to offer me the burlap mask back. "Make it through the maze first and then find me Monday. I'll tell you everything I know."

"And why should I believe you?"

"You're here for a reason," he jabs. "And that reason is to find out all our deep, dark secrets. Does that sound about right? I think you need me, or at least the information I can give you."

I hate that he's right. I despise the fact that I have no pull or autonomy in the situation. "Monday."

"Monday," he repeats, covering my face and carrying me deeper to the center of this labyrinth. My world is reduced to the shuffle of earth beneath my shoes and the scratch of burlap tickling the bridge of my nose as I breathe in.

I'm only gifted my sight again once we've reached the dead center of the maze and the largest clearing thus far. Calvin lifts the mask in time to show me the most gruesome orientation gift ever.

A knife. We're alone in the heart of the maze, and he's got a goddamn knife in his hands.

"I knew it!" I screech. "I *knew* it. You're going to kill me, too!"

He winces and with his free hand—the one not holding the *knife*, of all things—does his best to hush me. "Shhh."

"Don't you fucking shush me! I'm allowed to scream if you're about to stab me!"

"I'm not going to stab you!" he snaps, twisting the hilt of the knife around so that the blade is pointing away from me. "I want you to take it."

"You want me to take it?" I echo, and he nods, again lowering the volume with his hand like I'm the one being hysterical here. "And do what? Stab *you* with it?"

"*P-preferably not.*"

I swallow hard. Sure, it's got all the makings of a bad horror movie. A group of entitled rich kids, an unexplained murder a year prior, a convenient scapeghost. But I guess, hey, at least I'm the one holding the knife.

The blade glints in the moonlight. I idly twist it side to side to examine the hilt. It's simple black leather.

"It's part of the game," he says slowly, carefully, because, *hey, maybe being on the receiving end of a knife isn't that fun after all.* "They want you to prick your finger and recite a dumb oath. That's it. Here, see, I'm not making this up." He hands me a scroll.

I stare down at what is most definitely an incantation of sorts. Someone really had the job of tea staining this paper and scorching the ends like a Pinterest DIY.

"A couple drops of blood and then you read this three times and you're done. You'll be free to find the heart and figure a way out of here."

"Okay," I say, because I can totally do that.

It's the knife that makes me waver, but luckily, I think I'm up to date on tetanus shots. One drop can't hurt, right? I lower the top of the blade to the pad of my ring finger. It kisses the skin for only a second, the point slicing into the flesh. Blood wells on my fingertip before staining the page.

Em's pendant chafes against my clammy skin, hanging like a second heart above my own. I'm not superstitious in the slightest, but some baser part of me shoots warning signals up to my brain. I smother it down and force out the words on the page.

"Blood for blood, I do impart.
I invite you, Ana,
Come rip out my heart."

I clench my fists and say it a second time, then another, each repetition building in my throat. Louder and louder until the third and final chant feels like a Hollywood exorcist expelling a demon.

Nothing happens. Go figure. I square my shoulders in response, but Calvin jerks around like he's worried the words have already taken root.

"What now?" I ask as he sheathes the knife and puts it back in a satchel across his shoulder.

"Close your eyes and count to thirty. Then you're on your own," he answers, like it's that easy. His words are accompanied by the softening thuds of his footsteps as he abandons me there in the middle of nowhere with my eyes closed.

"One, two, three, four, *fivesixseveneightnineten*—" Screw it, I'm peeking.

He's gone. The moon swells heavy in the sky above me, partially entombed in a shroud of fog. What little light shines through casts a faint glow on my surroundings. The grass is parched and yellow beneath my feet, and four slabs of cold marble stand behind me on the lawn. *The mausoleums*, I realize soberly. I stare at the death date of the one directly behind me. The life cuts off at a tragically young sixteen, and I know without looking just who it belongs to.

Anastasia Hart.

Dear Diary,

I struggle to conjure a single second in my existence when my feelings have ever been reciprocated tenfold. I can't shake the sensation that I have cast this poor, beautiful boy under a spell. There's the ever-present fear that he might look upon Helen's face one day and he will be woken from his trance. If that fails to do the trick, he must only have a single conversation with my sister to discover the impossible valley between us. He will be charmed beyond return—if not by her fair looks, then by her sharp wit.

No, I simply can't let her steal him away from me. I spent all last night into the early hours tossing and turning and thinking of all the ways I might keep him forever. I've thought about it in my dreams, every moment while waking, and even pondered it whilst brushing my hair at the vanity.

It's only this evening that I received the answer I've been searching for all along. Perhaps I'm not casting spells yet, but maybe it is high time I learn.

—Anastasia Hart

9

Okay, so now it's officially a bad horror movie.

But I refuse to be the girl who dies first. Guilt gnaws at my gut as I remember what happened to Emoree, but I don't have time to dwell on her death. There are only three things that I need to do right now:

1. get that ridiculous heart they were prattling on about,
2. find my way out of this maze before the sun rises, and
3. track down Calvin so he can tell me what the hell is going on.

Having an agenda always helps. I can do this because I have to. I'm not the scared little girl I was at the county fair, trembling within a bunch of cornstalks.

I've come a long way since then. Or at least I think I have before I twist around in the dark and see I'm not alone.

"Jesus!" I hiss, my neurons taking way too long to fire between my eyes and my brain. When they've finally caught up, I've already scrambled an embarrassing foot away from an inanimate object.

It's not a monster but a marble statue of two sisters. But one of them has been beheaded in a clear act of vandalism. The decapitated head smiles upward at the night sky, and I know without a shadow of a doubt that it's Helen. There might be some legitimacy to the Anastasia story after all. I have no trouble picturing a heartbroken girl lopping off her statue sister's head in a fit of rage. The only confusing part is why the family never restored it.

Despite one of them being clearly mutilated, the girls continue to hold hands. They're identically portrayed, from their ringlet curls to their matching lockets.

I step back toward the path and pick up the flashlight left behind in the grass. It's not very strong, and I have no idea how I'll navigate my way out of this mess, let alone go on a scavenger hunt in the dark.

The light rain dampens my exposed shoulders as I walk, and my heels drown in the mud with every step forward. I hate to stick my feet in this mud, but I'd rather be shoeless and out of this maze than trapped here in heels.

The feel of the cool earth beneath my feet is familiar anyway. It whisks me back to childhoods spent running around, bruised, barefoot, and braver than I should've been. I remember the trees we'd climb and the old tires we'd swing on. Summers with Em were fireflies and tall grass and secret spots.

My thoughts break with a rush of movement to my left. It happens so quickly, I can hardly process what's going on. Seized by pure flight-or-flight instinct, I swivel on my feet, shoe poised like a weapon in my trembling hand.

It's a rabbit.

I smother a hysterical giggle. Here I am, clutching a kitten heel for dear life, and it's only a bunny. "Hey, buddy, you spooked me."

I bend down, but it rushes through the greenery, escaping quickly, out of sight. There and gone in a blink. Unfortunately, I can't follow it through the hedges, so I'm forced to stare down at the fork in front of me and make a choice. God, which way did I come in with Calvin?

Calvin.

A shiver courses through me. He recognized me even in a mask, and he chased me out from the ballroom, yanking me back in time for us to wind up tangled together in the rain. He hadn't seen Emoree, but somehow, some way, I had.

She'd led me out of the ballroom and through the hall, down the corridor and through the shadows, into a desolate room. There'd been the dead fireplace and the brush of her fingers, thoughtfully ghosting over the—

Wait.

She'd shown me the miniature of the maze. I take the heel of my shoe and lower myself to a muddy patch of the ground. I draw what I remember, which admittedly isn't everything but might be enough. The circular mouth of the central clearing split into a forked road, followed by a sharp right and then a left. Right, left, left, right.

I get up and follow the path as best as I can from memory, retracing my steps all while darting the flashlight left and right to keep an eye out for the heart. I take a sharp right turn, walls of greenery lifting beyond my head on either side of me.

"You can do this," I whisper to myself, because someone has to say it. I might not have the place completely mapped out, but what I saw in the study is enough to get by, and what I lack in memory, I make up for with muddy footprints in my wake. The storm has slowed enough to leave a path perfectly intact behind me. With each step forward, the hedge walls seem to grow tighter. I could've sworn a couple of steps ago

HOUSE OF HEARTS

that I could spread my fingers out on either side of me. Now my shoulders brush the tips of leaves, the space tightening like a clenched fist. It's like being swallowed alive.

I'm about to make another turn when a voice calls out from the darkness.

"Violet!" It's everywhere all at once, a disorienting echo in the night. Every part is enunciated, *Vi-o-let*, pitched like the voice of a windup doll. *"Violet, Violet, Violet!"*

I can't tell where it's coming from, but I know whoever is doing it is going to have a good laugh about it later. All a prank. A sick, twisted prank. Someone must be left behind in the maze to scare me, or maybe it's another pledge, trying to get in my head. That's all.

"Funny!" I shout, and the volume of my voice sends a black mass of birds shooting off into the sky. "Really, really funny, you guys. Absolutely hysterical."

It feels good to yell. So good, in fact, I continue to grumble under my breath as I storm forward.

The maze ahead of me hits a dead end, and I know I made a wrong turn at the last fork. Damn it, I guess I was supposed to go right all along. I let out another groan for good measure. I'd rather them hear me frustrated than terrified.

There's another rustle from somewhere in the distance. The crunch of soles imprinting in the dirt, the swish of a body twisting through the leaves

"Violet!" Here they go again. I'm getting sick and tired of hearing my own name. *"I need your help!"*

I freeze mid-step and whip around to search for the source.

Through the glow of my flashlight, I see her. Whoever is in front of me in the forked path just barely turns the corner before me. Before she disappears into the shadows, I see her hair flying out in an unruly tangle of blood-red curls. Her ivory skin is partially concealed by a stage-costume-esque gown, because of course we have an Anastasia Hart cosplayer in the mix.

If she thinks I'm going to run away, though, she has another thing coming. I charge toward her like a possessed bloodhound. I might be exhausted, but I'm also pissed off, which is currently stronger than a double shot of espresso.

"You're the only one who can help me." I don't see the girl, but I hear her again not far ahead. "I always played the damsel in distress, and you were the knight, remember?"

That makes me pause, remembering the games I used to play with Emoree. They can't be taunting me with a girl who died on campus a year ago, right? The bar might be in hell, but this is a new low.

"Do you know how long it takes for a body to fall and break into a million pieces?" The stranger's voice lifts from the gloom, and I see her moving ahead. The ivory shine of her skin in the dark. Like a body dissected, she reveals herself in parts. A flash of a wrist, a kicked-back heel, a strand of cherry-red hair. Her body is never stitched together, no full image for me to latch on to.

"What did you say?" There's no denying the comparisons now. My chest tightens, questions sloshing around in my brain, drowned by the rising tide of my bad thoughts.

She doesn't answer. She only keeps running, twisting and turning and leading me deeper. A quick lurch to the left followed by a sharp right. I'm panting trying to keep up with her. Sweat streaks a salty path down to my lips.

HOUSE OF HEARTS

"Six seconds."

The outer banks of the maze are a manicured, artificial green. Where she's led me is a mess of thorns and dead branches. They scrape against my skin, drawing blood. My legs ache the longer I run, and my sides cramp as I try to sprint even faster.

And then, all at once, she stops, with her back to me.

"I know this is all a part of some"—I pause to suck in air—"sick hazing ritual, but joking about a dead girl? Don't you think that's a little low, even for . . ."

My anger leaches from me immediately, making way for a terror so bone deep I worry I might collapse on the spot. For the second time tonight, Emoree stares at me. Her body is wisp thin and translucent in the dark. Not alive or dead but some miserable in-between.

"Remember what I said about ghosts?" she whispers, and even her voice is reedy and not quite there.

I can't speak. I can't blink. I can't do anything. The shock might've saved me back in the ballroom, but it feels different here in the maze. Horrifically real and impossible to wrap my mind around.

"Something really bad has to happen," she finishes for me, her voice tapering off with the rest of her until there's nothing left.

"Em!" I howl when she's gone, and fall to my knees. With my body collapsed against the earth, I hear a muffled sound beneath the dirt.

VioletVioletViolet, a voice sings. *I'm down here.* There's no thinking as I claw the ground bloody, dirt and debris digging beneath the tender beds of my nails. I pry the earth apart and tear through clods of soil. I don't know what I expect to find, but what I see before me breaks my trance.

A beating heart.

I freeze and stare at it, if only to prove to myself that I didn't see that correctly, that there's no possible way it's alive and moving, but it *thump-thump-thumps*, pulsating back to life before my very eyes.

Rip it out.

The words rattle through my skull, soft at first before building louder and louder, twice as loud as the heart.

Ripoutmyheart, RIP OUT MY HEART, rip it out, rip it out, rip it OUT!

I squeeze my eyes shut until tears spring in my vision and reach my hand out to give in and end this horrible night. It's still thrashing as I pluck it from the soil. I hold it in my hands, beating and bloody, and gasp as it dies with one final thump. With another blink, it's no longer real but plastic in my palms.

What the hell?

I don't get time to think about it before I hear an awful sound from the gate. Wait a damn minute. The gate? *The gate!* I can see it! I lift myself up, heart still in hand, and race to the entrance up ahead. They're all still waiting on the other end, the group of merry assholes kicked back on the lawn like this is some picnic and not the second-worst night of my life.

I send the plastic heart flying before I even emerge from the gate. It lands with a wet plop at Calvin's feet, and he startles at the sight of it. Good. If only he'd seen it when it was still alive.

"That's got to be a record." Calvin whistles, and he has the nerve to be standing there with a timer on his phone. If I still had the plastic heart on me, I'd send it flying at his face next. "Congrats."

I have no idea which other pledge might be joining me soon, but I'm entirely too exhausted to linger any longer.

HOUSE OF HEARTS

With his free hand, Calvin fishes out yet another card from his pocket. The Queen of Hearts stares me down in the dark. She's patterned like a typical playing card, in a gown with navy blue sleeves and a gilded collar. But instead of looking away, her eyes bore directly into mine.

"Monday," I snarl in Calvin's ear as I pass. I've had more than my fair share of nonsense, and I'm ready to get out of this dress, shake the loose twigs out of my hair, and bury my face beneath my blankets.

And if I'm lucky tonight, maybe I won't dream at all.

10

Birdie and I are twinning today, and it goes far beyond our matching set of fingerless gloves ("Trust me, they're on trend").

"Are you nervous?" she whispers as we walk up the front entrance to the House of Hearts. She's been jumpy for hours, and by hours, I mean the last forty-eight, when she ran into our dorm, red-faced and panting. Her dress was rumpled and her hair streaked with soil, but none of that mattered because she was holding up a Queen of Hearts card. The squeal she made when I showed her my matching card was at a frequency only bats could hear.

"No more than I was in the maze." It's not a lie, but it's not the whole truth either. What I'm feeling now isn't nerves. It's a beehive beneath the skin.

The storm stole what was left of summer, and Monday morning washed away the rest. The excitement from Saturday has faded to the dull monotony of classwork, glitter and gold party streamers swapped for number-two pencils.

That all changes now.

"Moment of truth," she whispers as we take the first steps toward the Cards' comically ominous front door Monday night. The panels are intricately decorated with linenfold designs, the wood carved to resemble arched cathedral windows with flourished hearts at their centers.

It swings open immediately after the first rap of the brass door knocker to reveal Tripp leering down at us.

"You're lucky, you know that?" he says before taking a hit off his weed pen. I know for a fact he's not allowed to vape on campus (some of us actually read the school rules before we break them), but I bite my tongue. "Should've seen the others when they got suspended. One dude cried like a goddamn baby."

I'm not sure if I feel lucky. I don't know what I feel other than haunted.

I offer my Queen of Hearts card to him now. "This is our door pass, right?"

He grunts before stepping aside to let us in. "You look like shit," he says, zero filter. "That maze did a number on you, huh?"

"Something like that." I can't blame him for the insult. My arms are littered with red scratches, cuts from where branches sliced through my bare skin, and I swear I can still feel the dirt crusted under my nails. I've left the maze, but in many ways, I feel like I haven't.

"Oh thank God, I'm so glad you guys made it." Mallory strolls our way with a swish of her hair. "Things were beginning to get boring. And, ew, Tripp, you reek. Hold still."

He grits his teeth and gags as she whips out a pink bottle and drenches him in an equally noxious spray of Tom Ford perfume. "There, you're welcome."

Tripp barks at us, *"Hurry up and follow me."*

I was expecting a lot of things: a medieval torture chamber where Tripp would say "gotcha" as he tied me to a wooden rack; a seedy,

Prohibitionist lounge where they all smoked cigars and talked exclusively about how rich they were; an Illuminati cult meeting with robes and pyramids and Gregorian chanting. I just wasn't expecting this.

"Sorry, it's a bit of a mess," Mallory says, which is a massive, massive understatement.

The room is a cyclone of news articles, pages strewn across couch cushions and stacked haphazardly by the mantel, newspaper cutouts pinned to corkboard-covered walls and photos circled in red ink. It feels like I've been thrown into a cliché crime drama, the perfect backdrop for a daytime television detective—*There's a method to my madness, officer, I assure you.*

Except I don't think there is one here. The only perk about this room is that none of the papers are oozing blood onto the floor. That definitely does some atmospheric heavy lifting.

"What is all this?" Birdie's the first to speak. She might be a mess herself right now, but even she sounds strained at the sight.

At least she can talk. I'm currently at a loss for words. I've never been so overstimulated in my life, my tired eyes darting past the chaos to the Cards members draped around the room.

Sadie scowls at us from a buttoned armchair; Oliver waves from one of the black-painted walls, his free hand pinning a new piece of information against a corkboard; Ash pats his knee like mall Santa, and Mallory sprawls disgustingly across his lap; Tripp takes another hit off his weed pen.

And Calvin stares directly at me.

"Sit down," Sadie instructs, gesturing for us to do as she says and shut up. The vintage Sorrento table between us is littered with papers, and Birdie has to push a manila folder out of the way to even sit beside me.

"First things first," she says, like a stereotype of a mob boss, "the information we tell you won't leave this room. Neither of you will say a word."

Fat chance of that.

My thoughts must be smeared across my face, because Sadie frowns in my direction. "And if you do talk, things won't be pretty. Scholarships revoked. Suspensions. Your parents blacklisted from all places of employment, be they corporate offices or gas stations. Make no mistake, we will find a way to ruin you."

My head jerks at the mention of gas stations. If the maze wasn't proof enough, this is no ordinary club and these people are way past serious. A flicker of apprehension slithers up my spine as I think of all the possible ways this could backfire on me: Losing my scholarship is one thing, but ruining my mom's job prospects is another. I always knew they were influential, but I guess it really is true that money has the power to make or break you. I'm over here sweating, and somehow, someway, Emoree actually *enjoyed* being in this weird club?

"Now, on the flip side," Sadie continues, sliding a fat check across the table. There are more zeroes on this piece of paper than I've ever seen in my life, and it's enough to give me heartburn. "The Lockwell family will sign a personal check to every club member if they succeed in helping us with our mission."

"Helping you with what?" Birdie blurts out. Her eyes are glued to the check in a way that suggests that this is an astronomical amount for her, too.

I swivel to meet Calvin's look as he clears his throat. His eyes are overcast, and his lips are pressed into a grim line. He dances around the answer initially. "We need your help breaking the Lockwell family curse."

"Your family curse," I echo, and even Birdie is struggling not to laugh. "Don't you think you've screwed around with us enough already? Besides, how does dancing in a ballroom and running amok in a maze suddenly make us good candidates for curse breaking?"

"We need people who don't shy away from the supernatural," Sadie answers, like it really is that simple. "Members who are willing to get their hands dirty and look in every possible avenue for answers. That's what we need. You two refused to back down from the start."

I brush the compliment off my shoulders and sneer back in Calvin's direction. "Are we talking poison apples or cursed spinning wheels?"

"Neither."

"True love's kiss, then?"

Birdie smothers a giggle with a nervous palm to the mouth, but she's the only one laughing. In fact, Calvin's gone deathly silent. *Almost like—*

"Violet's right." Birdie swivels to Oliver and crosses her arms over her chest. "Can't you tell us what's *actually* going on?"

Oliver winces and rubs a hand awkwardly on the back of his neck. "I know how it sounds. I reacted the same way when I was told."

"Seconded," Ash says with a lift of his fingers. "Though Mal and Emoree took the curse like champs. They believed it immediately."

I can totally see how Em lapped this up. Her world was held together by flimsy dream logic. Mom always said I was a bloodhound in a past life, but I think what I really am is anxious and obsessive. When I get a whiff of something, I won't rest until I'm dead. "You told me if I made it through that maze that you'd explain everything. Well? I'm waiting."

Sadie whips around in her seat. "What did you tell her?"

He slouches under the weight of his sister's glare. "Nothing!

HOUSE OF HEARTS

Nothing, okay? Calm down. She was asking me about her friend Emoree, and I told her I'd explain if—"

I wince at his wording, and if I had any hope under the sun that Birdie didn't notice, it's shot dead instantly when I hear her gasp. "What does he mean 'your friend' Emoree?" she blurts, her outburst overlapping with Calvin's defense. "Last time I checked, she was *my* roommate. You never even met her."

My cheeks burn hot. I don't know why the truth feels like Pandora's box; if I so much as pry the lid open, the world will devolve into Unspeakable Chaos. "I . . . lied."

"You *lied*?" she echoes. In the short time I've known her, I've only seen her frustrated once—flaring her nostrils and glaring out the dorm-room peephole as some girl burned popcorn in the shared kitchen and set off the fire alarm. "Why the hell would you lie to me? Who was she to you?"

"She was my best friend," I confess. "And the whole reason I came here."

"Don't you think you could've mentioned that while I was *crying to you at the lunch table*?" She scoffs, backing away from me like she's never fully seen me until this moment and now that she has, she's disgusted by the sight. "Were you only ever using me for information?"

I'm scrambling for an answer when Tripp's voice bellows to life, his frat boy accent a grating vocal fry. "EVERYONE SHUT THE HELL UP."

That successfully plunges the whole room into silence and gives Sadie the opportunity to regain control of the meeting. "Thank you, Tripp," she praises before throwing Birdie and me a harsh look. "If you two want to duke it out, do it on your own time. Keep it up and you both will be kicked out, got it?"

I attempt to catch Birdie's eye, but she's already treating me like I'm invisible. In case I'm not, though, I nod for Sadie's benefit.

Satisfied with our silence, Sadie beckons us over to the wall and gestures to the board behind her. "You all know the story of Anastasia Hart by now. Only it's more than a simple ghost story we scare the freshmen with. It's the start of something horrible that our family has endured for generations now. Ana was betrayed by her older sister, Helen, who stole Oleander from her. So, she cursed every eldest Lockwell in their family line to endure the same anguish she felt that day, to be completely and truly brokenhearted." She nods at a daguerreotype photo behind her; the portrait is of a young woman with her gown clawing up her throat and her sleeves scaling to the ends of her wrists. Youthful despite her slicked-back hair and genuinely frumpy attire.

"It all began with a girl named Mabel Beckwith. She was the soulmate of Helen's first son, Ezra Lockwell." Sadie rests against the wall, her shoulders slumping like the weight of the world is too heavy for her to bear. "Even back then, the family influence was large enough to pay off our own set of coroners and authorities. Because of that, 'official reports' say she died of a heart attack. Unofficial reports confirm what we know now: that she, like all the others to follow, died after being stabbed by a possessed Lockwell. The blade pierced directly through her heart."

My hands freeze at my sides, and I can hear Birdie breathing heavily next to me as Sadie continues. "The Cards were created with the sole purpose of breaking this curse to prevent passing it on to the next generation. They thought it'd be easy and that they'd be able to dissolve the organization immediately after 'saving' the Lockwell family . . . They'd soon realize what they were up against. This curse still stands."

HOUSE OF HEARTS

Beyond the girl's photo is an image of her grave, the dates cutting her down to sixteen years old. "It happened again. This time, it was a boy named Clifford Wallace, the lover of Ezra's firstborn daughter, Mary. Dead at seventeen. Again, a stab wound to the heart. Mary never married, so her younger brother, Edwin, carried the curse on with his eldest son, Charles."

Thus begins the procession of the dead: young lovers throughout the decades in yearbook photos with gelled pompadours and mullets, middle parts and side parts, all of them Hart students, all of them dating Lockwells. And all of them stabbed through the heart.

"And then there was last year. We invited a group of new members in after Joker Night, and to all of our horror, Percy realized that the girl we let in was his soulmate. It was a race against the clock to break the curse before the curse broke him."

Her finger glides across the board before landing on a face I know too well, a smiling, freckled Emoree Hale. Beneath it, a ripped-out newspaper article of the tower, the scene sectioned off with police tape and her mangled body covered with a black tarp.

Emoree Hale sat on a wall,
Emoree Hale had a great fall.

"I can see the pattern, thank you very much. So, you're saying Em dated Percy, and he murdered her for it," I snarl, stepping back from the corkboard graveyard.

Paranoia gurgles low in the pit of my stomach before raising the room several degrees hotter than it should be. A nauseous hot-and-cold wave ripples down my spine, and I don't like this setup at all.

The group shares a look that has me cursing myself for coming in here defenseless. I'm already envisioning my own forged autopsy and

105

all the countless ways they could shut me up for good and how I might look beneath the ground.

"I told you before, none of us ever wanted her dead," Calvin insists, his voice hitching in his throat halfway through. Behind him, Mallory is blinking back tears and fanning her cheeks, and Ash's cocky attitude has been swapped for a tense silence.

Calvin continues with a clench of his fists. "It was the curse, and her loss weighs on us every single day. Our club's whole existence is centered around breaking the curse, not continuing it."

"Bullshit." I have to laugh. It's sounds weird and strangled, and it makes me seem as hysterical as I feel right now. "Are you really going to act like a bunch of make-believe hocus-pocus killed her?"

Oliver clears his throat to intervene. "Magic is actually more scientific than people give it credit for. Personally, I rationalized the curse by inputting it into a formula. The variables being personal input, expressed intent, and—"

"You seriously believe that?"

"I'm not the type to subscribe to horoscopes and conspiracies, but this is actually happening, Violet," he answers, deadpan. "Anastasia was dabbling in the occult for years, so by the time she killed herself, she was well versed enough to know the impact of her sacrifice. She gave her own life to get ultimate revenge, and we're still dealing with the consequences today."

"You've got to be kidding me." I hiccup, more of that lunatic laughter bubbling from my throat. "You're not going to tell me this is about some dead lady. You, of all people, seemed rational, and now you're trying to get me to believe that the Lockwells are murdering their lovers because Casper the Friendly Ghost told them to? This is as far from 'scientific' as it gets."

Calvin's shoulders fall with a deep exhale. "Violet. You're telling me you didn't see anything in that maze? Or on the balcony, for that matter?"

I shudder in recollection and massage one of the scratches on my wrist. "I . . . It's not like I was a reliable witness Saturday night. Not after you had us all pregaming psychedelics as soon as we went in."

"If we did have psychedelics, do you think we would waste them on you?" Ash scoffs and shares a conspiratorial look with his girlfriend. "The party drinks were my idea, and I can assure you they were LSD-free."

I cage my arms together against my chest. "Even if I did believe this ridiculous story that my best friend just so happens to be dead because of a vengeful ghost, then—"

"Then where is Percy?" Birdie finishes.

Calvin's eyes rest miserably on the floor. "He's gone."

"Yeah, I'm sure he's hiding in Switzerland to wait this murder out, but I'd really like to hear from him."

Calvin drags his attention from the floor and blows out a measured breath. He levels his exhausted expression at me. His previously perfect face is marred by severe black eye bags I hadn't noticed before. "No, Violet, you're not getting it. He's *gone*. Poof. Nowhere."

Birdie sneers at Oliver. "What happened to him being at Le Rosey?"

"It was the only thing I could think of," he apologizes as he readjusts his frames on his face. "It wasn't personal."

She folds her arms to her chest, and for the first time in the last five minutes, she's looking at me again. "Do I have a sticker on my forehead that says 'Hello, world, please lie to me' or something?"

I know I should try to fix things with her, but my eyes are now glued to the photo before me. "Was the cause of Emoree's death a lie?"

The lenses of Oliver's glasses fog over with a hot breath as he gasps. "Last year shouldn't have happened," he chimes back in, methodically cleaning his glasses in lieu of looking up at us. He loses himself to the task, rubbing the same circle repeatedly without stopping. "It was an anomaly. Completely and totally unprecedented. It broke every part of the curse's formula. In a normal timeline, Emoree would've been found"—his composure breaks, and he pauses his hands where they are, staring down miserably as the words lodge in his throat—"in the maze with a fatal chest wound and Percy would've been beside her, shaking off the last bits of possession. In this case, E-Emoree actually *did* die after falling from the tower, and Percy was nowhere to be found."

Calvin picks up where Oliver leaves off. "Percy's not the type to get up and flee the country either. Even if he did, we would've seen a withdrawal from his bank or a flight ticket purchase or something. He woke up one day and was never seen again . . . and we have reasons to believe the curse is involved somehow."

Spurred by Calvin's declaration, Ash kicks his legs up on the end table and turns to him like he's been waiting for this part. "What do you say, Cal?" he asks, though he doesn't sound nearly as playful as he normally does. "Should we do a magic trick of our own and show them?"

Mallory might be gripping a mascara-blobbed tissue, but her eyes light up at Ash's question. "God, I freaked when I first saw it. You two aren't ready," she says with a final sniff.

Calvin grimaces. "I'm glad my brother's disappearance is funny for someone."

"No, mate, I didn't mean it like that—"

Sadie squares her shoulders and takes several steps to reach her brother's side. "He's right, let's show them. It's the quickest way to prove what we're talking about."

I watch as Calvin's shoulders lift and fall with a measured breath before he gives her a tiny nod and the two of them hold their phone screens out for us to see.

"Percival Vincent Lockwell," Sadie whispers, and for once her tone is soft and pleading like a little sister tugging on her brother's sleeve.

Calvin's voice wavers, but he joins his sister in chanting out his brother's full name. "Percival Vincent Lockwell."

It's only after the third round that their phones illuminate with a message, Percy's text flashing in unison on their screens.

I'm going to end this

That's all it says, and it's easy to imagine their snickering older brother in the other room, pressing send as soon as he hears the signal. The perfect parlor trick to scare us. Then the text sends again. The exact same message but doubled, tripled. Their wallpapers are eclipsed with the same words over and over again. I'M GOING TO END THIS on a terrifying electronic loop, several hundred messages spawning in a matter of minutes before a heat warning flashes and the phones power off.

"That was his last message to us," Sadie sighs, and with a tap of her finger, her phone returns to life. The screen is blank like the last two minutes never happened, and when she finds her group message with Calvin and Percy, there's only one iteration of his text.

And it was sent last fall.

Birdie clenches a hand over her mouth, but all I can do is stand there. Stubborn tears prick in the corners of my eyes, and I swat at them before they can fall. I can't do this. *I can't do this!*

I stagger back two steps at a time, wanting to place as much distance as I can between myself and this crazy situation.

"You didn't strike me as the type of person who's easily scared," Calvin says, and he's right, I'm not, but that's because there's always been an explanation. Logic hiding behind every bump in the night.

My own haunted message loops in my brain, *find Percy*, over and over and over again. What good will my revenge do if I'm finding a sack of bones and asking it to confess? And if this truly is a curse and not cold-blooded murder, there's nothing for me to prove and no way to get closure. How do you get justice when the culprit has been dead for over a hundred years?

No, no, it's not possible. It *isn't* possible.

"I'm not scared," I snap. "I'm just not the type of person who likes wasting time."

Sadie's the first to speak up again as I storm my way over to the office door. "Where are you going?"

I turn back with my hand gripping the knob. "Anywhere but here."

11

There's a mummy in the dorm hall.

Luckily, it's the toilet paper kind.

"Don't snitch to the RA," Amber says the moment I step inside. It's about a month too early for Halloween, but the decorations are already in full swing. She's got three bundles stolen from the girls' bathroom and she's currently in the process of mummifying her door in one-ply rolls. Her roommate—a girl whose name I never bothered to learn despite hearing it ten times—is assisting her with duct tape and moral support.

"You have my blessing to steal it all," I tell her as I rummage around in my pockets for my keys. I was in such a mad scramble to get out of the Cards meeting, but now that I'm back in the dorms, I've returned to the land of logic. Storming off and leaving has been replaced by a carefully laid exit plan: pack my belongings, call my mom to come and get me, and then discuss with the registrar's office how to get my transfer initiated. Once I get home, I'll plan out my next move.

Still, I can't help but feel wrong for it all. Emoree's face is forever seared in my mind, *find Percy* stitched beside her gap-toothed grin. My whole reason for coming here is muddied in a single instant.

"Where's Birdie?" Amber asks innocently. Her tone might've

fooled me if I wasn't so good at detecting the jealousy lodged in her throat. It's been there since Sunday morning when she'd loitered in our doorway in pink silk pajamas.

"Mom said she'd order pity brunch for us if you'd like to have a consolation-prize picnic today. Who gives a shit about the Cards, anyway?"

Birdie had wet her lips, her eyes shyly darting to mine before lifting a Queen of Hearts in the air. I had followed suit. "Sorry, Amber."

Amber's smile had wavered on her face, disappearing for only a second before it returned with strained force. "C-celebration brunch, then."

She's wearing the same look now: a flash of white teeth, a crinkle of her nose, smiling and yet looking utterly dejected all at once.

"Back in the House of Hearts," I answer truthfully, and she nods as if she expected that but still doesn't like the answer.

"That makes sense," she says, busying herself with a piece of Velcro on the door. "Totally explains why she hasn't texted back yet. I was going to ask if you guys wanted matching dorm decorations, but . . . another day, probably."

I'll be long gone in a week, but I can't fight the need to comfort her in some small way. Despite it all, Amber and Birdie have been nothing but nice to me—until I messed everything up with Birdie and torched our relationship to the ground. "I'm sure she'd love that. Your door looks awesome."

That seems to shake some of the jealousy away, and she beams proudly at her hard work. "Liz and I did a good job, huh?"

Liz—whose name I will promptly forget again in the next hour— flashes me a rubber band smile, her braces a bright neon pink. "I made it as historically accurate as possible."

"Yeah." Amber snorts. "My googly eyes were vetoed."

With that, she whips out her camera to snap photos of her door for the *Herald*. I'm not sure promoting your own arts and crafts on the front page counts as heavy-hitting journalism, but I can't deny it's front-page-worthy.

It's definitely well done. There are the four sons of Horus depicted in construction paper jars and Velcroed in place under the door handle. Back in ancient Egypt, they'd remove the stomach, liver, lungs, and intestines and leave only the heart intact—the core of someone's being.

My stomach is intact, but I think my brain might be in a jar somewhere.

It's the only explanation for why my clothes are on the floor.

The fine print here is that this is the third time I was absolutely, undeniably positive I put everything in my suitcase and the third time that my entire wardrobe has somehow ended up back on the floor. So I pack it all up again. But like clockwork, I blink or spin around or breathe wrong and boom, everything scatters on the ground.

"I really am losing my mind," I say, first to myself and then to a folded pair of socks I've just placed in my bag. I say it out loud like some sort of countercurse, and then I stand there and wait with my eyes wide open. A second passes. Ten seconds pass. I'm about to laugh to myself that I really *am* losing it, and then a dry gust of air hits my eyes and I blink and the socks are on the floor by my feet.

And this time the entire suitcase has not only tipped over onto its side, but it's been flung impossibly across the room and landed face-down on Birdie's bed.

This doesn't bode well for keeping it together. Forget the suitcase, then. I stagger back out of the room and scratch "packing" off my mental to-do list. I choose to hightail it out of there instead, swinging the door back behind me and ignoring Amber's confused calls as I stumble my way into the courtyard. The sun is low in the distance, but it's a welcome sight compared to the harsh fluorescents of my dorm room and the static crinkle of electricity.

The damp lawn squelches against my heels, wet grass soaking into my black tights as I maneuver off the cement path and trudge through the lawn. It's quicker to cut directly across to the main parking lot, and all I want is to be out of here this very second.

I cradle my phone to my ear and count the rings as I try to call my mom. Each ring has me gritting my teeth harder, my fingers clammy against the sides.

VOICEMAIL FULL

Goddamn it, Mom. I could be dying over here. I try again. Nothing. Knowing her, she likely skipped her break and chose to let someone else take her fifteen instead, which means I'm shit out of luck until her shift ends at midnight.

I'm ten seconds away from chucking my phone in the lake when I hit the wall. One moment I'm walking, and the next I'm flat on my ass, wincing as I recover from the impact. I guess that's what I get for not looking where I'm going, but Mom's going to freak out when I tell her I spontaneously want to go home this very second, and, oh, by the way, I've also got a black eye.

I hiss at the lingering waves of pain before risking a peek up at the wall that did me in.

Except . . .

Except there isn't a wall.

The space before me is a wide stretch of absolute nothingness. Open air for miles on either side of me. That's not possible.

I lift shakily to my feet and take an experimental step forward, and all at once I feel the sudden, inexplicable rush of air pulling me back. Just like in the dorm room. Again I step forward, and again I'm flung back. Gentler this time, like a child getting scolded for standing too close to a hot stove.

"Sorry I didn't catch you this time," a familiar voice says behind me. I turn, and Calvin is there, an infuriating shadow in the shape of a man. "You look..."

I gesture at the force field of pure nothingness before me. The words leave my throat in a sticky heap: "I was trying to pack my socks but they kept falling out of my bag and now there's this wall but it's air and I can't leave and I feel like I'm losing my mind and... and..."

I must look extraordinarily pitiful because Calvin lowers himself to the ground and offers me a hand I hesitantly take. He pulls me to my feet and steers me in the opposite direction.

"Where are we going?"

He uses his free hand to rustle through his hair. "Somewhere I always go to clear my head."

Nothing says "my daddy owns a yacht" like attending a private academy with a boathouse.

"This is where you clear your head?" I ask, staring up at the sun-bleached building at the same moment I register that we're still holding hands. I rectify that sin immediately and yank my arm away. Clearing my throat, I fight to keep my voice even as I say, "On a swan boat?"

"The alternative is lying on the ground, hyperventilating," he returns. "Personally, I prefer my panic attacks with a nice view."

"You're right, it's much better to hyperventilate on open water."

He doesn't let my sarcasm phase him. He yawns like he's tired of our banter. The end of his shirt lifts to expose his navel, and because I'm a human being with eyes, I notice his sun-kissed skin and the particularly hypnotizing freckle beneath his belly button. I make a point to look anywhere but at him.

"Fine," I say. "On to the swan boats."

The only living soul inside the boathouse is a Black woman in her late seventies. Her thin hands clutch a *Swimming World* magazine, and she regards us with a lift of her right brow. It's not lost on me that she's sporting a boatneck top in a nautical blue-and-white sailor's print, complete with a sterling silver sailboat pin.

"That's Ms. Austin, the boat keeper," Calvin whispers conspiratorially to me. "She swam the English Channel thirty years ago—I know that because she's told me nine times."

"Will she even let us take a boat out this late?"

"Believe me," he breathes, flashing me a wink. "I'm basically like a grandson to her."

He directs his attention back to the woman behind the counter and rearranges his face into an ear-to-ear smile. "Ms. Austin! Just the woman I wanted to see. You wouldn't mind if I took a swan out for a spin, would you? We'll be back before curfew, promise."

He's right, she does look at him like a grandson—specifically one she knows is full of shit. "Really, now, Calvin?" She plays along with a tap of her nails against the desk. "You'll make it around the lake and back in fifteen minutes?"

HOUSE OF HEARTS

He rests his elbows on the desk. "Of course. If you could swim the English Channel in, what, five minutes, you don't think I can paddle across this measly lake in fifteen?"

She scoffs, but I can see that in her mind she's wading through icy salt water, her chest heaving as she makes the arduous journey across the sea. "More like thirteen hours, young man."

I tune out their conversation, my eyes drifting beyond Ms. Austin to the wall behind her.

Despite the clearly new boats and dock, the boathouse itself is a relic. The brick wall behind Ms. Austin's back might be aged, but a black-and-white portrait paints a picture of when it was newly erected. There's a team of students standing at the forefront, each one with an oar in hand and their name scrawled in thin cursive.

Phillip Green, Martin Hoadley, J. Wellington Wales, Oleander Lockwell.

Oleander. Before he became immortalized in this school forever, was he really just another student?

Calvin's voice continues beside me. "You could swim it again this year."

She rolls her eyes. "With this bad hip? Not likely."

"Pat Gallant-Charette swam it at sixty-six. You could beat her record."

Her eyes brighten at the possibility. "I do miss it. Winds were wild that day, and not even halfway in, I was stung by a jellyfish. Don't even get me started on the dehydration—"

She's prepared to recount her story for the tenth time when Calvin interjects. His hand splays convincingly behind me, his fingertips hovering an inch above my skin. Heat radiates from his almost-touch, and

117

I stiffen to attention. "Ms. Austin, this is riveting, truly, but I hope you don't mind if we finish up next time? I'm not one to keep a girl waiting on a first date."

She reluctantly waves him forward, but shouts "no more than fifteen minutes" at our backs.

"I wouldn't dream of taking longer!" he replies, and something in my gut tells me we'll be at least thirty.

Ahead of us, two flocks of swan boats wait at the end of the runway to the pier. They're poised like ballerinas, their wooden necks arched gracefully my way. Calvin helps me into the first one on our right, and I glare up at him from the bench.

"Tell someone we're on a date again, and I'll send you overboard."

"You can always tell them it was the worst date you've ever had," he retorts sweetly, his eyes meeting mine beneath a canopy of dark blond lashes before he directs the boat away from the pier.

"You heard that one, huh?"

"I hear everything, Violet."

All around us, the world is alive in wet color—it's a painter's palette of leafy green lily pads, lavender water willows, and deep, shadowed water. I can easily envision a Shakespearean Ophelia draped in a garland of wildflowers, still singing as the water drags her under. The perfect canvas for a poetic death.

"It is peaceful out here," I admit.

"Percy loved it, too," he mumbles, shy suddenly now that he's not being a smug jerk.

For a long moment, neither of us speaks. The only sounds are a toad bellowing in the duckweed and the soft churn of our boat cutting through the water.

"I know that was a lot to soak in back at the House," he says. "It couldn't have been easy for you."

Huge understatement, but I don't fight him. I focus my energy on the space beyond his shoulder. The sun has melted into the silhouette of the trees.

"You know why I came here," I say finally.

He hums in response. "I assumed your mission was to personally drag me down to hell."

"A lovely thought," I acknowledge, "but no."

Against the storybook backdrop, Calvin looks like a prince. A crown of golden hair and a regal brow, looking down on me like I'm a frog he's supposed to kiss. "You did come to ruin me, right? Or at the very least, my family?"

I ignore the frenzied beating of my heart. "I wanted to haunt you, actually." I clutch the pendant slung around my neck. He tracks the movement with a bob of his throat. "I just never expected to get haunted in the process."

"As I recall, you don't believe in ghosts."

"I didn't, but—" The words are small through my teeth. "I had every intention of leaving this campus today, but Emoree wouldn't let me. She wanted . . ." I swallow and blow out a breath. "She wanted me to find your brother. That's what she sent along with this locket, but I don't know *how* I'm supposed to do that now or why, if it's true, he's not fully to blame."

He's fixated on the sway of cattails in the distance. "Our goals aren't so dissimilar, Violet. You want to find Percy. We want to find Percy. You want to get revenge for Em, and honestly, so do we. This curse has been tearing us apart for generations now. It quite literally forces us to hurt the ones we love the most."

My chest pangs at the idea of that. It's a world away from the picture I had of Percy a week ago: a conniving, two-faced killer ready to kiss her and discard her without a care in the world. It's nearly impossible to imagine him genuinely caring for Em.

I stare miserably at the water as it darkens minute by minute, burning away to a deep, fathomless black. "If Percy knew about the curse, why did he let himself fall in love with Emoree?"

"I don't think it works that way."

I shrug. "Doesn't it?"

"No," he retorts quickly, "that's why it's called falling. You'd have to be insane to jump in the first place."

I flinch at his wording, and it takes a split second for him to catch why. He winces apologetically before shifting directions. "I don't think Percy meant to fall for Emoree; it's all part of this curse business. The curse knows what's bound to happen before it even begins, and once it starts, there's no stopping it. Though it didn't stop my mother from trying to—never mind."

"To what?" I pry, turning back to face him.

He bristles like he's been snagged on a thorn.

"She was planning an arranged marriage," he explains, a stiffness to his voice. "Funny thing about being cursed, it doesn't stop your family from playing matchmaker. I think it might have incentivized it, actually.

"She knew there was no getting around the curse once in love, but she let herself believe she could end it. In a horrible way it makes sense, right? Mom picks out a daughter-in-law like a pedigreed broodmare, and no one has to die because Percy doesn't love her. A win-win. Except there's no dodging fate. Percy met Emoree when she transferred last year, and . . . well, you know the rest."

HOUSE OF HEARTS

We've reached the other side of the lake now, and Calvin expertly steers us back toward the pier. "I assume you've got a wife lined up, too? Or did your mom give up on that?"

He snickers. "Why? Are you interested?"

"In no way, shape, or form."

Calvin lets his free hand hang over the edge, his fingertips skimming across the water. "No, it was always 'the heir and the spare' with me and Percy. Percy is not only the oldest; he's also the smartest, the most talented, the most, well, everything—which means everything hinges on his continued success. The rest of us? *Psh.* As long as our mug shots aren't plastered on the news, the family doesn't care. But, for Perce, Mom had big hopes for him. And let's just say scholarship girls are great for charity and statistics, but they're not marriage material."

"She didn't like Em?"

He examines a speck on his sleeve. "She didn't like the fact that he was doomed to kill her—as most mothers wouldn't, I imagine. But even beyond the curse business, it was all about what Emoree represented. Her mother works at a laundromat. Her father, the mill. It was out of the question."

If this were a cartoon, you could count on me to have smoke out of my ears at this point. "So that's it, huh? She's not good enough for your family?"

He winces at my tone, but I'm not done. "Her mother slaves away at her job—wakes up at the crack of dawn to get to the laundromat and takes care of everything. The owners live out of state, and they don't lift a finger for that place. And if we're speaking of fingers, her father has lost two to the machines at his factory job. They're hardworking, good people; their jobs are a lot harder than your mother's. How dare she? How dare you—"

He lifts his hands up. "Don't shoot the messenger. I don't care how

121

many fingers the man has or doesn't have. It's my mother. She's obsessed with image and the 'betterment'—notice the air quotes, Violet; her words, not mine—of the family. I thought Emoree was perfectly lovely and I was happy for Percy.

"As long as it's a fling and nothing serious, she doesn't care. Percy was out here with heart eyes, and, trust me, no one expects *that* from me. No one expects anything from me at all, actually. I'm the resident fuckup of the family."

I'm still fuming, so there's no chance of me breaking out the world's smallest violin for him. "Excuse me if I don't feel bad for you."

Calvin looks at me like I'm not seeing him, or at least not the full scope of him. Like I've got some caricature in my mind.

"Don't worry, I wasn't expecting pity from you." He rolls his eyes and some of that stoicism washes away, and he's back to being thoroughly amused by the situation. "All I want is your help. If not for me or for Percy, do it for Emoree."

We're back across the lake when the wind picks up, and I know immediately that this night will be another cold one.

He's the first to get out, and when he offers a hand to hoist me up, I reluctantly take it.

"F-fine, I'll help. Only because I literally can't leave or pack my things or do anything and there's only one person in this world who would be trying to hold me back. It has to be Emoree. She wants me to figure this out." I dig my hands in my pockets and stare miserably at the pier beneath me. "Can you tell me something, though?"

He hums in approval.

"How much does the rest of the group actually care about Emoree?" I ask softly. "It almost feels like she's another face on the wall and not, y'know, *Emoree*."

HOUSE OF HEARTS

Calvin considers that as he looks back out to the lake. Water lilies reflect in his pupils, and I have a feeling that if I got even closer, I might be able to peer directly into the heart of him. "Em was a Card member, sure, but she was more than that. She was a friend, and what happened last year is something that none of us will get over for a long time. For Tripp and my sister, at least, they have a funny way of showing their grief, but if there's one thing that I've learned, it's that everyone has their own way to mourn."

I nod. I learned that the hard way.

Before I can say another word, Calvin shrugs off his crested jacket and flings it my way. It lands in a confusing heap in my arms, and I can't help the part of me that wonders if it will smell like him. Warm and sharp like spiced cider. "Huh?"

"I'm tired of hearing your teeth chatter," he says offhandedly. "Plus, you're no help to any of us if you get sick."

"Wow, chivalry isn't dead after all," I deadpan. My eyes dart between him and the red blazer and then back up again. "Y-you know it's a myth that cold weather gets you sick, right?"

He shrugs lazily and makes a move to swipe it back. "If you're not cold, I'll take it back—"

"Buuut on second thought, clearly curses and ghosts exist, so s-screw science. I'm freezing." Before he can reclaim it, I burrow into the jacket and relish in his residual body heat. The sleeves are comically long on me, and he snorts at the sight.

"You can give it back to me tomorrow at our first official club meeting. Five o'clock. I trust you know where to go by now," he teases, already walking away from me down the pier.

I wrap the jacket tighter against my shoulders. I was right; it does smell like him.

I clench my fists at my sides and call him with a taunting "Lockwell."

"Hmm?" he asks, twisting to look back at me over his shoulder.

"This was the worst first date I've ever had."

Dear Diary,

No one can know what I have created.

My grimoire is the child of several texts from my father's rare book collection and my own fiendish imagination. Night after night, I have worked diligently to scour through old Latin and keep my curses under lock and key. Not only would this secret be my societal undoing, but I fear the reactions of my family if they knew.

Mother would be devastated. Father, irate. And Helen? There was a time growing up when we were inseparable. We still wear the same lockets slung around our throats and whisper to one another during Father's "episodes," but we are no longer close by any stretch of the imagination. Still, I fear she would be hurt to know of the secrets I am keeping now.

None of that is enough to stop me.

Last night, I began my first spell to bind the maze to myself. With my father's vigilant eye and my sister's meddling, I need a place where I'm free to meet with Oleander without the nagging sensation of being watched. No one can follow me here unless I wish to be found. The maze will be my own corner away from the world.

The ritual was simple enough to perform. Under the pregnant swell of the moon, I slashed my palm against the hedges and watched, horrified and enraptured, as they lapped my blood up like a newborn calf. There was no immediate change—the world didn't burn blue with the tinge of black magic and the wind didn't whistle my name. Nothing happened, and yet there was that intrinsic *knowing* that it had worked.

I knew then that the maze was mine, and I knew it always would be.

—Anastasia Hart

12

I've been at this school for ten days, and what do I have to show for it?

A newfound fear of ghosts.

Several concerned texts from my mother (Are you making friends? When are you coming home again? Do you know where I could've put my keys?).

And a roommate giving me the silent treatment.

"Birdie, can you pass me the pepper?" I ask, pointing down at my already perfectly seasoned lamb chop. Flavor be damned, I'll bury my tray in salt and pepper if it means forcing her to look in my direction.

Emoree was never the "simmering, quiet rage" type. She was blubbering tears and rambling word-vomit, slammed doors and balled notes thrown at my back. Meanwhile, Birdie acts like I never opened my mouth in the first place.

"Pass the pepper, Bird," Amber says before volleying a puzzled look between the two of us.

Birdie pushes it to Amber, and Amber pushes it to me, and it feels like we're in the middle of a divorce proceeding, fighting over who gets to keep the house.

"Can I get some salt, too, Birdie?" I ask, fighting the impulse to say *You can keep the kids, too, I don't care.*

Birdie says absolutely nothing in response to that. She swirls a spoon in her Mediterranean couscous in lieu of looking at me. Amber opens her mouth to play mediator again, but finally Birdie groans and sends the salt skidding across the table.

"Will someone tell me what the hell is going on?"

Oliver shrugs from behind his open copy of *Clandestine Communication: The Art of Breaking Ciphers*. "Something petty, I presume." He flips a page absently.

"Here I was, happy that you guys didn't ditch me for the Cards table," Amber huffs, the type of anger I'm used to. She pushes her tray forward with a stubborn pout. "But now it feels like I'm sitting in the middle of a second Cold War."

"Which one of us is Russia?" I ask at the same time Birdie blurts, "We would never leave you, Amber."

Birdie throws me a dark look, but at least she's looking at me. "You're right, this whole thing is childish. Give us a second to sort things out, okay?" Then, to me: "Violet, do you mind?"

That's all the indication I get to grab my things as she storms out into the hallway. My rubber soles scuff the linoleum as I chase after, and this time, I know it's not my imagination when I feel eyes on my skin. Calvin cranes his neck to follow me as I leave, and his stare burns long after I've closed the door.

"Do you know how much I blamed myself for her death?" She whirls on me after a tense moment, her eyes wet with runny mascara. "When she transferred here, it was *my* job to take her under my wing and . . . and, God. I spent this whole summer thinking if I had been a better roommate, a better friend, that I could've saved her. No one even invited me to the funeral."

I open my mouth, but she shakes her head. "When you came, I wanted things to be different. I promised myself I'd be the best roommate I could, that I'd always be by your side and be a shoulder for you to cry on ... and ... and ... I want us to be honest with each other."

I lower myself to the tile and cradle my knees to my chest.

"I'm sorry," I say, and I hope she knows I mean it. "I wanted to tell you, I really did, but I was scared. I thought if I said the wrong thing to the wrong person, I'd be kicked out and I'd never learn what really happened to her." I paw at my own eyes now to stubbornly keep the tears from trickling down.

"She was like a sister to me, but near the end, there were times when she called and I would sit and let it go to voicemail because I was so stupidly jealous of her new life. If anyone should've been there for her, it's me. So, don't blame yourself."

Birdie wrings her hands, and her shoulders deflate with a sigh. "I get why you lied," she whispers, "but can you promise me you won't keep things from me again? I really do want to be friends, but I really can't handle a repeat of last year."

"Promise," I whisper, and her pinkie locks with mine.

And this time, I hope I can keep it.

"Am I interrupting a human sacrifice or something?"

The "or something" moment tonight involves Calvin splayed out on the meeting-room floor like a half-naked art model, his bare chest littered with strange sigils, and Oliver looming above him with an uncapped red Sharpie.

"Yeah, you'll want to come back later when I'm either levitating or dead," Calvin drawls. His composure disappears as soon as Oliver starts drawing on his chest, and he squirms like he's auditioning for another *Exorcist* movie.

"Why not both?" Ash deadpans from behind a monstrous stack of books. The texts range from Greek binding spells to Elizabethan-era magic.

"Good call, Ash. You're right, come back when I'm levitating *and* dead. That'll be more interesting."

"You'll only be dead if you don't stop moving," Oliver grunts, pressing his knee down on Calvin's chest to keep him from wiggling around. "You're making me draw squiggles."

"Sue me. I'm ticklish."

I bury my hands in my pockets. "I'm relatively new to the woo-woo scene, so would someone like to fill me in on what's happening here?"

"I'm testing out countercurse sigils," Oliver tells me, like it's really that simple. "It wouldn't take immediate effect since Calvin isn't the eldest child, but it doesn't hurt to try things out."

"And you think a Sharpie doodle will do anything?" I ask, wincing afterward at my own attitude. It's only day one on not being a naysayer, and old habits die hard.

"I was trying to tell you earlier," he says, adopting a lecturing tone like a weary professor. "I don't believe that science and magic are separate entities. I believe they run parallel. I mean, hell, look at math, for example. Irrational numbers were discovered by a Pythagorean cult—an entire group who believed the secrets of divinity lie within mathematics. I'm not saying we doodle $a^2+b^2=c^2$ on him, but maybe there is some stock in the belief that the supernatural world is more connected to reality than you think."

130

HOUSE OF HEARTS

I peek down at his handiwork. "So, if that's not the Pythagorean theorem on his chest, what is it, exactly?"

"It's a hexafoil."

"You told me it was a daisy wheel," Calvin sputters beneath Oliver's knee. His voice hitches at the end with another ticklish bout of laughter.

"I told you that because you wouldn't know what a hexafoil is."

"*Hey.*"

"Was I wrong?"

"...No."

Oliver caps his marker and stands up. What's left in his wake is a six-petal rosette in the center of Calvin's ribs. "It's a form of counter-magic typically found on buildings and doors to ward off evil spirits, but since this curse is affecting the Lockwell bloodline, I thought it might be worth a try."

"Enough with the hexafoil," Tripp whines from over on his laptop, which has—to absolutely no one's surprise—a *Saturday Is for the Boys* sticker. "I'm doing my own research over here."

"Speaking of that, what *do* you actually research?" Birdie walks in and does her best to sidestep a still-wriggling Calvin.

I appraise today's level of chaos. There are more books at Ash's side than on all of the ceiling-length bookshelves combined. Beyond that, even the checkered floor has grown more cluttered—emptied backpacks littering the Persian rug and spilling out onto the glossy tile beneath.

"Good question." Sadie beckons us over to the somewhat-organized center. The table sits in the eye of the storm.

"We like to divide and conquer so that we can cover more ground," she says, taking a sip of black tea before setting it back in the saucer.

The porcelain cup is bloodied by red Chanel lipstick. "Ash, Mallory, and Oliver are in the curse division. Since Ash is a polyglot, he's studying the linguistic component of spell work. Oliver's got his whole 'sacred geometry' thing going on and is using that to study sigils and runes. Meanwhile, Mal studies the anatomical elements of possession—basically, what happens to the body when a ghost hitches a ride."

"And, uh . . . what's Tripp doing in the corner?"

"Oh, he's on Reddit."

I can't help it. I laugh.

"Hey, man, don't fucking knock it," he jeers, pointing at us from behind a crushed can of Monster Energy. "I spent at least five hours in the subreddit trenches yesterday looking up the Grimaldi family curse. You're looking at someone who knows way too much about Grace Kelly now."

"What does Grace Kelly have to do with anything?"

"Love curses, dude. The Grimaldi family was cursed to never find happiness in marriage. Bada bing, bada boom, seven hundred years later and the whole family is still going through it."

I clear my throat. "So, if they have countercurses and Tripp has . . . Reddit . . . what does that leave for us?"

Sadie stirs a spoon in her teacup and drags her focus back to us. "I'm studying the founding family and gathering information on Anastasia Hart. You'll be joining me in that, Violet." Her eyes slice Birdie's way. "As for you, you'll be teaming up with Calvin to investigate the soulmate element, specifically constructing a file on everything we know about Em and Percy as our most recent—and best-known—examples."

Calvin starts to stand up, but before he can spend the rest of this meeting strutting around shirtless, I pull his blazer from my backpack and shove it against his chest. I draw my hand back immediately after

HOUSE OF HEARTS

because the last thing I want to do is catch cooties or the plague or whatever the hell he has that makes me unable to look at him for too long.

"And who is looking for Percy in all of this?" I ask in an attempt to shift my thoughts.

Sadie tenses at the name, her knuckles burning white against her thighs. "All of us. We spent all summer searching this godforsaken campus and couldn't find him. We've resorted to doing weekly séances in some of his most frequented locations. If he really is . . . d-dead, he'd likely want to linger in an area that meant something to him. We're planning on trying another one here tomorrow."

My brain balks at the idea of a Hasbro Ouija board, but I have to remind myself that logic's been thrown out the window. We're no longer in my domain. "Got it."

"Now, if you don't mind, let's not waste any more time," Sadie says tartly, her sour attitude a clever disguise for her watering eyes. She beckons me with a stern finger. "Violet, if you'd join me over here."

I throw one last fleeting look at Birdie before trudging toward my fate. Sadie sits primly in the corner of the room with a collection of old boxes and photos around her. She waits until everyone's occupied to whisper to me out of earshot. "Can I trust you not to run off again?"

My fists waver against my sides. "That was—"

She shuts me up before I can finish. "I don't care about your excuses. I care about my brother. Don't make me repeat myself again. Can I trust you?"

I nod.

She squints like she doesn't buy it but relents anyway. "Okay, then, let's get to work." God only knows how long we spend wading through research in near-total silence. The only times Sadie opens her mouth are when she's sliding something over to show me, and even then it's mainly her nail doing the talking.

This time, it's not a photograph she's tapping on but a rather complicated family tree.

"Ernest Hart only had two daughters, so in a sense, the academy was his way of carrying on his name." I follow the almond tip of her fingernail from Ernest down to his two daughters. "We all know what happened to Anastasia's branch . . . and as for Helen, she ceased to be a Hart the day she married Oleander."

Beneath her name, there's a bevy of children and grandchildren, and we follow the path from eldest child to eldest child until we make it to Meredith Lockwell-Kirkland.

"I didn't know your name was hyphenated."

Sadie shrugs. "'Sadie Lockwell' sounds a lot better than 'Sadie Lockwell-Kirkland,' don't you think? Plus, my mom says his name is a waste of space on the birth certificate."

I blink down at Arthur Kirkland and his alleged waste-of-space name. "Erm, is he your mother's . . . ?"

"Soulmate?" Sadie scoffs. "Hell no. They tolerate each other, but they're not in love by any stretch of the imagination. Her soulmate is dead. My dad was actually in the Cards when it happened"—"it" carrying the implied weight of supernatural murder—"and marrying Mom was his consolation prize for not breaking the curse . . . or his punishment, depending on who you ask."

We move past her mother's marital problems to photos of the school's construction ("Tripp thought it might be like the Winchester Mystery House") and, finally, the maze itself.

"It was relatively common to build elaborate graves before peo-

HOUSE OF HEARTS

ple died, though it had to have been unsettling to play in your own future cemetery as a child," Sadie says, pointing at the black-and-white images of standing mausoleums. A whole family of graves waiting to swallow up the dead: Ernest, Adaline, Anastasia, and Helen. "Oleander and the others are buried in a separate plot. I don't think anyone would have blamed Helen if she decided to be buried alongside him, but she chose to honor her late parents' wishes. Plus, she also felt guilty, I'm sure."

I pick at the skin around my thumb. "Speaking of Oleander . . . I saw his face in the boathouse. Was he a student here? Is that how this all started?"

She nods and digs through her stack of papers before retrieving a student acceptance form for him. "Hart Academy had recently made the shift toward becoming coeducational—one of the first boarding schools nationwide to do so—which meant he was a new student alongside Helen and Anastasia. According to Oleander's entrance interview, he'd lost someone close to him and needed a change of scenery. Plus, he was amazing at rowing, and Ernest Hart wanted to send their team to State, so he was an instant transfer for junior year."

I hum at that. "And he immediately decided to start dating the Headmaster's daughters? Plural?"

"It started with Ana, singular. A lot of guys on campus would've gouged out their eyes instead of looking at her. Not that she wasn't pretty, but she was the baby of the family, and breaking her heart was a surefire way of getting on the Headmaster's shit list. He met her in the boathouse, and she shoved this first letter in his hand the next time she saw him."

She passes me a stack of yellowed papers in a protective clear sleeve. I'm delicate with them as I lift the pages closer.

Dearest stranger,

My father says I should not engage the men at this academy, but you make it hard to abide by the rules. I hope you don't think of me as a flirt for this letter. I promise I'm not so vain that I am only enamored by your appearance (though I must confess you cut a rather striking figure whilst on the rowing team). More than that, I am besotted by your gentle-hearted ways.

What was perhaps a stray moment for you has illuminated my entire week. You were kind enough to help me into one of these marvelous swan boats. Not only that, but you called me beautiful, which I must admit I do not hear often. When many others ran with their tail between their legs at my father's behest, you did not. What good is a headmaster for a father if he acts more in line with a prison warden? Am I not a soon-to-be marriageable woman?

But you probably aren't interested in my familial troubles. You must be wondering as to the purpose of this letter. Perhaps it is untraditional for a girl to speak her mind so freely, but I have always been one to follow my heart. I have grown rather fond of you and I would be more than delighted if you would respond to my correspondence with your name. How else might I daydream without one?

HOUSE OF HEARTS

> Yours if you wish it to be so,
> Anastasia Hart

PS: If you so desire, toss your response over the
locked gate of the hedge maze. Only I have the key to
retrieve it.

It almost feels too intimate for me to read. Nothing is overly sensational—what was she going to do, show him her ankle?—but to have one's heart laid bare for people to see over a hundred years later? I cringe at the thought of it.

"Did he respond?"

"Yeah, right away, actually. For a while there, the two seemed to hit it off, which I'm guessing made the betrayal sting even worse."

I take the next sheet, and while it's significantly shorter than hers, it's ten times more gag inducing.

> Dearest Anastasia,
>
> Perhaps your father was right in some regard. You are enchanting enough to make the male populace at Hart lose their heads. I confess that my own research lay neglected in the wake of your arrival into my life. There is no sweeter subject than you. So, tell me, Ana, when might I study you again?
>
> A scholar of the heart,
> O

137

"That was brutal," I groan, letting the letter fall back with the rest. "Who knew being an incorrigible flirt runs in the family?"

"I heard that," Calvin quips from his end of the room at the same time Ash mumbles the Latin "incorrigibilis."

"Good. You were meant to," I snap before looking back at the paper. "How could anyone fall for that?"

Sadie shrugs. "She was pretty sheltered most of her life and also a die-hard romantic. I'm sure she thought it was charming."

"Plenty of people find me charming."

"No one's talking about you anymore, Calvin."

He grumbles to himself but mercifully shuts up for the remainder of the meeting. The next time I hear from him, it's when he's standing up and cracking his knuckles. "I'm going to call it for today. I have a Curtis audition I need to practice for—Mom's been grilling me on it. If you hear screaming and crying in the other room, it's me."

The clock in the corner says it's five past curfew, but I know one flash of my card will have the RA turning a blind eye when I get back. It feels like the ultimate hall pass, so much so that I cornered Calvin in the cafeteria earlier to hammer out the specifics. Surely there had to be *some* things off-limits, right?

"How is it that we can fling our card around and do whatever the hell we want, no consequences?" I questioned, my voice a hushed murmur in the lunch line.

He'd placed a waxed apple on his tray and thrown a shrug back at me. "When your mom's the headmistress, people have a habit of looking the other way. She's pulled some heavy strings in the background to keep us running and functional. Besides," he continued, sinking his teeth into the red skin and swallowing down a chunk. His voice lowered to a haughty whisper. "Who gives a shit about detention when you're fighting a literal ghost?"

As much as I hate being a smug card-waver like the rest of them, I can't leave all this information behind now. Like I'm in some sort of waking dream, I worry that the instant reality comes ringing, all this will fade away.

I'm clearly the only one in the room with that sentiment because the rest of them gradually leave one by one. Tripp yawns and dismisses himself for the night with a two-finger salute; Mallory leaves immediately after; Oliver winces at his phone screen as he leaves at the several missed FaceTime attempts from Amber.

Birdie stands up next, and I prepare for some excuse to leave her lips, but instead of heading for the door, she walks our way.

"I think you need to swap us," she confesses after a quiet moment. Her hand slides against the back of her neck, and she shifts her eyes to the floor. "I might've been Emoree's roommate, but let's face it, Violet knows more about her than I ever will."

"Are you sure?" Sadie asks like she's waiting for Birdie to change her mind.

"I'm sure. I'm better at history anyway. Violet should take my place."

Sadie deliberates over that with a strained wince. "I was worried about Calvin looking for any excuse to screw around and not work, but I can tell *you're* serious, Violet. Fine. You're right. We'll switch."

I have no idea what I'm supposed to say, but Sadie doesn't give me time to think.

With an exhausted rub of her eyes, she says, "Well, I guess go let him know."

"Where is he?"

"Didn't you hear? Follow the screaming and crying."

I do the second-best thing and follow the sound of the piano.

The overall composition has "Calvin" written all over it. Dramatic, consuming, maudlin. The pianist is so enraptured with his music, he doesn't pay me any mind as I slip inside. Calvin's eyes are closed as his fingers fly across the keys in a Dionysian riot. The notes are equal measures haunting and romantic.

Piano Sonata No. 8 in C Minor, Op. 13, "Pathétique," the sheet reads.

Somewhere within the third movement, the melody falls off. The piece collapses in on itself like a house of cards, and Calvin pushes away from the keys with a snarl.

" 'Pathetic' is right," he mutters under his breath before turning to look at me. "Are you here to laugh at my expense?"

"Shockingly, no. I'm here to tell you that Birdie begged to switch, so now you're stuck with me."

He couldn't look more disappointed if he tried. "You?"

"That would be what I said, yes," I grit back, ignoring the painful stab in my chest at his tone. "Is that going to be a problem?"

"No, I'm sure it will be as wonderful as a root canal," he mocks sweetly. "Oh, sorry, that wasn't very incorrigibly flirtatious of me. Allow me to try again. Ahem. Shall I compare thee to a summer's day?"

"I don't know, shall you?" I challenge.

He glances appraisingly at me and breaks out into a wicked grin at long last. "Hardly. You're more like a winter's night with a frostbite advisory."

HOUSE OF HEARTS

I take an experimental step forward, and his Adam's apple bobs strangely in his throat, his grin faltering alongside it.

"Oh, really? And here I was about to nurse your wounded ego and tell you your song actually sounded pretty good."

"'Pretty good,'" he echoes, "is precisely the problem."

"Would you rather it sound bad?"

Any trace of humor vanishes. "Anything less than excellent is bad. The acceptance rate for Curtis is abysmal. I'm not just going up against the classically trained—I'm going against six-year-old prodigal reincarnations of Frédéric Chopin. Oh, and if that weren't bad enough, my mother keeps reminding me how perfect Percy's recital was. Because God forbid I forget I suck for even a half second."

"Who cares if you're the next Chopin?" I take a step forward and bury my hands in my pockets. "The man's not exactly who I'd pick to be. He died before he hit forty, and they pickled his heart in a cognac jar. I'd rather be pretty good and relatively happy than a majorly depressed prodigy."

Calvin lifts a brow. "Do you think Anastasia's heart is in a pickle jar somewhere, too?"

"Frankly, I'm surprised your sister didn't slosh it around at me on initiation night."

"She would've if she had it." He runs a tongue over his broken lip. I need to stop thinking about what his mouth looks like kiss-bitten and bruised. How it might feel to tug his lower lip between my teeth.

He surprises me by scooting over and gesturing for me to join him on the bench. The black and white keys remind me of the chessboard floor beneath our feet, the innate feeling of being a pawn in a much larger game.

"Your mom seems . . ."

"Terrible?" he offers. "That's because she expects us all to fall in line with her carefully orchestrated life plans. She had big dreams for Percy, erm, post-sacrifice, and now all those dreams are being thrust onto me."

I settle my weight beside him and try not to notice his closeness. "And your dad . . . Where is he in all of this? Sadie said he was a Card member when they met."

"Well, for three hundred and sixty-four days out of the year, you can find him on the golf course, but then he magically swoops in on Christmas to leave us gifts and get into a drunken screaming match with Mom in the hallway. Typical Hallmark holiday." His attention drifts my way with a curious arch of his brow. "What about your parents? Perfect and hopelessly in love?"

"Parent," I amend. "And far from it. My father dipped before I was born. He probably fled the scene when Mom showed him two pink lines."

"I'm sorry."

"Don't be." It's an old wound. I prod at it occasionally to see if it will manifest into anything, but usually it lies dormant. "My mom took it hard, but hey, what's new? When she's not falling in love, she's falling apart, and when she's falling apart, it's my job to piece her back together again." I don't mean to sound like some wistful Grecian heroine, but I'm afraid that's exactly how it comes off.

"Guess the guys she picks aren't real winners?" he asks carefully.

"Understatement." I do my damnedest to sound nonchalant about it. "She's got a type, and it's called 'deadbeat assholes.' "

I force out a strained laugh, and I'm thrilled that Calvin doesn't push it. He gracefully changes the subject with a press of his fingers against the keys. "Can you play?"

"What, the piano? No. I'm awful."

I feel the warmth of his hands before I register him standing up and draping his fingers over mine. His chest presses into the planes of my back, and I shudder at the rush of his breath, sticky and hot against my neck.

"Wh-what are you doing?"

He guides my fingers over the keys. "Helping you. You don't need therapy if you have a piano. I would know."

"Is that so?"

"Believe me." His breath ghosts against my skin, his chin settling in the junction between my shoulder and my throat. "I wrote the playbook on familial trauma."

"Oh, did you?" Our fingers glide together as he begins to play a song from muscle memory. "Hell, I might've co-written it."

His chuckle tickles the back of my head. "That depends, do you have siblings?"

"Only child."

"Lucky." He hums the word, and I feel it radiate across my skin. "You've met Sadie."

I sure have. "She's . . . a lot."

"Understatement," he parrots, and I swear I can hear him smiling. "She didn't always used to be like this. We actually used to be pretty close, but not anymore. She idolizes my mother to a sick degree, wants to walk and talk and act like her."

"And Percy?"

"Remember how I said he was better than all of us?" he asks, his voice achingly soft. "My brother was kind, hardworking, talented, and perfect. I used to hate him for all that. So many times I used to daydream about him dying—horrible, I know. I was convinced that with him gone, I'd be useful for once. Now look at me. He's disappeared, and

143

all I can think about is getting him back. Not even as a brother but as a barrier between me and my family's expectations."

I don't know what makes me do it, but I thread our fingers together for a single moment. I squeeze reassuringly.

"Sometimes I wonder if our séances always fall through because of me," he confesses, his voice barely above a whisper. "That he knows all these treacherous thoughts in my head and doesn't want to come back."

"Where have you been conducting these séances?"

"His childhood bedroom at least five hundred times. The Winthrop music department. His old dorm room. We'll be doing it here again tomorrow. All the places he loved and might linger in."

I'm admittedly new to this supernatural world, but I know how it felt when I saw *her*. Emoree had been an electric current, my arms tingling with the sensation of lightning touching down in the distance.

Sitting in here now, I don't feel anything particularly *supernatural*. Nothing that would suggest a ghost was setting up camp in the vicinity.

He carries us back through the song, only this time in reverse. I clear my throat. "What are you playing?"

"A crab canon. Think of it as a musical palindrome. To get the full effect of the song, you have to play it in retrograde." His chin grazes the soft flesh of my cheek, and I feel the heat of him on my back.

Retrograde.

"You're tense," Calvin accuses.

Neurons fire off all at once. How many times has my mother lost something and the first question out of my mouth was "*Where were you last?*"

"I think I have an idea."

"About?" His question tickles my cheek.

"Tomorrow's séance."

13

Here's an equation. Multiply "locked clock tower" by "Calvin not having the goddamn keys" and divide it by "Sadie being their mother's favorite," and you get the following: the three of us walking up to the headmistress's home Wednesday evening, waiting to ask if we can go up to the locked upper wing of the clock tower and have a séance, pretty please.

The house is exactly what I'd expect of the Lockwell matriarch. It's *Better Homes & Gardens* meets Plymouth Colony—a colonial clapboard monster on the edge of campus with a thin trim of greenery confined to the herringbone walkway. Everything is meticulous. Everything is perfect.

"I'll do the talking," Sadie establishes with a roll of her shoulders. Then, in case there were any questions, she clarifies to Calvin, "Because I'm the responsible one, for starters. I'm—"

"Humble, too," he drawls. He's dressed down from this morning in class, his tie loosened at his throat and his collar buttons undone.

She sneers, her Van Cleef bracelet stack winking in the porch light. "That's another reason right there. I'm less of a smart-ass."

He's miraculously silent as she punches in the door code. "Mom's running late, but she'll meet us in her study."

The inside foyer is wallpapered in vintage green floral. Painted ivy curls in every direction, dark leaves guiding us down a narrow hallway and to a private office room. Beneath our feet, the hardwood flooring is draped with a Persian rug, and somewhere in the distance, a grandfather clock chimes the hour.

It's about as charming as being escorted into the depths of hell.

"Here we are," Sadie says with a twist of an antique crystal knob.

The door yawns open and transports us to an era of candle smoke and parchment paper. A Tiffany floor lamp cuts through the gloom and casts a beacon down on a large mahogany desk in the center. It sits like a caged beast between a set of leather chairs, and Sadie's quick to claim the one on our side.

"You should see her in a game of musical chairs," Calvin comments with a sweep of his thumb across his skin. "Cutthroat."

"Am I supposed to apologize for sitting down?"

"You? Apologize? That'd be a first."

I ignore their banter in favor of studying the desk in front of me. It's remarkably empty but for a few stray pens, a scratch pad, and an old picture frame perched in the corner.

Photo Calvin is posed with his brother and sister, a rare group selfie of the three of them where they don't look like they all actively hate each other. Calvin's eyes are bright, but his grin is even brighter, his arm slung over Percy's shoulder and his other hand making bunny ears behind Sadie's head.

Percy is the perfect gradient between Calvin's sandy blond and Sadie's sleek black hair. Brown waves graze the soft slope of his jaw and match the warm depths of his eyes, his baby-fat cheeks giving him an endearingly poetic look. Large round frames rest on the bridge of his nose, which only complete the scholar vibe he's got going on. He's far

HOUSE OF HEARTS

from the ridiculously chiseled prince on a white horse, but I can see how Em fell for him.

"This is the last photo we took together," Sadie says. "Before everything fell apart."

I remember her outburst by the tower, and it's clear she's showing a lot of restraint. She's yet another girl who refuses to cry. I can relate.

"Was there anything special about that day?"

"It was only special because there was nothing happening. Everything was perfect and normal. The world looked bright, and then . . ."

She fidgets in her seat and runs a frazzled hand through her hair. "When Emoree came, that all went out the window. He was jittery, anxious, always zoning out like he was lost in his own head. He'd go missing for hours, and we'd find him wandering aimlessly through the gardens. It went downhill like this," she says, illustrating the severity with a jarring snap of her fingers.

"And then he just disappeared?"

"Precisely," Headmistress Lockwell's voice says from behind me.

I turn to find her hovering in the doorway like a Victorian ghost. She regards us with a dainty arch of her thin brows before breezing past the three of us to take a seat at her desk. "I trust you'll make this quick."

"Of course, we know your time is very valuable, Mom," Sadie says, her answer immediately met with a gag from Calvin. Sadie's smile thins, but she continues as rehearsed. "We need the skeleton keys for the tower. It's for the séance."

Headmistress Lockwell frowns at that. "The incident is fresh in everyone's minds. You'll need to be careful not to draw unnecessary attention."

Sadie nods sagely, and Calvin does his part by not saying a word.

147

He leans against the wall and busies himself with a cuff link on his sleeve.

"What makes you so sure Percy will respond to you up there?" the headmistress challenges.

Sadie's eyes flick briefly to mine, and I ball my fists in my lap before speaking. "It wouldn't be Percy we'd be channeling. It'd be Emoree."

The full weight of her stare settles on me. "You think she would prove useful?"

I grit my teeth at the word "useful." "She would know a lot more about Percy's final days than we would. From what I've heard, last year was atypical."

"That's putting it mildly, but yes," she agrees, leaning back in her chair as she contemplates our request. "I am not opposed to it, but I need the group to be discreet. No marching around in plain sight with a Ouija board and heading up to what is still widely considered a crime scene."

Sadie dips her head. "Yes, ma'am."

"We're calling her 'ma'am' now?" Calvin questions with a curl of his lip. "What's next, 'Your Majesty'? 'Supreme Maternal Overlord'?"

"Calvin Peregrine Lockwell."

Peregrine, huh? Definitely storing that one in my brain for later.

"We'll be careful," Sadie reassures. "I have everything under control—annoying twin brothers included."

Calvin only rolls his eyes at that before focusing on something beyond his mother's head. I follow his line of sight to an impressive glass curio cabinet tucked in the corner. If you sat me down and had me guess what a rich headmistress might collect, I'd probably say fine china or antique pocket watches. Genuinely anything under the sun other than what's actually on display.

I have to blink three times to make sure I didn't spontaneously conjure it out of thin air. But no, the dagger is 100 percent real and tucked safely inside a glass frame. The photo beside it shows a young Oleander with his father, dead pheasants at his feet and the same knife plunged into one of their chests. Blood drips down the sides of their limp throats, oozing into a puddle at Oleander's feet. The accompanying plaque beneath the image reads HART'S MOST CHERISHED ARTIFACTS.

"Is that knife the one that . . . um . . ." I can't believe I'm even speaking but also can't stop the question from flowing freely out of my mouth. "The one that you used on . . . your . . . um . . ."

Christ. Save me from myself.

"The one that killed my soulmate?" Headmistress Lockwell speaks plainly. "Yes."

My mouth goes dry all at once, and I blurt out the most obvious question in my brain. "Why would you keep it?"

Sadie throws me a dark look, but it's too late for me to discover tact in this situation. If Headmistress Lockwell is offended by my question, she doesn't show it. She's a careful portrait of restraint, her hands clasped cordially across the table. "For starters, everything Anastasia touched has a nasty habit of lingering. I could throw this blade away several hundred times and it would still find its way back to us. Secondly, it serves as a reminder of what I've lost and the life I've gained. I didn't think I'd want to live after Isaac, but look at me now."

I squint in response. She meets my eyes briefly before casting a wistful look back at the blade. "It taught me what is truly important. When you sacrifice love, you see the world more clearly for what it truly is—a chessboard game of kings and queens where you lose a pawn or two to scale ahead."

My breath escapes me in a short, indignant burst. "You think Isaac was a pawn?"

Her veneer chips faintly. I see it in the quiver of her lips and the press of her nails to her palm. "He was the love of my life and my greatest heartbreak, make no mistake. I think of him every single day, and I have for the last twenty-five years. But through the grief, I realized what that loss afforded me. I'm one of the few people on this planet who can go through life with minimal distraction. If my husband is disloyal, it doesn't destroy me in the slightest. I have a fulfilling career and three children I wouldn't have had otherwise. In the place of love, I have so much more."

"Two," Calvin amends.

"Excuse me?"

He lifts his attention up from his sleeve to his mother's desk. "You said you have three kids. Percy's missing, so you really only have two."

"I have three," she snaps back. "He'll be found. Last year still has a chance to be rectified."

Calvin says nothing to that. With his chin resting in his palm, I recognize the beat of his finger tapping as the notes of the school anthem. It seems morbidly poignant at the moment, the lyrics floating through my skull like a missed warning.

Over a hundred years, our legacy kept alive
No matter what, we will survive.

Is this what survival looks like to them?

There's not a discreet bone in Tripp's body, but according to Sadie, we're dragging him along in case he needs to rough up potential witnesses (aka any students who managed to sneak out past curfew).

"You're right," I say as we approach the tower entrance. "Nothing says discretion like Theodore committing physical battery outside of a crime scene."

Tripp blows his vape in my face, and I choke on the fumes. "Jesus, man, you sound like my mother. Don't call me Theodore."

"Call him Grizzly, he likes that one," Ash tells me with a wink. "Griswold's a hell of a last name."

Ash is part of our merry band tonight: there's him, Calvin, Sadie, Tripp, me, and Birdie. Mallory's got a case of the sniffles, and Oliver's got a case of his girlfriend being suspicious of him disappearing at night.

The tower looms Rapunzel high above us. If this were a fairy tale, this is the part where a long braid would tumble down the side and we'd scale our way up the limestone wall. Since it's not one, Sadie quickly pulls out the skeleton key to let us in.

We disregard the TWO AT A TIME plaque hanging outside the door in favor of cramming inside in a single file line. Sadie trembles in the front, her hand drifting along the spiral railing. There's a chill to the air, courtesy of high winds blowing against the siding and a particularly gruesome draft. I'd probably be shivering, too, if my own paranoia wasn't lighting matches underneath my skin. It begins as a tiny prick in my stomach but catches quicker than a house fire. Spreading up my arms and throat and settling hot in the back of my neck.

The view out of the window beside me is blotted out by a thick gauze of gray webbing. A spider sits in its funnel, its legs like sewing needles, its thorax a copper button. I think of Aurora and the cursed spindle, pricking her finger and sleeping forever.

Not now. Not here. Not again.

Cool fingers cover mine, Calvin's presence stopping me before I burn myself down to the ground. His voice is gentle and low behind me.

"Focus on breathing. Can you do that for me?" he whispers, his thumb caressing a soothing path along my skin. "We've already established I'll catch you, but I don't need a third trust fall. I'm too young and beautiful to throw out my back."

I whip to face him. "You're—"

"Incorrigible?"

I nod mutely, though I can't admit that's not at all what I was thinking. There's one word coming to mind, and the realization is far worse than any panic attack.

Sweet.

It's a bedroom.

A dusty, ancient bedroom, but a bedroom. That's what's at the top of the tower. Furniture hangs inside like antique ghosts, the forms draped in moth-eaten white. They're shadowed by the night sky, starlight slipping through the cracks in the clockface window. I step inside the loft and am instantly greeted by the faint clicking of gears. Wheels whirring in place to keep the second hand ticking valiantly forward.

"Funny," I say offhandedly.

Calvin steps out from behind me and scrunches his nose as he's hit by a stray cobweb. "What?"

"I don't hear anyone playing the harp."

He arches a brow, so I elaborate.

"That's what you told me, remember? You said I can expect baby cherubs and pearly gates."

His eyes glint fox bright in the dark. "Oh, that's right," he says, playing along. "You can blame that on the budget cuts. Real bummer.

HOUSE OF HEARTS

We had to sell the pearly gates on eBay and kick the baby cherubs out on the street. What a tragedy."

"What would you know about budget cuts—"

"Can you two shut up for five minutes?" Sadie hisses, her face illuminated by the blue glow of her phone.

"Who lived up here?" Birdie's voice breaks from the back of the group. She's the last to straggle in, and her breath hitches at the sight.

I've got the same question whirring around in my own brain. I scan the room like its past owner might materialize out of thin air. There's a splintered hand mirror and a vintage tin of face powder, both of them thick with several months' worth of cobwebs. Littered around the rest of the room is a treasure trove of old junk. There's a collection of yellowed shawls and a single neglected kerosene lamp sitting on the counter. Everything's been left in a state of previously searched disarray.

"Helen Hart," Sadie answers, dragging a path through the dust with her finger. "She spent her final days up here staring down at the hedge maze, or rather, Anastasia's grave."

I glance back at the long staircase behind us. "I can't imagine an old woman climbing this every day."

"She didn't." Her chin juts in the direction of the canopied bed. The mesh billows out from the mattress like a banshee wailing in the night. "Everything she needed was brought up to her, so she never had a reason to leave."

"I don't blame the woman. It's got a real penthouse vibe to it," Ash declares with a sweep of his hand. "I can dig it. She even had panoramic views."

The aforementioned "panoramic views" showcase a direct vertical 161-foot drop. That's 161 reasons why I shouldn't look straight down, but because I'm a sucker for self-inflicted torture, I look anyway.

It's much higher than the last lookout, which nearly ended me. That was only a quarter of the way up, and now here I am at the tippy top.

The view is dotted with pumpkins and choked in lake fog. It's otherworldly from this high up, a certain type of sorcery in the air that you only find at midnight. It'd almost be beautiful if it wasn't for the dizzy rush of vertigo and the acid burning anxious holes in my gut.

Through the rising mist, my subconscious digs out a familiar rabbit hole. A sticky, dark vortex of grief. "Do you get the feeling that if you fell, you'd fall forever?" I whisper to Calvin beside me.

I can feel his eyes on me, but I don't bother to look up.

"I'd rather not test that theory, personally."

By the time Emoree died, our lives had already split apart like a seam tugged loose. Without me to mend her clothes, Em would always let things unravel. She had a habit of picking and prodding, ripping those careful threads apart. And this time, I hadn't tried to repair anything; I let it fall apart.

Which was why I was surprised she called the night before she died.

"Violet," she hiccupped. "I really need to talk to you."

A good friend would have listened and cared, but in this tale, I was no longer the fairy godmother. I wanted to trap her in her old life and keep her small.

"Sorry, Em," I said, and I meant it. I was sorry she left and sorry that it made me into such a jealous, hateful monster. "My shift is starting soon, I can't talk."

"Please! Percy and I found something we shouldn't have. There was this old desk and this book, but it wasn't really a book, it was—"

She continued to word-vomit, but it was too late. I hung up. Stared at the room around me. It was as miserable as I was: the shattered TV where Mom's last boyfriend had run a bat through the screen, the springy couch where I'd find her after their blowup fights, the grimy spot on the carpet where I'd sat with my knees tucked to my chest and wondered if this was all my life would ever be.

If only I'd known Emoree's would end hours later.

"So, are we doing this or what?" Tripp blurts with another puff of smoke. He's already leaning on one of the vanities, settling his weight on what could be (and honestly probably *is*) a priceless antique.

"Let me set the mood first," Ash insists with an unceremonious dump of his duffel bag onto the floor. In it, he's got a folded-up paper Ouija board, a guitar-pick planchette, and some candles he stole from Sutherland Hall's dining tables.

"Set the mood?" Tripp snorts. "What is this, prom night? You trying to get my clothes off after this?"

"Trust me, bruv. No one wants to see it," Ash taunts with a strike of a match.

What follows is a mad scramble to sit down and "get the atmosphere right." Lazy droplets of black wax roll down the sides of the candles around us. The flame eats away at the tapered edges, burning them down in strange stalagmites.

"How do we do something like this?" I ask, looking around the group for someone to chime in on Spirit Protocol 101.

"I've watched enough *Ghost Adventures* to get the gist of it," Birdie says before throwing a shy glance Sadie's way. "One finger on the planchette per person, right?"

She nods, and my stomach flutters strangely as Calvin's hand brushes against mine.

The firelight casts curious shadows on our faces, lighting us up in primal ways. Even Tripp looks nervous as he adds his hand to the makeshift planchette. He grimaces harder to mask the worry etched in his brow.

"Emoree Marie Hale, are you with us tonight?" Sadie asks the room with a small sniff and a clench of her fist against her knee. I strain for any sign of her, be it a tap against the windowsill or a jerk of the planchette. I'll take anything, anything at all, but nothing comes. "Maybe you ought to try, Violet. You were her best friend."

I nod even though all the moisture has wicked from my mouth and my stomach tightens with a nervous bout of energy. *I can do this.* "Emoree," I say, and my voice might be small, but I desperately hope it carries to wherever she is, "can you hear us?"

This time it's instant. All at once, I feel my finger moving upward. YES.

"Oh my God, it's working," Ash whispers with a shocked laugh. "Quick, ask her where Percy is."

"Shhh, I'll get there," I snap back, and my voice isn't the only thing that's trembling. My finger feels clammy against the planchette, my whole hand cold and slick with sweat. "Em, I've missed you so much. I should've been there for you, and . . . and I wasn't, and I'm so sorry for that."

"Emoree, side note, you still owe me five dollars," Tripp chimes in, and as if I'm not the only one irritated by him, the flames suddenly run sideways in a sharp burst. "Sorry, fine, you can keep it, Em. Hit me back in the afterlife."

"I'm here to fix things," I start again. "You wanted me to find Percy, and now I need your help to do that. Can you please tell us if he's still on campus?"

YES.

I wet my lips. Okay, good, we're making progress here. "Can you tell us if he's alive?"

156

HOUSE OF HEARTS

Everyone goes dead silent at that, the group of us holding our breath at once as if the first to exhale will break this spell we're in. I wait for her to guide our hands toward a damning yes or no answer, but the planchette gravitates down to the alphabet beneath.

I...N...B...E...T...W...E...E...N

There's a flurry of shock around the room—Birdie gasps; Tripp pretends to scoff.

Calvin continues staring down at the board incredulously.

"Could we try that one again?" he asks, his face ashen. "Preferably without speaking in riddles, Emoree?"

The planchette doesn't budge. No further elaboration comes, and after a second and third time asking, I worry it never will. Shifting angles, I switch my question. "Okay, fine, new question. You said he's on campus. Where?"

Finally we move again, but if I was expecting a coherent answer, I'm sorely disappointed the moment I piece together the words.

D...O...W...N...T...H...E...R...A...B...B...I...T...
H...O...L...E

"This isn't making sense," Tripp bemoans under his breath. "I swear she's just messing with us now. Some sort of ghost prank."

If I didn't know Em as well as I do, I could see myself siding with him at this moment. But I do know her, which is why I know there's no way under the sun that this is some paranormal prank. "Please, Em, is there really nothing else you can tell us?"

The planchette doesn't move, but the room around us does. With a flutter of a white sheet and a plume of dust, a flurry of sudden wind unearths an Edwardian writing desk waiting in the dark.

"I . . . think she wants me to go look," I whisper, and I'm aware I sound half-dazed, but this all feels like a strange waking dream.

"We've scoured this entire room before. What evidence could you possibly find?"

I shake my head. "I don't know, but it has to be a sign, right?"

The desk before me is solid rosewood, a genuine antique with delicate brass knobs, frieze-carved shelves, and glass inkwells. In an age before iPhones and safe-deposit boxes, there were false bottoms in desk drawers and secret compartments tucked away.

With the drawers already swung out, I move under the desktop itself and prod at the decorative panel in the center. It budges, ever so slightly, and from a rap of my knuckle against the wood it sounds promisingly hollow.

That's all the validation I need to keep going. It takes a good ten minutes of me mapping out the underside of the desk to find a hidden depression in the wood. I'm careful as I locate the wooden spring next and pop the concealed drawer out.

A leather-bound book sits inside with a single piece of paper resting on top.

> Please, Ana,
> Let this end.
>
>
> —Helen

Sadie's at my side in a heartbeat. "What is it?"

"Give me a second, that's what I'm trying to figure out," I gripe as I turn it over in my hands. It's a deep russet red with intricate gold tooling and a curiously shaped padlock. "It's locked."

Not only that, but someone's unsuccessfully tried to rip it open.

HOUSE OF HEARTS

It's clear from the significant wear and tear on the leather and the divots that someone took a screwdriver to the lock. Multiple attempts, but even more obvious than that, multiple failures. The journal stays locked.

"I've never seen a lock like that," Calvin intones over my shoulder. "It almost looks like a heart."

"It does, doesn't it?" I ask as a glint of silver metal flashes in my peripheral. My broken-heart necklace hangs from my throat, the pendant a perfect match to the broken-heart-shaped indent of the lock. I feel like "Goldilocks and the Three Bears," *too big, too small, just right*. With a wrench of my wrist, I place the heart in the lock, and smother a tiny gasp as the gears click to life and the front page opens.

"It's a book of curses."

"What?" Sadie is at my side in a second, but not before I get a better look at the first page. The paper itself is yellowed and blotted with stray flecks of ink, the text written in a cipher and punctuated with curious sigils and eerie runes. There's a lot of stuff that could be running around in my head as I hold a literal *magic grimoire* in my hands, but all I can focus on is the faded sticker stuck between the ripped pages.

Not just any sticker; it's one of the holographic hearts that Em would paste on her fingernails every week. They came in a cheap pack from Amazon, and they'd peel off constantly; I've lost count of all the times I found one of them in my backpack or on the floor, curled up on itself like a dead spider. She left them behind like her own personal breadcrumb trail.

And now there's one in Anastasia's old curse book.

"Guys, I think Em and Percy beat us to it . . . and they ripped out the first page."

14

Life doesn't play out like it does in the movies. There's no way on earth the main character would make an earth-shattering discovery like an ancient spell book only to spend the next several weeks cramming for an exam in multivariable calculus.

But, because real life follows no cinematic rules, that's precisely what I find myself doing. Anastasia's grimoire and Em's secret involvement play second fiddle to the rules of differentiation. I can hardly keep searching for Percy if I flunk out of school. I'm desperately trying to stay awake in class as my teacher reviews test material, but the chalkboard grows fuzzier by the second as I drift in and out of focus.

I couldn't tell you how the hell Oliver's managing between the Cards, school newspaper, and school itself. He's studiously taking notes on the opposite end of the classroom and even going as far as to raise his hand and participate. With the exhaust fumes I'm running on, I don't trust myself to speak coherently, let alone ask questions on the derivative matrix.

I'm not even the one working on transcribing the book in the first place. Oliver and Ash are leading that particular expedition. Oliver explained the harrowing process to me by referencing the infamous Copiale cipher.

"We're not the first secret society, and we definitely won't be the last," he said mid-yawn. "An eighteenth-century group of Freemason eye doctors—yes, you heard that right—wrote an entire ritual guide in code, and it took scholars years to crack. Researchers broke the symbols down and searched for letter pairs. After that, they eventually realized the original source language was German."

"You speak German?"

"Nein."

My head dips, and I jerk myself awake for the seventeenth time this hour. My pencil's scratched a graphite streak down the page. It's somewhat fitting given the messy state of my notes.

EXAM NEXT WEEK
THE IN-BETWEEN????????
RABBIT HOLE? IS THIS A CODE FOR SOMETHING? RABBITS BURROW IN THE EARTH . . . DOES SHE MEAN A TUNNEL?

It doesn't matter how much time I spend studying either subject—everything written on the page is an indecipherable blur.

"Word of advice, math class isn't worth premature gray hairs," Amber says that evening from the other side of the shower-stall door. "I can tell all those AP classes are kicking your ass."

"Thanks, I'll be sure to tell Mr. Bayer on exam day." My voice is drowned out by the chug of water sputtering out of the faucets and the screech of the plastic sliding on the metal curtain rod. "Sorry, sir, I got a zero on the test because my friend says I look ugly when I cram."

She snickers on the other side of the wall. "Hey now, I didn't say ugly, but otherwise? Damn straight. Tell him life's too short to spend it wasting away over tests."

My heart gallops at her words, but I'm getting better at not letting the panic kick in. She's not wrong. Life *is* too short.

For as much money as they pour into this school, the shower rooms lie neglected. A phlegmy pocket of yellow light flickers above our heads, and a run-of-the-mill shower divider cuts between us. Amber's baby blue pedicure shines against the grimy tile, her shower caddy filled to the brim with products.

On the flip side, she's got a view of my ratty sandals. They might be hanging on by the grace of God alone, but it doesn't matter because no one else is in here but her. Typically in the late evenings or early mornings, you can count on this room being packed with students; girls belting out song lyrics, blasting hair dryers, gossiping over the sinks as they brush their teeth. It's usually a competition of who can be the loudest, so tonight is a welcome respite.

"You've been quiet lately," she observes, her accusation followed by a squirt of conditioner in her palm. "You, Oliver, Birdie—the three of you have been weirder than usual. Don't think I haven't noticed."

I rub my scalp with the tips of my nails and massage the shampoo in. "I'm sorry. MV Calc isn't the only thing kicking my ass. The club's . . . taken its toll. Things are pretty heavy." It's as close to the truth as I can manage, but it still sits like a lie on my tongue.

"When it was Oliver, I could manage it, but the three of you? It's like you're speaking in code twenty-four seven and trying to figure out

HOUSE OF HEARTS

the best place to hide a dead body. And it's like, yoo-hoo, I'm literally right here with a shovel if you'd talk to me."

I deflect with an exaggerated "awwwww." "You'd help me hide a dead body? I'm flattered."

She chuckles. "I'll dig the hole and everything . . . It'd be more of a rabbit hole than an actual grave because I ditch PE, but I will bring the shovel."

My blood runs cold. "What did you say?"

"That I'll bring the shovel?"

"No, before that."

I hear her rummage noisily through her caddy. "Uh, that I have noodle arms and could only dig a rabbit hole? Even that's a stretch because that's still several feet deep. Let's throw them in the lake instead. Too morbid?"

I shake my head, then quickly realize she can't see that and clear my throat. "No, you just made me think of something. I promise we're not burying dead bodies, though."

She snorts. "Okay, good to know. I guess the Cards are more boring than I thought."

The faucet screams in protest as she shuts the water off. I go to follow suit, but she stops me with a reach of her hand beneath the stall. "Here, use this."

"What is it?" I ask, staring down at the mystery goop squirted onto my palms.

"A hair mask. You'll want to leave it in for like five or ten minutes. It's really good, but it smells like cherries, and I hate that . . . Also your three-in-one hair-care bottle is borderline satanic. I swear I cross myself every time I see it in your bag."

I work the product through my dead ends before tying my hair

163

back in a bun. "'Satanic Shampoo' has a ring to it, though. You should patent that."

"I'll get back to you with a SWOT analysis," she replies with a swing of her stall door. I listen to the soft pads of her retreating footsteps until finally I'm all alone.

I relish the hot water raining down my skin. I've always been careful to take quick showers at home so I don't rack up a huge bill or make the next bath freezing for Mom. Here, none of that matters.

The only thing that does matter now is doing what I came to Hart to do. And even that's morphed and shifted in the short time I've been here. No longer the tangible takedown I'd planned for. Some masked killer I could cuff and send to jail.

No, now I've got ghosts to summon.

Curses to break.

Rabbit holes to find.

Amber's words sift back through my skull. Could the rabbit hole really be referring to a grave? Some deep burrow in the earth where no one could ever hope to find him? There's no way he could be *alive* if he was buried beneath the soil.

Hmm. I'm once again reminded of my night in the maze. Standing there in the dead center with the moon winking overhead, the Lockwell mausoleums surrounding me like an army of the dead. It feels wildly far-fetched, but perhaps he's not *literally* buried. Maybe Em meant he was hiding inside one of the family tombs? Could there be some special passageway? It's one thing to explore the tower, but breaking into a family grave is a pretty heavy extracurricular activity.

I could almost laugh if the situation weren't so massively grim and messed up. Of course someone like Em would get herself into this mess. Using your heart over your head has always been a bad move in my book, and that's all she did. Applying to this school was reckless and impulsive. She had starry-eyed dreams of opera houses and sold-out concerts. She was a dreamer, even if her life ended in a nightmare.

I clamp down on my lip and try to smother the thought of her terrified. For all our disagreements, she'd been like a sister to me, and I knew her better than my own blood.

I squirt some of my three-in-one gel into my loofah and scrub my skin with more force than necessary. Emoree knew I'd go to the ends of the earth to find the truth. Not for the first time in my life, though, I wish I didn't have to. I wish my love didn't need to be danced over hot coals. I wish I could live without the knowledge that I was put on this earth to look out for everyone around me at all times.

"You're so grown up for your age," Mom would say through sniffles when she'd use me as a glorified therapist at ten years old. "You always know what to do."

"You'll always protect me, right?" Em blubbered in the sandbox. "Do you promise?"

Everyone's savior and yet I wasn't able to save everyone. The girl who depended on me most is gone. Dead.

I growl under my breath at the same time I hear a shuffle of feet.

"Amber?"

No response. Okay, awkward, it's not her. I shut my mouth and contemplate the minutes left for this mystery hair mask. Three? Would Amber even know if I washed it out early?

I brace myself for the stranger to blast music and start belting along to it. Honestly, with the rate my thoughts are going, maybe I need something to drown my mind out. I cast a quick downward glance at the opening at the bottom of my stall door. She's barefoot. That's a bit ballsy considering the chances of contracting athlete's foot or ringworm.

The girl is intensely pale, enough to make my own pallid skin look like I've gotten a spray tan. She's borderline translucent, a whole spiderweb of blue veins on display beneath the surface.

I'm aware I'm still staring as I decide to rinse my hair early.

As if she's aware I was looking, she swivels to face me from in front of the shower barrier. It's jarringly abrupt. One second she's facing forward, and the next she's directly facing my stall, her body unnaturally still as she stands there.

There's absolutely no way she could tell I was looking at her. She'd have to be psychic or actually peeking above the divider, and she's nowhere near that tall.

And of course she starts singing. *See,* I rationalize, *she's just a normal girl in the shower room, and I'm being incredibly rude staring.*

Her song begins wordless, a soft vocalization in the back of her throat. It's as hypnotic as the rest of her, a striking siren call between us. It's only as I'm about to shut the water off that I hear the first lyrics.

"Goosey, goosey, gander, whither shall I wander?"

Weird start, but okay. I don't think this made it on the Hot 100. But some strange, buried side of me seizes up like a gazelle at a watering hole, and I strain to not make any sudden movements.

My hand rests on the shower knob; I can't bring myself to turn it off.

"Upstairs and downstairs, and in my lady's chamber." Her singing voice is haunting in the echo of the empty room. It bounces off the walls and carries back to me like a choir. I recognize the nursery rhyme, a morbid little song with a gruesome ending. "There I met an old man who wouldn't say his prayers. I took him by the left leg—"

HOUSE OF HEARTS

I know where this goes, but I still wait in anticipation for the ending. My heart constricts painfully behind my ribs.

"—and threw him down the stairs."

The song ends. She's still facing me. I'm still facing her. My hand is still clamped tightly on the knob. We're locked like that for way too long, and I'm no Em, but my mind's run away from me. A horrific daydream plays out in my imagination; it starts with the water staining orange before deepening to a violent shade of scarlet. Blood circles down the drain, and I see her nails, long and black and talon-like, slip over the top of the stall and tap.

Tap . . . tap . . . tap . . . like a faucet with a leak. Then she peeks over the top and I see her and—

Nothing happens. We're in this standstill for a moment longer before she twists away from me and leaves. I stay frozen until I'm positive I'm alone and finally shut off the water. It's grown cold.

I square my shoulders as I leave the stall and force myself not to take the entire door down with me as I scramble out. I whip my head left and right, but I really am alone. She's gone, but with the stall door swung open, I see she's left something behind for me.

It's scratched into the paint of the shower wall like knifepoint graffiti. I see a jagged letter carved by hand, one single message left behind for me.

O

Dear Diary,

What a silly notion Mother has, that a young woman might be deflowered. On the contrary, I bloom with Oleander's touch. There's ivy in my ribs and petals in my heart. I will always remember the two of us in the hedge maze, the sunset a bright peony pink overhead.

"I'll marry you," he whispered, his roots tangling together with mine. "I promise you, my love, I will."

And in that moment, a garden grew.

—Anastasia Hart

15

New fear unlocked: a ghost jumping me in the shower.

To be honest, I'm not even sure if that *was* a ghost, but I damn well wasn't going to stick around and find out. Whatever it was, the memory of the potentially haunted shower stalls has been lingering with me all week. As soon as I beelined back to the dorm, I immediately off-loaded every terrible second onto Birdie and made her promise to buddy-system with me to brush my teeth the next morning. Even with her beside me 75 percent of the day, I can't help but be suspicious of shadows in far corners and peer over my shoulder for our entire club meeting. Oliver and Ash spend the hour bemoaning their limited progress with Ana's grimoire ("It's all useless! Half of it is for shit, like hair care and studying spells, and the last page is an indecipherable mess"), but I can't shake the sensation of being watched.

It's ten times worse as I walk through the Little Garden Halloween night. Emoree always believed Halloween was a bridge between the living and the dead, and I hate to admit I'm starting to believe that, too. After recent events, it doesn't seem all that far-fetched to believe there's a thin veil between both worlds, that someone might easily pull back the curtain and cross to the other side.

The whole campus shivers with the late-October chill. There are fog machines spurting thick mist in a variety of wild colors, bright pink burning into neon orange. Paper lanterns illuminate the outdoor walkways, and streetlamps are festooned with cornstalks and ribbons. Every street features stacks of pumpkins, their faces carved out with the jagged edge of a knife.

"The Cards went all out this year," Birdie tells me with a swish of tulle. She's a dead bride tonight, her skin tinged an asphyxiated blue and her eyes hollowed in black. Her costume might be straight out of a Tim Burton movie, but her image sends me back to the ghost in the shower room, her skin bloodless and strange.

"*You* went all out this year," I shoot back, gesturing at the product of nearly two hours of work. I'm intimately aware of how long it took to assemble her outfit because I was there for every second of it. From the slathering of paint on her arms to the white streaks of exposed ribs, fake bone curling out from a sheared hole in her gown.

"Do I look terrifying?"

I've seen terrifying plenty of times at this academy, and I can safely say she's not even close. I give her a thumbs-up anyway. "You look amazing."

Quieter now, she leans in to ask the real question. "Are we going to talk about your plan?"

My plan has been tweaked several times over since I first brought it up in the clubhouse, but the morbid essence of it remains the same: Halloween night, when the campus is a riot of strobe lights and fog machines, we'll use the distraction to get into the Hart family mausoleums and scour the grave sites for Percy. It's not the best look to go in as a large group with shovels, so we'll be splitting up.

The bulk of the group will be on "distraction duty," and Sadie, Birdie, Calvin, and I will split up between the four mausoleums to see what we can find. Which, unfortunately, could be nothing at all.

"I have no idea what Tripp has arranged, but I'm willing to bet it involves contraband fireworks and God knows what else." I snort. "'Illegal explosives' has his name written all over it."

"All he said was 'You'll know the sign when it happens,' which is infuriatingly vague," Birdie says as she adjusts her wig. "I won't lie, this whole thing is freaking me out a bit. Between the séance and you seeing ghosts and all this paranormal stuff. I know we signed up for it, but, God."

She leads me through the Little Garden, and all around us, the air is alive with the smoke of a bonfire. Kids swarm around, their outfits ranging from cheap gags to all out masterpieces. A toilet paper mummy sits beside an impressive Frankenstein; a realistic siren saunters past a Party City Wednesday Addams.

Our whispering is cut off by the sound of Amber's real-life banshee wail when she sees us. She's in full Big Bad Wolf attire—a white granny wig, old-lady curlers, and a whiskered "snout" of brown and black eyeliner. Oliver's eyes are (*finally*) shot with exhaustion, but he's still putting on a good show of matching his girlfriend. He's her very own Little Red tonight, with an exaggerated long hood and a wicker basket in his hand.

"How did I just *know* you wouldn't be in costume?" Amber jabs an accusatory finger my way and points out my incriminating red-and-white-tartan skirt and black tights. "One of the few nights you can ditch this uniform, and you're *still* in it? On Halloween, of all nights? Have you no shame?"

"I have a lot, actually," I argue, with a poke to her inflated cheeks. "Which is why I'm not borrowing another outfit from you. If you recall, the dress from Joker Night was trashed at the end of it."

"So? Dry-cleaning exists," she tuts before rummaging around in her bag and whipping out an eyeliner pencil. "Here, make yourself a cat or something. This is ridiculous."

"Fine, yes, Mom," I relent, uncapping the black pencil and quickly streaking three cat whiskers on each cheek and a black dot on my nose. "Happy?"

"It's half-assed, but at least you're not completely costumeless."

Music floats up from an army of outdoor speakers; it's a classic playlist composed of songs like "Monster Mash" and "Thriller." Whoever is DJing for the night is hit with boos as a censored song blasts over the speakers—granted, the boos are coming from a kid in a white ghost sheet, so it's hard to tell whether he's actively pissed or super in character.

The next thirty minutes are spent entirely at Amber's whim. There are seven thousand group photos in a Halloween-themed photo booth, followed by a traumatizing attempt at bobbing for apples in a steel tub (hello, transmittable germs). It's only when Amber tries dragging us to make bonfire s'mores that I'm able to break away.

"Actually, do any of you know where Calvin is?" I ask, and no matter how nonchalant I try to sound, my question is still met with a jostle to my ribs and Amber's "*ooooh!*"

"I think I saw him at the gazebo," Oliver answers beneath his red cape. "He's so loud he's usually hard to miss."

If I had any humor left in me, I might chuckle at that, but with the shower nightmare still lingering in my mind, the only thing I can think of is the plan ahead. I'm careful to not draw suspicion as Amber turns around, giving Birdie a silent plea to come find me when she's able to. Once we're all assembled, we can wait for whatever wild thing Tripp has planned for his "signal."

It doesn't take long at all for me to find Calvin sitting inside a crowded gazebo. The ceiling is draped in ropes of ivy tangled up from the latticework sides and a string of fairy lights hanging from the rafters.

Calvin's dressed for the weather as a vampire in a red velvet fitted coat, a billowing cape, and ruffled sleeves. The costume suits him too well. His eyes skirt over mine in the dark, and I ease into the empty space beside him.

"You make me feel overdressed," he jokes, and his gaze lingers a little too long. "A cat, huh?"

I sniff to mask my embarrassment. "Don't ask, Lockwell."

"Claws out already?" he taunts. "You're in luck. I like it when a girl is feisty."

"That's too bad because I like my men silent." I retract my imaginary claws and ball my fists against my knees. "What made you choose Dracula tonight?"

"There's something alluring about becoming someone else for a night," he answers wistfully, tipping his head back to soak in the moonlight. "I'm sure if you asked Sadie, she'd psychoanalyze that statement and rip me to shreds, though."

"I could, too, if you gave me a minute."

His lips curl wryly. "I know better than to give you a second."

His eyes are trained on me as I hear the ring of a cocky junior blowing into the mouth of a dumped-out glass Coke bottle. "All right, spin the bottle. Who's first?" the guy taunts, puckering up for the air. His fake kiss has some other guys breaking out in laughter.

"What are we? Twelve?" a girl taunts with a roll of her dark eyes.

"Twelve and a half." The original guy grins. He scans the crowd desperately before his shit-eating grin lands on Calvin.

"Cal, why don't you kick us off? C'mon, man, that will get the girls to stay."

Calvin throws me a sheepish look, his Casanova attitude momentarily set back to an expression I've rarely seen on him: anxiety.

"I . . . I'm not sure." He winces, wiping a bead of sweat from the back of his neck.

"Calvin, Calvin, Calvin!" The circle has started chanting for him like a guy at a college frat party being told to chug.

"Worried about your girl being upset?" someone jeers, and now I instantly recognize the emotion on his face. Horror. The disgust of anyone assuming I'm of any importance to him.

"Thought you lived for this kind of thing," I retort icily. What was it that he said back when we first met? *I'd never dream of kissing you.*

My cheeks burn, and my throat feels horrifically dry all of a sudden.

"Anyway, if you're going to do it, do it fast. We need to be out of here when Tripp gives the signal."

He arches a brow, and it's clear he's searching for something in my eyes, but for what, I couldn't say. Whatever it is, he seems to reach some final verdict and nods grimly to himself, gulps, and then plasters his typical playboy persona back on.

"All right, then," he announces with a cocky gleam in his eyes. "I'll bite."

He probably does, a wild part of me muses, and I've never been so relieved that my thoughts are trapped in my head.

HOUSE OF HEARTS

Some girls I don't know chitter like a flock of lovesick birds. Preening and fluttering in hopes of catching his eye. It's a record-scratch moment as he leans in and grabs the bottle, everyone frozen in anticipation and pleading with the gods that it will point their way.

It spins and spins and spins some more, and when it finally lands, it's so close to me that even I need to catch my breath.

But it isn't me. That's clear from the sharp gasp and giggles to my left. The chosen girl smooths a wayward strand and tucks it shyly behind her ear. She's pretty—warm, sun-kissed skin, hair in an immaculate fishtail braid, her face painted with iridescent mermaid scales.

He cradles her cheek, leaning in only after she gives a shy nod. It might be all of five seconds, but it lasts a lifetime in my head. I'm consumed by the sight of his lips pressing against hers and the brush of his fingertips against her face.

I have no reason to hate her, I have no reason to hate him, but hate is all I feel.

More than anything, I hate how these seconds won't pass. And when they finally do, I hate the dizzy satisfaction spread across her face as she draws back with parted lips and flushed cheeks.

"Satisfied?" Calvin asks the group, and he's far too casual about this whole ordeal. *Of course this would be casual for him.*

"All right, moving counterclockwise, Violet, it's your turn," the junior announces with a wink. His interest is completely unreciprocated, and yet it still has me pushing back my shoulders, emboldened by the possibility that anyone here might *want* to kiss me.

Calvin clears his throat. "You don't have to play the stupid game. We can get out of here."

I should take his advice. I shouldn't be ruled by this horrifically petty part inside me. There are a million things I should be doing instead of grabbing this bottle.

"No, it's okay," I insist, flashing him a smile I don't mean. "I'll play."

His brows knit, but there's no time for him to argue. There's no time for anything as the bottle spins and then slows in front of a lumberjack senior in my study hall. He's handsome enough in a boy-next-door sort of way.

I think his name is Landon, but it's the last thing on my mind as I lean in. He wastes no time smashing his lips to mine, and it's an unwelcome sensation, as unpleasant as a shower gone cold. He's sloppy, his mouth missing mine and his hands hovering awkwardly in the space behind my back.

His eyes might be squeezed shut, but mine stay open. I tell myself I don't know what I'm looking for, but that's not true. I immediately lock eyes with Calvin.

All he does is stare. Stare and stare and stare. It's funny how quickly a brain can draw parallels: same blond hair, same wide-set shoulders. If I squinted, maybe I'd never know the difference, but I'm not squinting. I'm staring right at him. I'm kissing Landon even as Calvin's eyes sear hot onto my skin.

Calvin staggers off, his legs trembling like he's forgotten how to walk when he'd desperately like to run. I can't think why he's this upset. Unless he's so utterly repulsed by the sight that he's going to go throw up in the bushes.

I don't know what compels me to follow him, but it has the circle jeering yet again. They laugh at us, smack their lips, but I can't seem to care.

He doesn't stop walking until his back is pressed against the wall

HOUSE OF HEARTS

of the dorms, his hand twisting furiously through his hair. He grinds his teeth together, squeezing his eyes shut like he might block out the memory of what happened if he focuses hard enough.

I try to softly approach, but a leaf crunches underfoot, and he stiffens at the sound of it. He raises his head, expression stricken at the very sight of me. "You shouldn't have followed me," he says, words barely making it through his teeth.

"Why not?" I challenge, and his gaze darts to my swollen lips. A brief, infuriated stare.

"I'm sure Landon will miss you," he barks, and there's no denying the heat in his tone.

Hold on a minute. The realization hits me hard and fast, my subconscious unscrambling his expression and realizing I made a major miscalculation back at the gazebo. I test my new theory by leaning in, and surely enough, his breath catches strangely in his throat. He lets out a horrified little hiccup, but that's not enough to stop me. Especially not as his lips part and his gaze goes half-lidded.

That wasn't disgust I saw in his eyes. It was desire.

"Oh, I get it," I whisper, my accusation skipping along his skin as I loop my fingers around his neck.

"Get what?" he asks, his voice ragged and his pupils blown wide. He regards me with sick fascination, terrified yet enraptured.

"You're jealous."

He shudders at the accusation, and there's not a casual bone left in his body. It's oddly alluring getting under his skin, so much so that I sweep a thumb against his throat. He gasps, and the bob of his Adam's apple is far more tantalizing than it should be. I wait for the stereotypical markers of a first kiss: the tentative brush of lips, the hitch of shared breath as his lips part, the dizzy leap in my stomach.

None of those happen. What does happen is an emotional sucker punch to the gut.

"You think I'm jealous?" he scoffs. Any desire I thought I saw is quickly extinguished. His features have rearranged themselves in seconds, and the face he wears now is one of pure shock and horror. "Violet, I'm sorry. Whatever you want from me, I can't give to you. Don't you remember? I'm the worst man on the planet. An incorrigible flirt. You don't want this."

I'm not wearing face paint, but I'd bet anything my cheeks are a horrible, cartoonish shade of red anyway. "A simple no would have sufficed. Shit, forget it. You're right. Pretend this didn't happen."

He has the gall to look *pitying*. "I really don't want to hurt you."

"You didn't! I don't care. Blame it on stress-induced hysteria. A brief lapse in judgment. Whatever."

He opens his mouth, but I'm spared the "it's not you, it's me" monologue by a series of loud cracks in the sky. Fireworks glimmer overhead like a pop of champagne before waterfalling down among the stars. That can only be the signal that Tripp teased. It might be beautiful if things were different.

Right now all I want to do is disappear into the earth. I break away from Calvin, already beelining for the gate. "That's our cue."

"Violet—"

"Already walking! Try and keep up!"

It's a good thing we're going to a grave site, because this awkward silence might kill me.

I'm trying my hardest not to look at Calvin, or speak to Calvin, or accidentally brush against Calvin, because if I do, I'll be forced to acknowledge the most mortifying thing I've ever done, and I truly can't handle that right now.

Thankfully, Birdie must pick up on this strange tension, so she mercifully fills the silence. "How did Tripp smuggle fireworks on campus in the first place?"

Sadie trudges forward with a shrug of her shoulders and a swish of her cape. She's a witch tonight, with a pointed black hat and gnarled black broom. "You can always count on Tripp to know a guy. And if he doesn't know a guy, he knows a guy who *knows a guy*."

On cue, another firework crackles overhead and casts the hedge walls in neon blue. This sort of thing would be a major write-up for any other student on campus, but I already know Tripp will get let off with a slap on the wrist.

"You make him sound like a glorified mob boss," I say as I realize we've finally made it to the center of the maze. The Lockwell twins know this place like the back of their hand. I almost have to wonder if the route is etched in the family DNA.

"No, he's just well connected," she retorts before gesturing at the four mausoleums in front of us. I stop to read the inscriptions as we pass each tomb. Calvin flashes a light on each one and briefly brings the words to life. DEARLY BELOVED, DEPARTED TOO SOON, REST IN PEACE. A whole family alive and dead like sand sifted through your fingertips. "All right, here we are."

The silence returns. The only noise comes from a bat chirping overhead and the buzz of a fly spun in a spider's web. We're alone and yet we're surrounded, this maze teeming with all sorts of nocturnal horrors. And I have the distinct, horrible feeling that more are yet to come.

"Hypothetically, would you say this counts as grave robbing?" Calvin asks finally.

"By definition of the word, it doesn't count as grave robbing if we're not robbing a grave," I argue, breaking off the silent treatment. "We're grave peeking, which is ethically questionable, but not as bad."

"All right, grave peeking. That's loads better," he says, sucking his lips into an anxious, tight line before digging the key into the lock. "All right, then, who wants to call dibs on Anastasia's grave?"

I grit my teeth. No turning back now. "I'll do it."

If this were a low-budget horror movie, this would have the whole audience groaning and pelting popcorn at the screen. It's the kind of self-sacrifice that gets you killed first. "Dead Girl #1" in the credits.

"Violet, are you sure?" Birdie asks.

"Someone's got to. Let's split up and get this over with before anyone notices, okay?"

Birdie looks at me like I'm using a Disney FastPass to get to the front of the execution line, but she doesn't argue, and just like that, I'm alone and staring down the entrance of Anastasia's tomb.

My imagination has already painted the scene of what I might find inside: a macabre mix of the Parisian catacombs and the royal vault at Windsor Castle.

Surprisingly, the room inside is neither. The crypt might be cold and uninviting, but it's not some eighteenth-century hovel constructed out of femur bones. Similarly, the alabaster chest tomb is beautifully embellished, but the surrounding room is so musty and dank, the royal family would roll over in their graves at the thought of being buried here.

I throw a queasy look at the casket and remind myself that there actually *is* someone buried here.

She's not one of the plastic skeletons on display at school, either. This is a real person, and perhaps that's more terrifying than any ghost or zombie or make-believe monster. Someone who lived and died and was buried here to slowly decompose.

Horrifying mental image aside, there's nothing all too damning about the tomb from an evidence standpoint. No satanic sigils on the ground or *HELP* written backward on the wall in blood. It's a simple marble crypt with a stone floor and a sealed casket in the center and really not much else.

Maybe I misunderstood what Em was trying to tell me. "Down the rabbit hole" could mean literally anything. Or, if Tripp is to be believed, it could mean nothing whatsoever. Another dead lead in an unsolvable case.

I'm about to abort the mission when I feel the prickle of something brushing against my leg. I stumble back in a panic and land my ass on the cold hard ground before seeing it was a centipede.

It's only as I'm struggling to sit my bruised self up that I feel *it*. A pale stone juts out strangely on the floor beneath me, not quite grouted like the rest of the tile. It wiggles in place beneath my fingers, and that's all the incentive I need to shimmy the stone free. Tile by tile, the floor comes apart beneath me, the stones pushing back to reveal a wooden trapdoor.

I take it back. *Now* we're in horror-movie territory. No sane individual would open a secret door in a haunted mausoleum, but here I am doing it anyway. I expect to find a lot of horrible things—a portal to the underworld or an Indiana Jones snake pit.

What I don't expect to find is Percy.

16

Hart Academy might be storybook material after all—we have our very own Sleeping Beauty. Percy Lockwell is a slumbering Aurora inside Anastasia's tomb, his expression waxen like a Tussaud model of himself.

Apparently if you let out a bloodcurdling scream from a tomb in the vicinity of other people, they all come barreling toward you. Which is flattering, if nothing else.

"Violet." Calvin's by my side in a second, his hands gripping my shoulders, his eyes more worried than they have any right to be. "Violet, what is it?"

But I don't even have to answer him. Sadie is the first to follow my trembling finger downward, and she echoes my scream with a terrified "PERCY!"

That gets everyone's attention, and soon we're all gaping down at the third Lockwell sibling. Sadie shakily reaches a hand down to his wrist, her fingers pressing for a pulse. "H-he's alive."

There's no spindle prick on his finger, but Percy lies in wait anyway. If he's hoping for true love's kiss from Emoree, he'll be waiting forever.

Birdie shares a fleeting horrified look with me. "How is that possible? It's been"—she counts on her fingers—"ten months. You

HOUSE OF HEARTS

don't sleep for ten months without . . . some sort of assistance, right, Violet? I've seen your grades. You know more about this than I do."

All I can do is shake my head. "It's not possible, but . . . is anything at this point?"

"Percy! PERCY!" Calvin digs his nails into his brother's shoulders and shakes, but no amount of pleading wakes Percy up. There's not a flutter of a lash or a wrinkle of his nose. Percy lies frozen, miraculously immortalized as if by divine intervention.

"Why was he in here?" Calvin asks. The question splinters in his throat, and the last word gnashes through his teeth. "Why the hell did he lock himself here? In this goddamn tomb?"

He stumbles away from his brother's body and pounds a fist on Anastasia's casket. "Why him?" he seethes, tears freely streaming now. They spill messily down his cheeks and drip off the bridge of his nose to the floor. "Why any of us? A broken heart isn't worth this. Fuck!"

He's not the only one crying. Sadie's eyes swim with fresh tears, and her expression breaks into a silent outburst. I don't miss the way Birdie's hand instantly finds her shoulder and the wide-eyed stare Sadie gives her in return before leaning into her touch.

Meanwhile, Calvin's slumped to the floor, and from a cursory glance in his direction, it looks like he's attempting to enter a coma of his own. He stares vacantly at the ground and pitches forward. His expression is blank for several minutes before his gaze wanders back to his brother and the dam breaks, his emotions getting the best of him once again.

I don't lie and tell him it will be okay. Nothing about this is remotely okay.

Instead I focus on what I can do. My mind's already rolling out the blackboard and the stub of chalk, ready to go. I've never been good at feelings, but I'm the best at stripping a scenario down into logical parts.

Part #1: location. If you think about it, this is actually a pretty good hiding spot. We've got multiple barriers in play here—right now, Percy is not only hidden beneath a trapdoor, but also inside a closed tomb within the confines of a locked hedge maze. That makes him about as far away from Emoree as he can be. It also makes sense for him to want to be in Anastasia's tomb since she's the one who started the curse in the first place. Part #2: Percy himself. He might look peacefully asleep, but his hair and uniform are disheveled and mud-splattered. Streaked like he ran desperately through the maze in the rain, was caught by stray branches. The stitching on his blazer is frayed and loose, partially concealed by the cross strap of his brown leather satchel.

"I... I want to check something, if that's okay," I say before lowering to my knees and leaning to undo the top clasps of his bag. I peer into the canvas-lined interior before gently lifting it up and rummaging through it. There's a small journal tucked into one of the pockets, and upon further inspection, I recognize the handwriting as Anastasia's.

"Holy shit," I whisper, and I wildly flail my hand at the group to get their attention. "It's a diary."

I blink down at the pages, shifting between Anastasia's diary and her two living, breathing descendants next to me. Calvin's eyes flicker to mine, and I'm quick to look away. We scour through each entry before lingering on the last page. It's a hastily scrawled letter that had originally been ripped out before being shoved back into the book:

> Dearest Diary,
> I fear this shall be my final entry.
>
> My wretched sister is probably with Oleander now,

HOUSE OF HEARTS

laughing over her devious plot to steal him away from me. What a fool I've been! I let her trample over my emotions and make a mockery of my heart. How could I have been so naive to their secret trysts?

If they wish to wed, so be it. Let the families come pouring in to offer them good tidings and blessings, but I shan't be here to celebrate.

I have already ripped this infernal locket from my throat. My mother gifted these necklaces to me and my sister when we were young. She said they represented our sisterhood, a stronger bond than all else. It was supposed to forge a timeless connection between the two of us, but I intend to take mine to the grave.

Yours eternally,
Anastasia

Beyond that page, another ripped piece of parchment slips out from the back cover. It's identical to the pages of the grimoire the Cards found, folded several times over and torn violently at the edges. The spell is transcribed in the margins in Emoree's handwriting. She might not have been a master cryptographer, but most of our childhood was spent creating secret languages together. Even the letter she sent about Percy had been coded. I grip the page tighter and read the translation under my breath. It might only be four lines long, but it knocks the wind out of me all the same.

185

In this labyrinth of hedge and thorn
My heart is broken, my grief is born
Either ~~eternal~~ sleep of eldest prior,
Or true love's heart I do require

"Sleep of eldest prior," I whisper, the puzzle pieces clicking together. I bolt to my feet and pace several steps back. "That's what Em meant by Percy being in between. It's like some magical coma he put himself in. A loophole where he wouldn't have to follow through with the curse and cut out Em's heart."

Calvin goes perfectly still. "If only she knew that she would still die anyway."

I chew my lip. "I still don't understand that part." My voice wobbles. "To be honest, I don't understand most of this. When I came to this school, I . . . I figured it would all be cut-and-dried. One of you had killed her. I would expose you to the police. It would've made sense, and there wouldn't be ghosts or curses or dead girls with vendettas."

Calvin doesn't say anything to that for a long moment. He's too mesmerized by the sight of his brother and the steady rise and fall of his chest with every breath. I search through the satchel for anything more and find Percy's phone. It's the only other clue left behind, but of course it's dead.

"I guess magical sleeping spells don't apply to cell phone batteries," Calvin mutters to himself.

"We should take it anyway," Birdie insists, swiveling to face the rest of us. "We'll grab a phone charger back at HOH. We should bring it along, right?"

Sadie gestures down at her brother. "What about Percy? We can't just leave him here in a graveyard!" She swats uselessly at the tears welling in her eyes. "Shouldn't we at least try to lift him out of here?"

Calvin has begun pacing circles, but Sadie's question has him skidding to a halt. "You really think dragging our lifeless brother out of the hedge maze on a Friday night is a good idea? Tripp's distraction aside, not everyone gives a shit about fireworks and you know what's more interesting? Percy Lockwell being paraded around like deadweight."

Sadie sniffles, and as much as she tries to seem older, right now she really does look like a little girl who misses her brother. "We could c-cover him with something."

"Even better! Roll him in a rug and make it really look like we're carrying a dead body out of the maze. I don't want to leave him here, but I don't want to make a spectacle of him, either, and I'm scared we'll hurt him if we try to move him." He shakes his head. "Birdie's right, we need to bring this to HOH."

Sadie gives a tight nod and wipes the remnants of tears away. She locks all that's left of her in a box, and I see the moment she swallows the key and stands up, clear-faced and determined. "All right. Emergency meeting. Grab everyone."

This has got to be the weirdest "Situation Room" moment of all time.

We're crisscross applesauce on the floor of the House of Heart's parlor room. Everyone aside from Ash, that is. He's lounging across the grand staircase like *The Creation of Adam*, which is fitting given that he's marble streaked in strokes of gray paint. Mallory beams up at him with a headful of snakes and kiss-smudged lips.

"I'll have you know I was enjoying the fireworks," he laments, then, turning to Tripp with a wink: "Mate, you really know how to put on a good show."

Tripp lifts his Freddy Krueger mask and flashes him a cocky grin in return. "I did pretty good, didn't I?"

"This isn't the time to talk about fireworks." Sadie gets up and starts furiously tapping her heel against the checkered floor. "We found Percy."

It's the verbal equivalent of an atom bomb, the room stunned into absolute silence. Tripp sobers in the aftershock of it all, his eyes widening. "You're serious?"

"You think I'd joke about that?" Sadie seethes. She's got her mother's expression mastered, the purse of her lips and the narrowed slits of her eyes.

He scratches his cheek. "When . . . when you say 'found' . . . is he dead?"

Calvin answers with a vague swish of his hands. "Not really."

"What the hell does 'not really' dead mean?"

Sadie tells them precisely what it means, relaying the last half hour in excruciating detail. Then the questions really start.

"Do we bring him to a hospital?" Mallory blurts, her phone whipped out and ready to dial 911 as soon as someone gives the A-okay.

"And tell them what?" Calvin volleys back. His head rests against the front door, and his chin tilts up to the ceiling. "That he's in a magical coma?"

"I don't know! We'd tell them something! Did you at least try CPR?"

"What would CPR do at this point?" Oliver weighs in with a sardonic lift of his brow. "His heart is beating."

"What about true love's kiss?" Ash offers uselessly. "That always works in the movies."

"Too late, asshole, his girlfriend's fucking dead," Tripp shoots back.

He throws us a sheepish look after that, but Birdie's cheeks burn with a flash of indignation.

"I don't see *you* throwing out ideas. Also, can you not talk about Emoree like that?"

I give her an appreciative nod before turning to glare at Tripp as well.

He wipes his lips with the back of his hand. "All right, here's an idea. Ash and Oliver translated Anastasia's magical grimoire. Why don't they hocus-pocus Percy awake?"

"I'm not a wizard, for starters," Ash argues. "Also, like we said last meeting, most of the pages were useless. You want clear skin? How about getting a boy to notice you? Hit me up. Otherwise, you're screwed as far as the spells in there go. We still can't translate that final page, so God knows what that one's talking about. There's a reason Em and Percy ripped out what they needed and left the rest behind."

No one says anything to that for a long time. In the silence I swivel to check how far we've gotten Percy's battery charged to. Ten percent, good enough for me.

"What's the code?" I ask, and Sadie's smile is solemn and half-broken.

"Zero, two, two, zero."

"Emoree's birthday." I hiccup. The group crowds around me as I tap out the four numbers and the phone clicks to life. I scroll through Percy's group chat with Calvin and Sadie, passing the I'm going to end this text as I work my way to the top. Several weeks before that, I see a drunken selfie of Calvin in the back of a Bentley Mulsanne, the background a blur of city lights and red leather seats.

you're missing out, dude

He winces in my peripheral, and for his sake, I exit the app and navigate to the camera reel. Beyond lovesick photos of Em and Percy kissing and textbook snapshots, the rest of the album is a disturbing downward spiral: selfies zoomed in to show the dark bags beneath his eyes, distorted angles of the hedge maze magnified and cropped to show fuzzy silhouettes. Several of them have been marked up in digital red pen, the text overlaid in all caps: SHE WAS HERE.

I wince before opening the Notes app.

It's a world away from the usual grocery lists or bullet-point to-do lists. It's a frantic array of thoughts, his mindset deteriorating with each additional note.

October 28, 1:21 AM
I can't sleep. I see her whenever I close my eyes. She's always there.

October 31, 11:00 PM
i need to hide. i need to stay away. i need to keep em safe. i need to wrap my fingers around her neck. i need to press until she turns blue. i need to rip out her heart.

November 3, 12:00 AM
RIP OUT HER HEART RIP OUT HER HEART RIP IT OUT RIP IT OUT RIP IT OUT RIPITOUT

The battery dies once more and the screen burns black, and Calvin lets out a strangled noise.

"I think I'm going to be sick," he says before he quite literally charges out the front door and empties his stomach into the bushes.

HOUSE OF HEARTS

The campus party rages on in the distance, and the strobe-light flashes illuminate the arch of Calvin's spine.

"Are you okay?" I ask, following him outside. My hand tentatively rests on his arm, and his skin is cold to the touch.

"I'm fine." His voice is an uncharacteristic growl in the back of his throat. He wipes his hand against his mouth and glares at me, the golden light extinguished from his eyes. Burned down like the amber glow of a candle giving way to a black puff of smoke. Then, to the rest of the group standing in the doorway: "I'll see you all later. I've had enough for today."

The rejection should sting more than it does. All I can think of, though, is my mother's stricken face on orientation day, the same question leaving her lips and the same lying answer leaving mine. *I'm fine*, I said, over and over again.

But I was far from it then, and if you asked me now, I'd say it couldn't be further from the truth for Calvin. Neither of us is fine, and I have a horrible feeling that the worst is yet to come.

Dear Diary,

My sister is a great many things, but she isn't daft. She is cunning, calculated, and far too perceptive for her own good.

"You're spending a lot of time in that maze," she commented out of nowhere this evening. It was more an accusation than observation. She was sitting in the drawing room with two knitting needles in hand, crafting something that looked an awful lot like a trap.

I was measured with my response. "I enjoy the solitude it provides."

She hummed. "That's the funny thing, Ana, I don't quite believe you're alone in there."

Helen didn't look up from her handiwork. If she had, perhaps she would've seen the way I stiffened in the doorway. "What makes you say that?"

"It's curious, that's all. You enter in the early dawn and you leave at dusk, flushed and disheveled . . . and I could swear sometimes I hear another voice in there with yours."

"What are you insinuating, sister?" I asked icily.
I inherited my father's temper, though it flares
differently in my chest. There are times when his blazes
hot enough to heat the whole estate. Mine is frigid; my
grudges chill me down to the very marrow.

She shrugged. "I'm not insinuating anything, but it's
curious, wouldn't you say?"

"Perhaps you ought to be examined for sun sickness. I've
had a bout of it myself in the past, though I can't say
I've ever had these hallucinations."

Helen paused over her work. "I know you're seeing
someone, Ana. Is he a student at this academy?"

I didn't dignify her question with an answer.

"Be careful," she warned when the silence between us
persisted. "You have seen our mother's marriage. Some
men know how to burn a girl down and leave nothing but
ash in their wake."

—Anastasia Hart

17

Monday is a gloomy affair. The whole campus has grayed out over the weekend, grown stiff and cold like a funeral procession. The streamers have been picked off the ground and the gourds have been thrown in the trash and the madness of Friday is overtaken by the monotony of the several weeks until Thanksgiving break.

Dr. Sampson might be prattling on about Ovid's *The Art of Love* in class, but I can't focus on Ovid talking about hunting women like stags and getting them to sleep with him in 1 BCE. The only note written in the margins of my journal is *sleep of eldest prior*.

Graphite digs a hole in the page, and I groan to myself. Is this curse really that hard to parse? I feel like the answer is infuriatingly in reach, but I'm this close to slamming my head into the desk when Calvin waltzes in late, per usual.

His tardy arrival shouldn't be anything out of the ordinary, but he's acting incredibly off. Calvin is the type of guy to strut into a room and bask in everyone's attention like his very life depends on it.

Right now he seems like a paranoid husk of himself.

"Is he okay?" Birdie whispers from our balcony seats. "He looks..."

She doesn't need to finish that thought as he scrambles his way

HOUSE OF HEARTS

up the steps and trips over his own two feet in the process. He's not looking where he's going because he's busy looking everywhere else, scoping out all the corners as if he expects a hit man to be waiting in the wings. When no one takes him down in a mafia-style assassination attempt, he manages to secure his seat, and even then, he searches the room frantically.

Tripp throws him a weird look, but even he must understand that finding your brother in a magical coma does this to a guy.

Class continues like that. Our professor prattles on while Calvin gets jumpier by the second. His paranoia reaches a boiling point mid-lecture and manifests in the snap of a pencil between his fingertips. The pressure splinters it in two and the eraser half thunks into a girl's head in front of him.

Dr. Sampson's stub of chalk drags a screeching path down the blackboard, and the sound has Calvin erupting from his seat. He flies up in a worried frenzy, his chair skidding back as he rises to his feet before it tips backward onto the floor.

The class has gone deathly silent, the only sound the flustered panic of Calvin throwing his belongings haphazardly in his bag, papers flying all around him and his expression distant and horrified.

He doesn't say a word on his way out, just takes the stairs two at a time and escapes the room with a ragged breath and a slam of the door behind him.

The auditorium breaks out in a whispered chorus of gossip. "What the hell was that about?"

For the first time ever, even Tripp seems thrown off as he looks up from his phone to our balcony seats. He doesn't need to say a word as he meets our eyes because it's written all over his face.

Something is wrong with Calvin.

It continues like that all week. The next incident falls on Tuesday morning in Sutherland Hall. We briefly make eye contact across the dining hall, and he promptly freaks out. There's no warning as he drops his untouched food, tray and all, into the trash and runs out.

"God, what's his damage?" Amber asks, first to Oliver and then to the rest of us when her boyfriend only shrugs. "He was like this in study hall with me, too. He was so weird, it actually inspired me. Okay, follow me here, guys. Full spread in the *Herald*. Title: 'Lockwell's Lost It.' How does that sound?"

Oliver crunches a celery stick between his teeth and uses half of it to point at her. "It sounds like a lawsuit."

"A lawsuit for what?"

"Libel."

She huffs. "Is it libel if it's true?"

Cafeteria-gate isn't the last Lockwell incident. It happens again as I'm racing to Shakespearean Lit. The class is hardly worth racing for when I have a Queen of Hearts card in my pocket, but I hate using it and I hate being late for anything most of all.

I run into Calvin outside the English building. He's muttering to himself while walking in a frantic circle. Cracking his knuckles, chewing on his nails, messing up his already-messed-up hair.

I know I should force myself to walk past him and make it to class, but my legs have another agenda entirely. Before I know it, I'm standing at his back, tugging on his sleeve.

"Calvin?" I ask, and that simple word is all it takes to break him from his trance.

It zaps to the core of him, and he quickly stumbles away, staring at me in what can only be described as an unflattering blend of shock and horror.

He shakes his head. "I'm late."

"Calvin!"

He's running now, taking off like the spooked hare in the maze. "Sorry, I'm late! Can't talk!"

His silhouette retreats hastily in the distance, farther and farther until he's a lost speck in the landscape.

Rain has returned to Hart. It rampages against the windows and summons the worms up from the earth, where they lie waiting and writhing.

That's how I feel, too. The mattress groans beneath my weight, and I pull the duvet up to my throat. Birdie might be a typhoon at the best of times, but there's something comforting about hearing her toss and turn.

"I can't believe he didn't even show up to our last meeting," she gossiped while slipping into pajamas before bed. "He's taking everything really, really hard... which is fair, but... I don't know. Sadie still comes to meetings." She shook her head and turned to me. "What do you think?"

"I think..." What did I think? That his mind was a mess after the graveyard? That he was still revolted from our almost-kiss? "I don't know."

But neither of these feels like the reason for this behavior. There's a puzzle piece missing from the board, a gap in the equation rendering it unsolvable. Something is wrong, and for the life of me, I don't know what.

It's still on my mind as Birdie mumbles into her pillow. I can't say how long I lie there, staring up helplessly at the ceiling, before exhaustion finally catches me. Sleep sinks into my bones, dragging me under the second I least expect it.

I dream of a woman in white.

She's a young bride opposite my easel, her beauty captured on canvas with each stroke of my brush. Her lacy sleeves billow against her wrists, and her train hangs behind her like a gauzy blur of lake fog. She looks achingly like Calvin. The same Cupid's bow lips and firefly eyes, the same chiseled jaw and prominent cheekbones. I know who she is immediately.

Helen Hart.

Which makes the man beside her Oleander Lockwell. He's an indiscernible shadow of gray, his dream-self a murky smudge in my mind's eye. Helen's the only one in total clarity here, her forced smile wavering in place on her lips as I paint.

I dip my paintbrush in fresh color, but before I can paint her bouquet, she shakes her head. "Violet."

What?

I open my mouth, but it's not my voice I hear. I'm merely a spectator in someone else's skin. "Pardon, miss?"

"Paint me with violets instead."

"Whatever for?" Oleander's disembodied voice asks.

She doesn't dignify his question with an answer. Her voice is pleading when she returns to me. "Violets, please."

I do as she asks, swishing my brush in vibrant purple rather than the orange of the marigolds she's holding. It's only as I finish the last petal that the windows shatter in a sudden spray of glass. The couple

HOUSE OF HEARTS

sits unfazed even as the wind rips their portrait off its easel and the rain melts their image away. Helen's still speaking, but her words are riddled and strange as the storm drenches me down to the bone. "There's fennel for you, and columbines. There's rue for you, and here's some for me."

Rainwater trickles down my cheek, slipping a path off my brow and down my nose until it finds its way to the crack of my lips.

It tastes like rust and salt.

The dream fades with the very real feeling of droplets splattering against my skin. Sleep crusts in the corners of my eyelids, and I whine as I wake up to the sensation of something wet.

Likely a leak. We'd get those back at home all the time. I rub my eyes and blink into the darkness, anticipating the next drop.

Except it's not rainwater.

A bloodied woman hovers in the air above me. Anastasia in the flesh, a waking nightmare from the dream that was her sister. She's a fury of curls, her hair as dark iron red as her blood. It drips from the horrible hollow in her chest, the tip of a knife piercing through her rib cage. The hilt of the blade appears to be decorated with a cursive initial, but the letter itself is shadowed and indistinguishable in the dark.

She stares down at it, aghast as the blade sinks deeper and deeper yet. Pushed in by an invisible hand, frighteningly close to my own skin. Her thin, featherlight brows lift in terror, and her mouth gapes like a fish on dry land. I make a soft noise in the back of my throat. The start of a question. The rest of it dies on my tongue.

I clatter around for the lamp on the bedside table, unsure if I want to see this woman—this ghost—in full, horrifying detail but knowing I can't face anything in the dark. Yellow light floods the room, chasing her image away like a sputter of smoke.

With a cupped hand to my mouth, I muffle my scream before it can fully leave my chest. Birdie is still blissfully asleep on the opposite end of the room, her arms flung up to the headboard and her chest rising and falling in measured beats. I could wake her. I should wake her. Except when I open my mouth again to call out her name, nothing comes out.

Panic has robbed the air from my lungs and buried this room several feet under. I'm left with a pocket of air, each shallow gasp depleting the oxygen further. I breathe in what I can, and it's as unpleasant as a mouthful of soil, heavy and dry on my tongue.

I need to get the hell out of here. Logically, I know I'm not buried alive, but my nails are seconds from clawing at the walls, splintering my fingers down to jagged stubs of plaster and paint.

I have no idea where I'm going when I slip out of the girls' dorms. My feet carry me on a path my brain doesn't know. Wet leaves crunch underfoot, and I dodge bare branches. I'm lucky the rain has ceased, but the storm has left a nasty chill to the air and I shiver with it. I cup my pink-knuckled hands to my mouth and shiver with the cold.

Floodlights burn a beacon forward; they're attached to a shadowed building a couple of yards away. Through the gloom, I recognize it as the school chapel. I can't imagine it'll be open at this hour, but my body carries me toward the somber building regardless. I'm shocked to find that the door swings open at my command. Stepping into the shadows, I'm greeted by miraculous warmth. And then I see a portrait I know all too well now.

Perhaps when this building was first constructed, there were portraits of saints adorning the walls and weeping statues of Mother Mary. Now there's a gallery of the dead. My dream hangs on the wall in the front entrance, featuring Helen's solemn expression and her bouquet of violets. Her husband stands tall beside her, his palm possessive on her shoulder.

Violets, please.

She was adamant in my dream, imploring me to paint over her bouquet. "Flowers convey what words cannot," that's what my mom always told me. That was how she felt about violets. They're a symbol of loyalty, modesty, and humility. All perfect traits for a wedding, and yet, I don't understand why she was so insistent. *There's rue for you, and here's some for me . . .*

Her words come spiraling back to me, and they're no longer a nonsensical ramble but a quote. I've heard it before in my Shakespearean Lit class, the teacher assigning a popcorn-style class reading of *Hamlet*. A guy in the front of the class had squinted down at the book and recited a stilted, monotone passage.

> *There's fennel for you, and columbines. There's*
> *rue for you, and here's some for me. We may call it*
> *herb-grace o' Sundays. O, you must wear your rue*
> *with a difference. There's a daisy. I would give you*
> *some violets, but they withered all when my father*
> *died . . .*

Sure enough, I look back at the portrait, and the flowers are subtly painted beyond their prime, their stalks bowing in a limp bouquet.

This isn't a picture of a happy couple.

This is a woman mad with grief.

I don't know what to do with this information, but I don't have long to dwell on it, either. The chapel's tranquil silence dies, and the atmosphere is reborn with the haunting rumble of an organ. It's a violent whirlwind of blaring pipes and slammed keys, a villainous concerto by Johann Sebastian Bach.

I follow the notes as if hypnotized. The arcade arches above me are enveloped in darkness, and the path forward is streamed silver with moonlight. The stars wink off the golden pipes and illuminate the arched spine of the player hunched over the keys as I approach.

Calvin is swept away in his playing, each note striking harder than the last. His profile paints a severe portrait. He's split apart at the seams, no longer the paragon of perfection but untethered from the world as we know it. Like a monarch gone mad, the beautiful and dreadful King of Hearts.

"Calvin?" I try, but he can't hear me.

The playing grows louder, more discordant and unrefined. It's horrifically shrill and out of key, like the frenzied, wild strings at a bacchanal. That moment when one transcends their humanity and enters their most primal and unrestrained state.

I make the mistake of pressing my palm to his shoulder. The music stops all at once, breaking off in a violent clash of keys as he stiffens on the bench. He's quiet beneath me, so perfectly frozen I wonder if he's alive at all, before he whips around.

I hardly recognize him. "So, let me guess," I say to diffuse the tension. My voice sounds funny in the air and not quite my own. "You're a vampire, aren't you? Handsome, perfect, doesn't need to sleep. You sit here all night, playing the organ like some brooding, bloodsucking monster."

He curls a lip to show me his teeth. "Not a vampire, just an insomniac. On really bad nights I can't stand to be alone in my room, staring up at nothing, so I come here to play." He sits with that answer before adding, "It feels like praying for me."

"I didn't think you'd be the religious type."

"You think of me often?"

"Only that you strike me as some sort of heathen."

In the light of the stained-glass window, he's a fallen angel, his beauty a sin in itself. Some gorgeous abomination.

"You really shouldn't be here." His voice rumbles over me like the swell of a passing storm.

"Why shouldn't I?" I challenge, but my voice shakes when it leaves my lips.

It happens too quickly for me to register. The tiniest fraction of a second where I'm hunched over him, my palm pressed to the broad plane of his shoulder, and the next where he's got me pinned beneath him, my back crashing a melody of its own into the keys.

The weight of his body falls over mine, and I feel the cage of his arms on either end of the organ. He leans into my throat and shudders as he feels my rampant pulse.

Exhaustion has turned the whites of his eyes red. "B-because I . . ."

He cuts off abruptly. I stop breathing as his knuckle charts a path up my ribs to my throat and finally to my lips. The groove of his finger curls longingly against my lower lip, and he swallows as I exhale. "Because I can no longer trust myself around you. Every time I see you, all I can think about is kissing you, and I ca—"

I don't hear the rest. He's rigid as I lean all the way forward. He's gone statuesque, Medusa-turned by my kiss.

"Violet?" he muffles against my lips. When I don't respond, he shifts with a sigh and pulls me closer. It starts off gentle enough. A tentative brush of his mouth against mine. The careful conquest of my lips, delving deeper as his fingers comb through my hair.

When his teeth graze against my lower jaw, it's like a bolt of lightning in my veins. He offers an approving noise as my hands find his hair, a low groan that dances along my skin. I hum against the kiss, and that propels him even further.

A dam bursts at that moment. He kisses like a man starving, like he might feast on this moment and last the winter off the memory.

I wonder if this is how all the other girls felt. Diving in the deep end and quickly realizing you can't swim, but it's okay, you want to drown in him anyway. Should we be doing this? I'd be a liar if I said I hadn't thought about it again and again and again, in all the quiet moments staring at the ceiling and whenever my gaze lingered on him too long in class.

My name is a prayer. *Violet, Violet, Violet,* like I'm some great and terrible saint, a woman worth worshiping.

When we finally pull away, I gasp for air. His lips look good swollen, the type of mouth meant to be kissed. I marvel at the sight of him.

Except it isn't longing I see on his face. "We shouldn't have done that."

"Why?"

Horror burns in his eyes, fathomless and deep. "Because I'll kill you."

18

I don't know what it says about my rapidly deteriorating mental state, but I immediately start laughing. It's not a little giggle, either. My laughter ricochets off the vaulted ceiling and echoes back like a canned laugh track when I ask, "Melodramatic much?"

He's not laughing. He's staring ahead at the altarpiece with grim determination; I imagine if Calvin actually were religious, he might be asking God for the right words to say now. "Anastasia's going to make me kill you," he confesses finally.

That's not the punch line I was expecting. "Don't even joke about that."

Dust motes play in ribbons of moonlight overhead, their speckled bodies floating in the night air.

"Do I look like I'm joking?" he asks, and okay, admittedly, he doesn't. "I didn't tell you before because I wasn't completely sure, but I think we're—"

I cut him off. "Please tell me you're not going to say what I think you're going to say."

He's horribly, tellingly silent, and I wait for him to utter the words and ruin everything. He doesn't disappoint. "We're soulmates," he whispers, and the truth drapes over everything. It weighs my world down and consumes it.

I brush a thumb across my mouth, the intrinsic fear building in me as I think of the ghosts only I can see and all the little moments avalanching over one another. "You don't even know my middle name," I say like it's some magical rebuttal, an ace slapped on the table that will end this conversation. "You're not in love with me. There's a million reasons not to be. I'm cold and unpleasant and, as you saw back at the gazebo, enormously petty. I'm also broke, and a boy in eighth grade told me I act like a robot and—"

He finally rediscovers his own voice. "Your middle name is Alice, not that it matters."

Screw my ace.

"Wh-what?" I sputter. "How did you *know* that?"

Embarrassment colors his cheeks, but he doesn't let it dissuade him. "You're not the super spy you think you are. When you were playing FBI and scrolling through my Instagram, you accidentally liked one of my photos from two years ago. I . . . might've looked up your page as well. You've got your middle name in your bio. Aside from that and some old selfies, your page was pretty boring."

I don't have it in me to deny the Instagram-stalking accusations. "O-okay, fine, you know my middle name, congrats, but that doesn't magically make you in love with me," I relent, taking a step backward until I hit the organ keys once more. I jump as the sound reverberates through the chapel. "How does Anastasia even know we're . . . whatever it is that we are? I've only known you for a short while, and besides, you're not the oldest child, so it doesn't count, right?"

He toys with a signet ring, twisting it anxiously around his finger.

"The curse relies on fate and some cosmic concept far beyond our understanding." His knuckles bleach white as he balls his hand into a fist. "When Percy cast himself out of play, apparently it switched hands to the next eldest. I'm thirty minutes older than Sadie, so here we are."

My voice is too small in my throat. "How long have you known?" He doesn't answer immediately, so I ask again, slowly, deliberately. "Calvin, how long have you known this?"

He looks anywhere and everywhere other than at me. "Part of me knew the moment I first saw you in the crowd at orientation," he confesses when his eyes finally catch mine. "I saw you and suddenly the world disappeared and you were the only thing that seemed to exist."

"Why didn't you tell me?"

Barking out a dark laugh like the Calvin I know, he asks, "How would I have done that? Should I have gone up to you and said, 'Hi, nice to meet you, we're soulmates, and by the way, I'm going to kill you for it'?"

"Okay." I wince. "Not great."

"Besides, I thought I was wrong. I wrote it off as a crush on a pretty girl with a sharp tongue." He swallows; his eyes dip back down to my lips before he remembers himself and shakes the feeling aside. "I never wanted to fall in love in the first place. I was always going to be the good-for-nothing flirt. The player. The heartbreaker. A far better alternative than carrying on this god-awful curse."

My breath is ragged, and I hate that he's right. This is more than a crush. It's a death sentence. "That's why you were being so weird this week? You finally admitted to yourself what was happening?"

He nods and worries at his split lip as the wind howls outside. "And now I think it's for the best if you stay away."

"You know it's not that easy. Everywhere I go or turn or look, you're always there." It's only dawning on me now, but it's been like this the whole time. Swiveling around to find his eyes on me in the dining hall, seeing him walking toward my dorm as if entranced, drawing me here now like a fly to a spider's web. A wall, trapping me here. "Wait, that's why I couldn't leave campus, isn't it? It wasn't Emoree. It was . . ."

"That damn curse," he finishes for me. His voice is a strange ripple of contradictions, fear and hate and bone-deep sadness swirling into a monstrous pool inside him. "I tested it myself yesterday. I can't leave, either. We're stuck together until everything plays out."

"By that, you mean we're stuck until you cut out my heart?" I clarify. My legs go weak beneath me, and I slump onto the organ bench.

"I'm not going to let that happen." His words lodge in his throat, and he has to avert his eyes to the floor, like the sight of me might drive him mad all over again. "I'm going to tell the others. If everyone in the group knows, they can keep you safe."

"Has that ever worked?" I ask, and before he can even answer, I continue. "I don't want the group to know. Not yet. They're going to lock me up in a room and keep me from solving this. There's got to be something I'm not seeing here. A solution that Percy and Em were so close to grasping. I need time to figure it out."

"There's nothing to find. We're screwed," he seethes, gripping my arms and forcing me to look up at him. "I'm going to go absolutely insane and kill you. What part don't you get?"

"The part where you want to give up. I can handle myself."

His nostrils flare at that, his mouth curling into a grimace. "You're stubborn," he corrects, "but you're not Superwoman, and you're not going to be able to brainstorm your way out of a knife in your chest and

HOUSE OF HEARTS

your heart in my hands." He continues, "Percy was right to do what he did. It's a far better alternative. I think it would be better for everyone if I also . . ."

"It didn't fix anything, though," I shout. "Em still died."

"There's a difference between an accidental fall and being killed by your soulmate because they're possessed by a poltergeist."

Now I feel like I might throw up. I'm certainly queasy as I retort, "Does it matter? Dead is dead."

His jaw slackens at that. "Have you considered that I don't want to kill you?" he asks, and his eyes are pleading and wet and far more terrified than I ever recall them being.

"You won't," I insist, but we both know it's a lie. "I have time to figure this out."

He catches the quiver in my voice and rubs his cheek with a frustrated palm. "You can't even say that like you believe it, Violet. Let's learn to cut our losses when it's time, okay? You and I both know all of this was a mistake, and now we're paying for it."

I suck in a steadying breath. I can do this. Fixing is what I do. I'm always the one putting my nose to the ground, unscrambling everyone's problems and coming up with the clear solution.

"Give me two days, okay?" I plead.

"Two days might be too late."

"Please. You can't tell the Cards or your mom or anyone. This has to be a secret," I insist, and while I don't elaborate, the rest of my thoughts hang heavy in my mind. There's no definitive reason to believe his mother can't be trusted, but I remember the hard set of her eyes back in the office, the belief that despite the death of her soulmate, her life remained perfect in the end. "Two days. That's all I'm asking."

He looks like he might say something more but thinks better of it. "Two days," he whispers. "You get two days, and I can't even guarantee that at the rate I'm going."

"I'll fix this," I promise, and the second half of my statement goes unsaid in the air between us. *Or I'll die trying.*

It's not immediately clear when I wake up if last night was real. All it takes is one horrified look at my neck the next morning to remember. Beyond the embarrassingly obvious trail along my collarbone, there's an inexplicable chain of blisters beneath my necklace. The pendant is hot to the touch, and the skin scabs like an allergic reaction around it. I tug on the chain, but it doesn't come off.

"You've got to be kidding me," I whisper, pawing at the necklace in vain before realizing it's probably another lovely side effect of the curse I'm under. That sentence alone is difficult to wrap my mind around, but there's no denying it. I might not have a physical timer hanging over my head, but hours count down on the back of my eyelids nonetheless.

Giving up, I slip on a tartan scarf and down some Tylenol for the pain.

"Did you go anywhere last night?" Birdie asks from the depths of her walk-in closet. She's a ghost of white fabric, her head hidden as she slips on her button-up. "You weren't there when I woke up."

Her question from weeks earlier has left an imprint of its own on my mind. *Can you promise me you won't keep things from me again?*

I make eye contact with Birdie's antique Georgian brooch instead of her. She probably thrifted it at an estate sale. It's a lover's eye encrusted in pearls and stitched with diamond tears. Immortal and ever watching, just like Anastasia. "Were you going to see anyone?"

"No . . . I, um, I needed some air," I say, which isn't a lie but is most definitely not the full truth, either. *I'll tell her*, I rationalize to myself, *but not yet.*

"And you didn't stop and talk to anyone while you were out? It felt like you were gone for ages."

I force out a strained chuckle. "Are you my mom?"

With her intense stare and the brooch she's sporting, there are three eyes glaring down at me when she says, "No, just a concerned friend."

My throat bobs. "You don't have to worry about me, Bird."

"Somehow I don't quite believe that."

Too bad Hieronymus Bosch is long dead; he probably could've used my day to draw up another portrait of hell. We're missing bagpipe-playing demons, but otherwise my schedule is complete with a whole host of horrors beyond comprehension.

It begins with breakfast.

"So, it's a hard no for my Lockwell article?" Amber asks through a spoonful of oatmeal. Swallowing, she shifts direction and uses her spoon as a pointer at Calvin's empty seat. "He freaked out for days, and now he's mysteriously out sick. C'mon."

Birdie's gaze cuts sharply to me, but she stays silent as Oliver fields his girlfriend's questions. "What would you even write in your article?"

Amber's eyes gleam. "Hypothesis number one: mind control. I saw a hypnotist once with my family in Vegas, and he got a woman onstage to think she was a parrot and—"

"Good thing this isn't Las Vegas," he retorts, then: "Also, do you hear him squawking like a bird?"

"I'd have to listen to him longer," Birdie offers unhelpfully.

They keep talking, but I'm not listening. The conversation bleeds away in the background while I'm distracted by the plate beneath me. I could've sworn I put a croissant on it, but that's not what I see there now. It's a *heart*, just like the one I saw back in the maze.

I whip around to see if anyone else looks even remotely horrified, but no one so much as bats an eye. *That's because it's not real*, I remind myself. I prod it experimentally on my tray. It's meatier than I expected, all muscle and no gelatinous fat.

The room is suddenly sweltering as anxiety flames in my gut. I grip the handle of my water glass for dear life and try to get a hold of myself. This is all a product of my imagination. Some sick illusion making me feel like I'm losing my mind. I can't just *not* eat. I have to find a way to stomach it—

The organ twitches, and suddenly there's one on every plate. The cafeteria is a rat-king chain of hearts, all of them alive and throbbing. The chorus clatters the silverware, rattling the table beneath its weight.

I squeeze my eyes shut until tears spring up. *It's not real. None of it is real.* This is what nightmares are made of, terrors that only your mind can cook up. But what I feel next is very, very real, and I gasp at the flare of pain as glass cuts through my palm.

I didn't even know I was gripping my cup for dear life until it explodes in a sea of shards on my tray.

I risk opening my eyes, and not only has the world returned to normal, but everyone is staring. Gawking. The appropriate response when someone is actively losing their shit in public and breaking glasses.

HOUSE OF HEARTS

"Christ, Violet, are you all right?"

It's Amber.

I take stock of the scene. The heart is no longer a heart at all but a croissant on my plate, crimson blood reduced to a jam spread along the side.

I cradle my hand to my chest. "I-I'm sorry," I respond, sounding anything but stable, and to be quite honest, I'm not sure I *am* stable.

"You're *bleeding*."

"I'm okay, I'm just lightheaded," I lie, and when I go to stand up, I realize that's true. My legs buckle beneath me, and I have to grip the table with my good hand to keep from falling.

"You're most definitely not okay," Birdie snaps at the same time Amber whispers, "Mind control," under her breath with ten times more conviction.

I don't wait to listen as I scramble out of the cafeteria. It's almost, *almost* a relief to be out here in the crisp autumn air and away from the deafening chorus in the dining hall. Unfortunately, that lasts all of five minutes before a hot new horror enters the villa.

19

I'm surrounded by the dead.

Shadows wade in and out of focus all around me, their spectral forms born from thin air. Anastasia is the first to float along the lawn, her bare feet bent at an impossible angle and her toes barely grazing the ground. She stares at me like an owl, eyes a wide, milk-foam white. There and gone before Oleander replaces her.

He strides purposefully my way, his figure aging as he walks. Over several steps, he transforms from young student to graying Headmaster. His expression is the one constant: a grim determination thinning his lips and a haughty lift of his chin in the air.

I'm frozen in place as his astral form breezes *through* me. I flinch with the icy gust of a spirit cutting through mine, and it's enough to send me running. As soon as I find my strength, I'm sprinting through the academy's open-air corridors, outrunning the hearts in the cafeteria and the ghouls waiting for me around every corner. *Was Calvin right? Is there really no hope here? Am I doomed like Emoree was, fretting over an unsolvable problem?*

I'm no closer to figuring any of these questions out as I slide down the stone siding of the Winthrop Music Hall to catch my breath. I crane

HOUSE OF HEARTS

my neck around the side of the building and search my surroundings for students and spirits alike.

Satisfied that I'm well and truly alone, I sacrifice my scarf and use it to staunch the bleeding on my palm. Then I whip out my phone and scroll to Mom in my contacts list. Her smile in her profile picture might be weathered from a lifetime of labor and lost love, but despite it all, her eyes remain childishly hopeful for the future. I wish I had her optimism.

I wage war with the part of me that would throw away my phone and go back to hyperventilating on the ground. In the end, the sliver of me that misses my mom wins out, and I cradle the phone to my ear. I'm prepared to give up on the fifth ring when her voice crinkles through the speakers.

"Honey? What's up, is everything okay?" She might be miles away from me, but with her voice in my ear, I can easily pretend the two of us are together on the couch.

I do my best not to sniffle. "Yeah, everything is fine. I just miss you, Mom."

"Aww, I've missed you too, honey," she hums softly on the other end. It's such a strange feeling to be the broken one.

"How are things at home?" I ask, and I wonder whether she's eaten today. Whether the fridge is stocked and the bills are paid. I worry if she's back at her typical dating haunts, plucking terrible men out of obscurity and shoving them in the hole in her heart.

"G-good, things are good," she mumbles absently, her mind clearly elsewhere. I listen to the groan of creaking wood and the telling squeal of cabinets. She's pacing in circles, yanking out drawers and rummaging frantically inside.

"Are you looking for your keys again?" I guess, and the familiarity of it all is strangely soothing.

The noise stops all at once, overtaken by a trill of shocked laughter. "I swear you're psychic."

"Psychics don't exist," I say before remembering I'm literally *cursed* by a *ghost*, so God only knows at this point. "If they're not in between the couch cushions, they're on your bedside table. If they're not on the bedside table, there's a decent chance you left them in the fridge."

Hell, maybe I am psychic. I'm in a whole other state, and I can still picture the moment Mom storms over to the kitchen, swings open the freezer door to rummage around in the frozen peas, the smothered gasp when she brushes against cold metal, and the jangle of her lanyard as she pulls it out.

"That's my girl," she marvels, but the tail end of her voice is lost to static. The sound stretches out longer than it should, devolving to the shrill pitch of a whistle.

"Did you hear that?" I ask, wincing as I put distance between my phone and myself.

"Hear what, hun?" she asks, but the words are warped and underwater.

"My phone's acting up," I explain, but there's a *knowing* deep in my bones that tells me otherwise.

"Violet." Mom's voice is more than distorted. It's wrong. I sense it down to my marrow, feel it running in the currents of my veins. This isn't my mother. "It's all in your head."

I'm surprised I can speak at all. "It isn't," I manage to say, but the words tremble on their way out.

"It's all in your head." The voice flows from the receiver, spilling

HOUSE OF HEARTS

along my shoulders like a shawl of morning mist. "Or maybe it's not your head; maybe it's your heart."

I hitch in a staggering breath, and there's no mistaking what this is about now.

"Don't worry, you won't have it for much longer," the voice says, and that's *it*.

I throw my phone against the wall and let the screen shatter into a million horrible pieces. It doesn't matter; the static continues to erupt from broken speakers, humming in my ears like a biblical swarm of locusts. I abandon my phone there on the ground, my mother's face cracked and distorted, the screen splintered where her eyes should be.

I don't even have a moment to catch my breath before I see Oliver and Birdie around the corner. If I had any question about whether I was still cursed, all I have to do is watch as they storm across the open lawn, chattering hurriedly to themselves until they make it to the woman waiting for them.

All my bad luck has manifested into a single person: gray hair swept tightly to her scalp, overplucked brows, and a monochrome beige pantsuit.

"It's about Violet," Birdie says, and I instantly forget how to breathe. Headmistress Lockwell listens intensely, her body rigid as Birdie continues. "I followed her last night into the chapel and overheard her with Calvin—"

The rest of the conversation is hushed to an indiscernible whisper, but I don't need to hear any of it to know what she's about to say: that if I don't figure this out ASAP, I'm joining the Lockwells' long list of the dead.

A phantom slips through the veil and rips my attention away from the trio. It's Emoree. She is all consuming, her auburn hair cascading down her back and her gap-toothed smile transcendent even in death. She cranes her neck to look at me before beckoning me to follow with a slight incline of her head.

Common sense would say *Girl, for the love of God, don't follow your dead best friend again around campus* . . . And the key word there would be "again" because the first time didn't go so hot. But since I'm not in my right mind and I haven't been for quite some time, I go scampering off at her heels as she leads me around the back of the building.

We cut through the campus, and thankfully the final destination isn't *Final Destination*. She instead leads me to a house I've been in only once before. Headmistress Lockwell's campus residence sits empty, and when Emoree turns to me next, she fades through the door.

Unfortunately, the odds for quantum tunneling are one in a hundred billion, so I can't follow her that way. I'm left with the only mortal route available: breaking in. The front door boasts an impressive keycode panel, and it's going to alert someone if I screw this up.

I can't have that. I'm already in hot water; I don't need to switch the temperature to boiling. C'mon, think, *think*. I know the code is Percy's birthday because Calvin wouldn't stop griping about it the whole way over to her office. *"At least make it a little less obvious you have a favorite."* What the hell is his brother's birthday again?

I squeeze my eyes shut, concentrating with everything in me on all the inane conversations I had with Em about him. She was relieved he was a Taurus, wasn't she?

"I got lucky, he was on the cusp. Two days away from being a Gemini."

"And that's a problem?" I asked, failing to see the importance of astrology.

"Obviously!"

Two days from the cutoff. That would land him . . . when? I do the math in my head, running along the dates she prattled off before rushing to punch in the four-digit code. Gemini begins on May 21, so that would place him on the 19th.

0519

The half second stretches achingly long before the green light flashes and I can push the door open. It's bizarrely normal to see Emoree waiting for me inside.

She'd always hang outside my last class once the bell rang. Totally lost in her own head until the moment our eyes met; then and only then would a smile explode on her face, and it was like seeing someone's soul from the inside out.

"Thank God for the zodiac," I tell her, and my heart pangs as she doesn't smile now. "I'll never make fun of it again."

She's entirely blank-faced as she turns, gliding across the familiar hallway and toward the headmistress's private office. I'm ditching class and breaking into the headmistress's house—both things that would've given me a stress rash before Hart. Now I'm relieved that the study door is unlocked so I don't have to kick it in.

Emoree floats over to the curio cabinet, and I follow her eyeline to the knife perched behind the glass. It was ominous before, but seeing it today has me wanting to crawl out of my own skin. The baser part of my brain recognizes what the rest of me refuses to. I'm in danger and Calvin's right. There will come a time when Anastasia gets her wish and the curse has me perilously close to death . . . a time when I'll need to fight back.

"Is this what you wanted me to find?" I whisper, but she disappears on the heels of my question. Her image blows out like candle smoke and fades into nonexistence. I'm all alone as I unlatch the frame and free the blade from its prison.

The weapon is blackened with a century's use, and it reminds me of the redcap fairies in Emoree's stories. The ones who would dip their hats in the blood of those they'd slain, wearing the ichor of the fallen like a war trophy. The leather hilt is beautifully engraved with the letter *O*.

I've only just cradled it in my hands when I hear the click of heels striking against a hardwood floor. I hadn't heard the door open, but there's no mistaking the sound. I only have seconds to sheathe the blade and tuck it away in my pocket before taking cover beneath the headmistress's clawed desk.

"You know what needs to happen." Headmistress Lockwell's voice permeates through the silence, noxious and thick with faux understanding. The door hinges open, and I hear the shuffle of two other bodies entering behind her. Through the narrow crack in the opening of the desk, I recognize the pair as Sadie and Calvin. "There's no use in delaying it further."

The headmistress approaches her son like he's rabid, inching toward him as if one wrong move will spell disaster. He's darkened with sleep loss, and when she dares to get too close, he darts back with a sharp gleam of his teeth.

"Calvin!" Sadie cries, but her mother only shushes her with a lifted hand.

"Your brother isn't well, Sadie. He is in the throes of the curse. I know the feeling." The desk shifts faintly as she lowers her body onto it and crosses her legs against the Persian carpet. "It consumes you from

HOUSE OF HEARTS

the inside out and makes you feel like a spectator in your own skin. Isn't that right, Calvin?"

He doesn't need to say a word because it shows in every aspect: the mismatched buttons of his dress shirt, the stubble spreading across his jaw, the frantic darting of his eyes in every direction. Even his signature cologne is traded for the sharp bite of espresso.

"I wasn't vigilant enough when it came to Percy. I should've overseen that night to make sure he did what was necessary. Now look where we are! Two deaths in a single year? Tsk. The optics will be horrendous." Headmistress Lockwell paces in frantic circles before turning to one of her many shelves and freeing a bottle of bourbon and a Swarovski crystal glass. She fixes herself a drink and takes a sip. "We'll be proactive this time. Hide the body and call her a teenage runaway. We can say Violet was troubled and came here out of grief and—"

My name sends Calvin to the floor. He buries his face between two shaking palms and mutters a long nonsensical whisper through his teeth. "I can't . . . Don't make me . . . Violet, Violet, Violet . . ." He reminds me of a wild animal locked in a cage—hissing and gnashing its teeth—or perhaps it's more like a boy who knows his fate is sealed.

Sadie grimaces, horrified. "Mom, this isn't like you."

The headmistress harrumphs. She goes rheumy-eyed in memory in memory. "You'll learn soon enough that this curse, in its own sick and twisted way, is a blessing. It doesn't look like one now. Trust me, I know that. Isaac begged me to stop. He pleaded, but I . . . I couldn't stop myself, and damn it all if that memory doesn't linger with me today. It took years to see through the fog and realize I was better off. With this girl . . . it's a tragedy, I understand that, but perhaps a necessary evil. We need to ensure this sacrifice goes as planned and we dispose of all evidence afterward."

"You can't be serious," Sadie argues, lowering down to help her brother on the floor. "What you're talking about isn't a curse, it's premeditated murder."

"This is survival." And I think Headmistress Lockwell really means that. Conviction strikes in the harsh clatter of her drink against the counter. "Until the curse is lifted, this is our hand in life, so you'll do well to play your cards right."

Sadie blanches at her brother's side on the floor.

"Calvin would never forgive you." She speaks as if he isn't there, and in many ways, he isn't. "You know that, right?"

"I don't need his forgiveness," she answers simply. "I don't need yours, either. I need your cooperation and your understanding that I know better than you at this moment. Hate me forever if you must, but know I'm the only one who has lived this before. It's called a curse for a reason. The ramifications are ugly, but there's no fighting the tide, so it's better to swim alongside it."

Sadie doesn't get the opportunity to argue. In one awful moment, her eyes drop beneath the desktop and land on mine. Time stands still as recognition flares across her face.

"You're right, Mom," she admits with a solemn dip of her head. "I don't know what this is like, and I guess I'm still reeling from Percy and now this. It's a lot to process, but I actually know where Violet might be hiding."

Shit. I come up with ten new curse words on the spot as I wait for her finger to lower and fall upon me. Headmistress Lockwell will haul me out kicking and screaming, and Calvin will carve into my chest with his bare hands. I'll die here on her ridiculously overpriced antique rug, and then she'll scrub me out of the fibers.

HOUSE OF HEARTS

"I think she's in the House of Hearts. She told Calvin she wanted time to look for a way to break the curse, so we'll probably find her in the archives."

Headmistress Lockwell nods sagely. "Good girl. I can always count on you to do what's right. Grab your brother and let's do our best not to make a scene on the way over."

Sadie slings Calvin's arm over her shoulder and half drags him through the doorway.

I wait for the door to click and their footsteps to soften in the distance before I breathe again, and I immediately scramble for the window latch of the office. I can't be in here a second longer, not with the walls pressing in like a bruising exhale, squeezing me tighter and tighter until I'm perfectly coffin-shaped.

Lifting my body over the ledge, I topple over into a thorny patch of rose briars. They leave their mark in a dozen bloodied cuts, and with my still-bandaged hand, I know the picture isn't a pleasant one. All I'm missing is an open knife wound to the heart now.

There are a million places I could go, but none of them would matter in the end. I can't flee campus, and Birdie would innocently offer me up to the headmistress all over again. Sadie probably can't save me twice. So instead of hiding anywhere, I head to that same elm tree Oliver and Amber sat under the first day, its canopy mostly skeletal, the colored leaves in large piles on the ground.

I didn't know it was possible to feel like a pumpkin rotting on a porch, yet here I am. All scooped out. There's no escaping now. Soon I'll be one more dead body to join the rest.

"It wasn't supposed to be like this," I growl under my breath, letting my head fall against the hard tree trunk.

223

My hair snarls in the splintered wood, but I don't bother to untangle it. I finally figured out what killed my friend, and I can't do a goddamn thing about it because I naively thought I could outsmart a love curse. That I could use my brain against a matter of the heart. If I had understood the strange threads connecting me and Calvin earlier, maybe I would've had time to solve this, but here I am, resigned to die.

The tears come, one by one, and I can't stop them. They multiply, and I burrow in on myself, heaving alone. Alone, alone, alone. I haven't cried like this in ages. I've always lived in a black-and-white world, worshiped at the altar of knowledge and kept my heart in a box under lock and key.

It all seems so useless now. If Anastasia wants my heart so badly, she can have it. It's not like it's done me any good.

I bang my head against the trunk of the tree and debate what I'm even feeling anymore. Anger. I'm angry at the world. Angry at the shitty luck that got me here; angry at Emoree, who couldn't have just listened to me and stayed home; angry at myself for opening up to Calvin; and angry at Calvin for seeing something beyond my prickly, uninviting exterior.

And most of all, angry at Anastasia, because some foolish part of me wishes this whole thing could blow over and I could show up at Calvin's door and have an honest-to-God relationship with him.

That would never work, I tell myself resolutely, standing upright to stare at the maze. Even if there was no curse, there's a world of difference between the two of us. Calvin's an entire planet, and I'm only a moon trapped in his orbit.

I swallow and it hurts. I have no idea what to expect as the seconds tick onward, the threat of Anastasia's wrath growing more real by the minute. What's waiting for me inside the maze? A monster stitched from scraps of stories, a jagged patchwork quilt of a girl with black eyes and a cavernous heart.

Undead and hungry for what she no longer has. The Queen of Hart's.

I don't have an heirloom key, but that can no longer stop me. It's my life on the line. I have nothing else to lose, do I?

Divot by divot, I climb until I drop right into the maze.

Dear Diary,

I dreamt last night of Oleander.

That part wasn't new. I have dreamt about him for the last several months, but never like this. Last night he wasn't a man, he was a vine, twisting around me in tight, bruising spirals.

I couldn't fight against his embrace, had no hope to break free as he kissed me. With each kiss, he breathed me in deeper and stole the air right out of my lungs. I gasped for it, my skin a strangled lilac blue, but he didn't stop. Wouldn't stop until I felt myself go cold. It was then that he began to dig an earthen plot in the soil. The exact dimensions to bury me.

"I've planted every seed in this garden," he whispered, his hand coming to rest on my cheek. "And you, my dear, will be the prettiest flower of them all."

—Anastasia Hart

20

"Intuition" isn't a Magic 8 Ball squished between my ribs or an old lady fortune teller whispering prophecies in my ear. There's science behind the mysticism, a subconscious survival instinct built upon a series of somatic markers. And what it's telling me now is that even beyond the obvious curse, something is terribly wrong.

I notice that wrongness immediately after recovering from my fall. The rough landing tears my tights, ripping the black fabric at my knees and exposing the bruised skin beneath. I hiss at the impact and smear the cuts clean with the sleeve of my blazer. After the last twenty-four hours, I'm sure my body is a Rorschach inkblot of bruises beneath my clothes. I don't have time to check, though, because the instant I sit up, I take stock of the bizarre world around me.

The hedges are the same, but there's a dizzy lurch in my gut and a strangeness sticking to everything I see. It begins with an otherworldly ripple of the grass and continues with the gate behind me, padlocks clattering a discordant melody against the bars before everything goes silent. I look up, and even the sky is wrong. The sunset is long gone, stars flickering like stop-motion animation, constellations rippling past in a blur. And then it's sunrise, the sun a bloody cough against the white fringed dawn.

This can't be happening.

Except it totally is, and I have no choice but to grip the ever-changing gate behind me to keep my wobbly legs upright. My body rebels against all of it—the changing sky and the world slipping between my fingers. I make the mistake of looking back out through the bars and immediately want to throw up.

It's my high school, but it isn't. It's stripped down from a century's worth of modernization, the streetlamps replaced with old-fashioned gas lamps; the flag banners winked out of existence. Second by second, the campus molts beyond my recognition. Buildings broken down and remade, the tower yet to be built.

It all gives way to a vast stretch of nothing and no one. Thick fog rolls in from the left and blankets the campus in gray. I narrow my eyes and squint into the gloom. The fog swallows what's left of the campus until there's no world beyond the maze, no north or south or east or west. Only here.

Here stretches on forever. It's like being trapped within a cloud, a shapeless blur until images lift from the mist, appearing before me like memories playing out on a vintage projector. Two strangers meander down a beaten path beyond the maze, their bodies corporeal and yet fuzzy around the edges.

They stroll closer toward me, but neither person acknowledges my presence in the slightest. They're both swept away in conversation, speaking as if I don't exist beside them.

"His name is Oleander Lockwell, is it not?" a young woman's voice pries. "The lover you're meeting with. He's a student here."

My entire body goes tense. For a dead girl, Anastasia Hart is very alive right now at her sister's side. Rosacea colors the apples of her cheeks, a bright flush of pink against her ivory skin. She's more than an urban legend. She's tendons and flesh and bone; a girl my age, alive and breathing and oblivious as to what's to come.

"What of it?" she sniffs, her wide-eyed stare giving her face an ethereal, Renaissance quality. Her bright red hair is bundled high atop her head, crowned with a series of intricate braids. She's beautiful, but her shoulders slump, her fingers toying self-consciously with a loose curl.

"Did you know he was engaged once before?" her sister asks. "The girl died."

Helen couldn't be any more her opposite. Everything about her is confident, vibrant, electric.

Anastasia wrings her hands helplessly at her side, her mouth thinning into a severe tight line. There's a tense beat of silence between them, an unspoken challenge flaring hot in her eyes. "Is a man not allowed to experience tragedy?" she asks after a telling moment.

"I never said that, but it's odd for him to have fled town after and then pursued you, don't you think?" Helen challenges, her expression a mingled mess of desperation and steadfastness.

"It's odd for you to concern yourself with him," Anastasia replies tartly, her eyes darting briefly to mine, but apparently seeing nothing beyond the rustle of greenery. I shiver all the same. "You don't know him."

"It's my duty as your sister—"

"To spoil my happiness?" she snaps, her hands balled tightly and her nostrils flared. "Is that your great familial duty?"

Helen captures her sister's fists in her own hands. "My duty is to keep you safe, Ana!"

Tearing herself away, Anastasia gestures dramatically at her body, her fingers a flourish from top to bottom. "Do I look harmed? Do I look as though I might be in any sort of danger? I'm happier than I've ever been, and you'd do well to stick your nose elsewhere."

Helen blows a measured breath between her teeth. "Any other man. Go for anyone else other than him. He's bad news. I need you to listen to me."

Ana's expression teeters beyond rage and sends her into a deep, watery-eyed chasm. She sniffles, and the high planes of her cheeks color further. "Who would you have court me? Christopher McNally? Oh, wait, yes, that's right, he's smitten with you. Bernie Hawthorn? Hmm, no, that's right, he also favored you. It's easy for you to look for another suitor when you have the whole world vying for your attention."

Helen balks. "That isn't what I meant."

"No, I know what you meant, sister. I finally found my own slice of happiness, and you wish to dash it. So what is it now?"

"He is only with you for your inheritance!"

Anastasia leaps back like she's been struck. "You're right. How on earth could someone ever love me without motive? Impossible, I'd wager."

Helen's eyes widen, and her lips curl back into a grimace. "That isn't what I meant!"

But Anastasia doesn't linger long enough to listen. She storms out of focus, their forms dissipating into wisps of smoke.

I stagger away from the scene and wring my hands nervously. It's one thing to hear about the sisters, or even catch ghostly glimmers of them throughout campus. Seeing them here in the flesh is another matter entirely. This is really happening, isn't it? What will I find when I get to the center of this maze? Ana's still-warm corpse, her heart freshly carved out of her chest? Or is she somewhere inside now, waiting for me to arrive?

Wherever she is, I'm not showing up empty-handed. My fingers twitch at the stolen knife in my pocket, and I brandish it now, letting the cool silver of the blade shine through the gloom.

I won't go down that easily.

With the fog limited to the world beyond the gate, I might have the advantage of the sun inside the maze, but that doesn't make navigating it any easier. The greenery high above my head eclipses me as I walk the path. I feel microscopic in the face of it all, no different than an insignificant blade of grass rustling below. I wade through the maze as best as I can, but either my memory has grown murky or the paths have shifted position. The latter seems more likely as I round the corner and am immediately spat back out to where I was several steps ago.

The paths aren't the only things changing. Time moves differently, and clearly we're not in the twenty-first century anymore. I'm not even convinced we're in the nineteenth century, really. It's a forgotten fairy-tale hour, the thirteenth strike of a clock where we slip between worlds and logic ceases to exist.

I throw a look over my shoulder before rounding the next corner. I can't shake the creeping, crawling sensation of being watched. This is typically the point where I'd talk myself out of my fears and chalk it up to paranoia, but in here? Logic's out the window. Through the thicket of dark green hedge, I imagine a set of eyes blinking through the gloom. Some hidden audience trained on every wrong turn I make, laughing to themselves as I lose my direction and my sanity all at once.

I'm met with another fork in the road, and I suck in a sharp inhale as the trail rustles behind me. It could be nothing, but I swivel around regardless. Alone. Of course I am. I flood my lungs, hold the air, and push it out. Slow, methodical, a testament to the fact that I'm still alive. Every inch of this place is a twisted illusion, spinning me in desperate, nauseating circles.

I flash back to my Ovid lecture hall listening to Dr. Sampson prattle on about princesses and Minotaurs. I feel like Theseus. I wanted revenge, and now here I am, in the belly of the beast. I'll stab my way out.

My thoughts drift to the words our teacher left us with. *"It only takes two facing mirrors to build a labyrinth."*

What did he mean by that? I never had the time to pause and figure it out, and by the time the next class rolled around, I'd been too absorbed in my own issues to pay his lesson any mind. Frankly, I'm surprised I haven't run into my own twisted reflection in this madhouse.

It's horrifically quiet, every crunch of earth beneath my feet almost deafening in the silence. The only other sound is the beating of my heart. I press a hand to my chest like I might be able to stifle the noise. This is the same frozen-over fear I had as a child, my head beneath the blankets, a monster lying in wait beneath the bed, but this time the bogeyman isn't a figment of my own childish imagination.

This time it's real.

The silence doesn't last long. The sound begins with a howling uptick of wind and then moves to a rustle in the grass. Branches sway, and footsteps squelch in my wake.

"Violet!" a voice calls out, and I'm reminded of my very first time in this maze. That night felt like a ripple in time, a flickering candle that blew in and out with the breeze. The maze wasn't ready to spirit me away yet, with its two worlds sitting parallel to one another.

"Violet!" My name is called again, and I recognize the voice. It's

HOUSE OF HEARTS

fantastical and dreamlike. It's Calvin, and yet . . . it isn't. Just how I knew my mother wasn't the woman on the other end of the line. "Violet! Where are you?"

I'm all goose bumps as I twist around to see if I'm still alone. I can't help the nervous chatter of teeth and the live-wire trip in my veins.

The thought of Anastasia Hart possessing Calvin has me shivering. I can see it all in my mind—the moment when she overtakes him, lifting his body and dragging him here to this strange upside-down world with me. Anastasia is a cat with a mouse, not content with simply killing me. She'd rather throw me in the air and bite my limbs off one at a time before scooping out my heart.

I tighten my grip on the blade. I'm not completely helpless, but I still feel horrifically vulnerable in this moment.

My name comes from all directions now. It rumbles beneath my feet, echoes from my left, and launches from my right. The hedges— once a uniform, never-ending stretch of green—pulse with new life. There's a taunting splash of pink and purple against the dark foliage as violets bloom all around me. Their petals unfurl like a hundred tiny mouths, all of them wanting to latch on to me, to kiss, to bite. Vines lasso around my legs, and I nearly trip in my attempt to break free. I squash the petals beneath my heel for good measure, and it's then that an idea takes root inside me.

I don't have the time to weigh the odds. I only have time to lay the bait.

"Where are you, Calvin?" I shout back, my grip clammy on the hilt of the knife. I inject as much naive concern into my voice as I can. "Calvin! Help!"

Everything crashes to an abrupt halt. The violets rot, petals furling inward before burning black and crumbling into ash. The maze stops twisting and turning; the hedges stop pulsating like a beating heart. And Calvin's stolen voice goes quiet. We sit in horrific, anticipatory silence, the only noises my jagged breath and the deafening pulse in my throat.

I don't have to wait long.

Just as quickly as it all ended, it ripples back to life.

"Violet!" The voice has returned, but it's distorted like a broken record. It shifts and takes shape in the air, growing closer and closer until all the little hairs on my body prickle to attention. I don't need to turn around to know I'm no longer alone.

Every inch of my skin begs me to stay rooted, to not turn and give life to my monster under the bed. Against all instinct, I have to look.

"There you are, darling."

21

There's a stranger in Calvin's skin.

He's all predatory feline grace, his eyes devilishly dark as he stalks my way. He sizes me up like a conquest to be made or a throat to tear out with his teeth. Even though fear swells like a tidal wave inside me, there's still that dizzy, lovestruck flip of my heart.

He grabs my free hand and presses kisses to the mountain ridge of my knuckles. I shudder at the sweep of his thumb against my wrist. He holds me there for far too long, measuring my pulse. Breathing me in.

I can't help it. He's devastatingly handsome in the morning light, his jaw limned with dappled sunlight, his blond hair aglow. There's no trace of his earlier exhaustion. Either this maze is deceiving me or he got a razor and some heavy-duty undereye cream. Contacts, too, because those amber eyes of his are unnaturally bright in a way no human's should be.

In another life, I could see myself offering my heart gladly. I remember the first time I laid eyes on him—the curious, horrible realization that he could bite off my head and I'd let him. I obscure the blade from sight, wedging my arm behind my back and gripping it tightly.

"I was watching when you left my mother's office," he tells me, and it's not a whispered confession, but the start of a hunter's tale. His fingers splay mine apart, stretching my hand like we're comparing palms. He grins down at me like he's wondering how my head might look mounted on his wall. "It's so strange, these thoughts in my head. At first," he says, his lips gravitating to my ear, "I was thinking about how beautiful you looked."

"And then?" I ask, and my voice is tight between my teeth. He laughs at my question. A low rumble trembling against my collarbone.

"And then . . . hmm . . ." he trails off contemplatively, letting the sentence linger. He doesn't answer immediately, choosing instead to brush his cheek against mine, his body so very close. He hums softly before he switches angles. "You want to know what I love the most about falling in love?"

I make a strange noise in the back of my throat, and he chuckles.

"The thrill of the chase," he whispers, and I stagger back, finally seeing the full extent of him. A scream threatens to peel from my lungs.

I dreamed up a great number of horrible things, but my imagination has nothing on reality. Ana's spirit manifests over Calvin's body like a murderous marionette. She's a gruesome shadow, too tall and too thin, limbs all muscle beneath tight stretches of translucent skin. Her body has grown gaunt, her chest flayed open and her bones jutting out like a repulsive set of splayed wings. There's a cavernous black hollow in place of her heart, flanked by a twisted tangle of hungry arteries. From here, they look like starving mouths wanting to latch on and feed.

She's a dead thing, but I am not yet a fresh corpse for her to tear apart.

She steps closer, and her shadow body propels Calvin's legs to follow. Each crack sounds like the crunch of bone; each pop is a joint

HOUSE OF HEARTS

snapping in and out of its socket. How many boys and girls have fallen victim to this? How many Lockwells have lost themselves completely? Too many, and I refuse to lose another one now.

"Th-this isn't you," I stammer, brandishing the dagger in my hand and tightening my hold on the hilt until it feels like an extension of my own body. "Ana's gotten into your head, Calvin. This isn't *you*."

He might not hear me, but he most definitely sees me. His attention snags on the blade in my hands, and I don't have long to process as he lurches forward, one hand angling for my throat and the other grappling for my knife. I only have a split second to react before he reaches me, and self-preservation yanks ahold of the reins.

Possessed by my own will to stay alive, I breathe in, steady myself, and swing the blade down. Anastasia's body is all smoke and mirrors, and the knife fails to make impact on her. If she were a *Night of the Living Dead* ghoul, I could hope to cut her clean away from Calvin like a nightmarish parasite. But instead, the blade bypasses her entirely and grazes against Calvin's face before slipping from my fingers. It falls onto the grass, and I'm forced to stand back and take in what I've done. A thin streak of blood cuts along his cheek, sending him staggering.

He brushes at his face, blinking as if breaking free from a trance. The edges of his fingertips are stained, and he examines them in slack-jawed horror.

"Violet," he whispers frantically. "*Violet*. You need to get the hell out of here."

I squint at him, unsure whether this is a clever trap or a rare moment of lucidity. He proves it's the latter by taking the blade from the ground and lodging it into his leg. The glint of silver disappears into the meaty muscle of his calf, and red gushes from the wound in volcanic spurts. Calvin starts to howl, his eyes welling with fresh tears, his agony disrupting the maze's perfect illusion of him.

"Calvin!" I cry, rushing toward him. "What are you doing?"

He throws himself away from me, the abrupt lurch only causing him even more pain.

"What does it look like?" he pants through clenched teeth, squeezing his eyes shut in a futile attempt to stomach the pain. I'm not the most well versed in ghost logic, but this must be a way to thwart possession, like how Percy trapped himself in a magical coma. "I'm buying you time to get the hell out of here! You need to find Percy!"

"Percy? He's . . . here?" "Here" being code for . . . whatever this place is. A weird limbo beyond the planes of reality, a purgatory.

Calvin nods, his skin pale from the blood loss. Behind him, the faint shadow of Anastasia grows clearer by the second. It won't be long until she's taken him over yet again, ripping the blade free and chasing after me with her human puppet. "I can feel him. He must've followed us here in this weird limbo. Find him and figure out an escape. *Now run!*"

I don't have a choice. I'm forced to abandon him as Anastasia returns to his body. It begins with his eyes rolling back in his skull and ends with a tremor running through his veins and propelling him upward. I run past him, immediately hitting a forked devil's-tongue path. Anastasia is howling my name, blood still geysering from the wound.

"Violet!" His voice no longer sounds lucid but wild and disembodied. The sound of my name is followed by a horrific, off-putting screech in the air. "Violet! Violet! Where are you?"

I hastily decide on the left path and chuck one of my shoes to the right to throw him off. It thunks in the distance, and a minute later

HOUSE OF HEARTS

there're the lumbering footsteps of Calvin's possessed form darting after it. Anastasia drives him forward despite his wound, my name growing more and more warped in the distance.

My chest heaves, and my body is alive with nerves. "Terrified" is a massive understatement. "Terrified" was back when I was stumbling through this maze the first time, my imagination playing hellish tricks on me in the dark. Now that I know what's truly waiting for me inside, I want to curl up and disappear.

A cowardly part of me wishes I could find a place in this maze to ride out the storm, hide in this labyrinth until starvation kicks in. It would be a kinder death than what's waiting for me. I rack my brain, feeling like a little girl all over again. Like I might not actually make my way out of this mess.

My name is a shrieking wail in the distance. I wait another agonizingly long moment before fleeing down another split path. With the way this maze keeps twisting and turning, for all I know, my next step might chew me up and spit me out at her feet. That's not a thought I want to entertain.

I need to find my way into the heart of the maze, but how do I navigate anything when the maze keeps folding in on itself?

It's only then I notice the first few flecks of red. Calvin's blood stains the hedges, marking a gruesome Hansel and Gretel trail in his wake. He's left a purposeful trace through the maze, and I know immediately that it's not one for me to follow. It's one to avoid like my life depends on it.

He's trying to help me, even now, despite everything. He's in there, no matter how deep.

My heart pangs, and I wish I could crawl my way back in time to the other night. The moon overhead and his lips on mine and everything fleetingly perfect.

I continue at a careful pace, not wanting to speed ahead and launch right into Anastasia, but not wanting to be a sitting duck, either. The maze might want to play tricks on me, but I'm one step ahead, and that will have to be good enough.

I keep my gaze straight ahead, my nose to the soil like a bloodhound. If this mirror-world is anything like reality, Percy is waiting for me in the mausoleum. I hold on to that tiny hope, as fickle as it may be, and I close my eyes to will the clearing into focus. My mind paints a visual of marble walls and a slumbering boy, and I channel all my energy into breaking through the last of the maze's illusions.

Peeking an eye open, I'm relieved to see that I can reassert logic back in an illogical situation. The path opens up, unfurling like a flower in the face of the sun. I step into the clearing, and it's everything I remember.

The Hart crypts sit in a half-moon sickle against a wide stretch of barren lawn; beyond it, there's a stone bench planted in the center, and the statue of the two sisters. In this timeline, Helen's yet to die and Ana's yet to carve out her own heart. Even their marble renditions are still intact, both sisters still wearing matching necklaces just like the one I'm wearing and holding hands, the eldest one's head still attached to her body, not sitting in the dirt.

My stomach sours at the sight. How difficult would it have been to talk it out? Why make heartbreak and a petty siblings' quarrel all our burdens to bear? My fingers twitch, and in a fit of anger I rip the locket off, no longer constrained in that aspect of the curse. I don't want to die with a glorified BFF charm strung across my throat, especially not when it belongs to the person trying to kill me.

HOUSE OF HEARTS

Banishing it to my pocket, I turn back to the mausoleum. It's not silent like it was the other day. It's a nightmare. The slab doors are pounding violently from the inside, the ground trembling alongside them. It's as haunting as the sight of a cemetery bell ringing above a grave. And then a voice cries from inside.

I'm hesitant as I lower my hands to the door, my breath catching as I pull it open. A different scene awaits me from the last time I entered this tomb. There's no lifeless body slumped in the corner, numb to the world around him. I see a familiar face from old photographs: wild, disheveled curls, punctured glasses splintered in the left frame, and warm brown eyes. And this time they're open and looking right at me.

Percy.

22

Admittedly, I look horrible. I'm drenched in sweat, covered in blood that's only half my own, and I'm missing a shoe. For as terrible as I look, I don't think I'm anywhere near horrifying enough to warrant Percy's response.

He gawks at me like *I'm* the ghost.

"You're Violet," he says breathlessly. He devolves into a broken hiccup, and his hand grapples against the wall for support. His lips pull back in a clear grimace, and he stumbles so far back, he lands on his ass on the ground. I offer him a hand, and he hesitantly takes it.

"You know me?" I take a careful step forward, and he tracks the movement with a skittish adjustment of his glasses. They slip down the bridge of his nose again, and he's quick to correct them.

"Of course I do," he says, and his voice is so much deeper than his baby face would suggest. "You're Em's best friend."

It's almost heartwarming—almost. The heartwarming part is overshadowed by his horrified gulp and the sentence that comes next. "But . . . but if *you're* here, that means Emoree is . . ."

"Dead," I finish, and I hate being in this position. The same one my mother was in when she cradled the phone and got the news, her eyes going wide, her voice breaking in a horrified gasp. She didn't need to open her mouth for me to know what she was about to say. The truth was written so plainly over her face, and I'll never forget the way the world was ripped right out from under me that day.

His fist strikes the marble, and he stifles his cry before it can alert Anastasia to where we are. "It wasn't supposed to be like this," he whispers, and I can see it in his eyes that he really means it. There are a fair number of things in life I never put much stock in before, and the eyes being the window to the soul was high on the bullshit meter. But when I look at him now, I think I might just see his soul after all. "How did everything get so messed up?"

His expression is unerringly genuine. I don't know how I ever doubted his innocence. There's such an outpouring of love in his eyes, mingled deep with pure, unadulterated heartbreak. Love and grief are two sides of the same coin, after all. I've learned that lesson the hard way.

"Have you been here this whole time?" I ask, waving at the strange world around us. "Whatever this place is."

He nods. "Mm-hmm. I've been trapped in this godforsaken limbo since I uttered that spell in the maze."

"Was that the plan all along?" I ask, and I've been dying to know how they stacked everything up before the inevitable, brutal fall.

He wets his dry lips and stares at his nails. They're bloodied, dirty half-moon crescents caked with slivers of soil. From a cursory glance around us, it's clear he went from pounding on the slab doors to digging a trench where Anastasia's future grave would someday lie. He managed to carve a hole several feet deep in the earth.

"To be trapped in a hellish time loop forever?" he scoffs, running his nails along his scalp. "No. There was a spell I found in Ana's book, and I thought if I surrendered myself, that Emoree would survive in my stead and that I would be the only one affected. I knew what I was offering, but I still had no clue what it would mean. I thought it would be like dying or falling asleep. I didn't think I'd come *here*."

He clears his throat and continues. "I didn't tell Emoree the full truth. I scratched out the word *eternal* in the spell and let her believe that if I surrendered myself to the maze for a single night, that I could 'ride out the curse,' so to speak. I told her I was locking myself up in the mausoleum and she'd hide away in the clock tower. She really thought that when Anastasia's ghost disappeared, it would mean we'd properly outlived the length of the curse. I let her believe that she could come and wake me up after and everything would be okay again." He sniffles, averts his eyes. "She had no idea that I planned to stay like this forever. I would've sacrificed my life to keep her safe."

I wring my hands helplessly, and he finally asks the question I've been waiting for in return. "How did she die?"

"She fell."

The scene plays out in my mind. A million little clues finally pieced together into a fairy-tale tragedy—Emoree waiting in Helen's old room, alone and terrified for Percy. Searching the maze for a glimpse of him, chest pressed too close to the railing, the wind swirling.

It's so easy to imagine how the maze might've played tricks on her even from afar. She could've seen the silhouette of a woman. Maybe Em saw Ana follow Percy into the mausoleum, or maybe Anastasia simply stood there, staring up at the tower, beckoning for Emoree to lean in and look closer.

And Em did just that. She strained over the railing, the perch under her feet slippery from a rain-heavy winter. A sharp wind and a fall.

HOUSE OF HEARTS

Emoree Hale sat on a wall,
Emoree Hale had a great fall.
Six seconds.
And then nothing—nothing at all.

"If she's dead . . ." he attempts to say, the words a choked cry. He looks nauseous at the very idea, and it takes him two tries to even finish his thought. He rubs his eyes like this is all some lucid dream he can shake off. If only it was that easy. "If she's dead and you're here, in this world, then that means the curse has extended to you and . . . Calvin?"

I nod, and even the sound of Calvin's name in the air is enough for me to crumple in on myself. A nervous half giggle gurgles up his throat, echoing the delirium I feel.

"Well, shit," he says, and it's such a heart-wrenchingly normal thing to say that I almost forget where we are. We could be two friends sitting in the school courtyard for lunch, swapping poor test grades and shrugging it off with a muttered curse.

"Yeah, 'well, shit,'" I repeat.

Percy's expression sobers up, and he looks achingly broken.

"This has gone on for too long," he snarls to himself, and it's not difficult to match his anger. Thinking of Calvin alone out there in the maze, bloodied and stripped of any free will, makes me want to punch a hole in the wall.

"How many hearts do you think she's stolen?" I ask even though I'm not sure I want to know the answer.

"Too many," Percy says, wiping the beginnings of tears with the back of his hand. "It needs to end. I won't let Emoree die in vain. I won't let Calvin get roped any further into this mess. We have to end it."

"How?" I ask, looking around us at the mausoleum. Nothing about it seems like it's equipped for curse breaking. There's nothing but sterile white walls and . . . *the hole he dug.* "Wait a minute. We could lure her in here, couldn't we?" I whisper in a daze.

With the door stuck behind him, Percy had been trapped inside Ana's mausoleum and had resorted to trying to dig his way out. Is it possible to trap her now while she's corporeal?

Percy throws a disparaging look back in the direction of the hole, but nods. "You might be onto something there. We can have her—or, my brother I guess—chase us into the mausoleum. If we could somehow get them to fall into the hole, it'll buy us time to trap her and work up a counterspell. We'll need to cover it, though, so she doesn't see what's directly under her until it's too late."

"Not sure with what," I say, scanning around for a convenient camouflage tarp. Unfortunately for me, the maze is fresh out. It's just hedges and dirt and more dirt. "There's nothing here."

He considers that, and I watch him do the same miserable sweep of our surroundings. Finally, his gaze lands on my shoulders and he nods in my direction. "Your blazer should do."

With as many falls and tumbles as I've taken today, my blazer very nearly matches the raw floor in color. I shrug it off my shoulders and do just as he said, covering the hole and staking my sleeves on either end with two thorned branches. "All that's left now is the bait."

I throw an anxious glance to the distance to make sure we're still alone. We seem to be for now, but I don't trust Anastasia not to come barreling out of nowhere. I smother the naive rush of hope in my chest at this plan. I'm not foolish enough to think we'll escape alive, but I know I'll go down swinging.

"It's risky taunting her out in the maze," I say, weighing our odds.

HOUSE OF HEARTS

"There's a chance she could draw us away and lead us deeper into her labyrinth."

Percy tightens his fists and steps away from the trap. "That's why I'll be the one to bait her. No use risking *both* of us."

I scoff. "Over my dead body."

"That's what I'm worried about."

I narrow my eyes into slits. "There's no way I'm letting you face her alone." I lift my chin defiantly and take a step forward until my finger wedges against his chest. "I wasn't there for Emoree when she needed me most, and I refuse to make the same mistake again." I gulp and wet my parched lips. "We'll go together, and when this is over, we'll find a way to free Calvin."

He smiles somberly. "I can see why you're his true love. You two complement each other well. Okay. We'll both do it then. If she gets too close to one of us, the other will need to shout out to distract her."

He offers me a hand, and we shake on it.

"Time to put an end to this once and for all."

Actively taunting a monster in her own domain has got to be a new low for me. What felt like only thirty minutes ago, I was chucking my shoe and trying to stab her just to get away. Now I'm here, missing a shoe, missing a weapon, ready to whistle through my fingers like she's my long-lost dog.

Percy gives me an encouraging nod as we reenter the maze. The plan is to not go very far. We can't risk getting completely lost, but we need to get far enough to entice her. I tremble with every step and whip around like she might jump out in Calvin's skin and yell "boo!" Or worse, given her track record.

With the opening to the center clearing just visible behind us,

247

Percy stops in his tracks. I know it's time before he even signals with a silent lift of his hand. Ready or not, here we come.

"Anastasia!" I cry, and the world seems to ripple with the name. Percy winces at the sound but gives me a reassuring nod. Somewhere in the maze I know she must hear me. She's been listening and waiting and now, finally, is her chance to strike.

Every little neuron in my brain is firing with "bad idea." I scream her name in the wind again at the top of my lungs, "ANASTASIA HART!"

Percy follows suit so we're both shouting. It feels bizarrely like being at a sleepover and chanting "Bloody Mary" three times in the mirror for the hell of it and then being surprised when she actually shows up covered in blood and drags you kicking and screaming into the glass.

But in the beginning, wasn't Bloody Mary someone, too? A woman before she became a monster? Em's words echo hauntingly in my mind. *Ghosts don't appear for no reason! Something really bad has to happen to bring them back.*

It's not long before I hear the rustle of a branch and the hiss of someone's breath, which is more than enough to shut us both up. We stop to listen, and there's a shuffle of footsteps against soil. She's coming. And she'll bring Calvin's body with her. She'll use his hands to press into my throat and his nails to dig through my chest and tear out my heart.

I can't help the lick of fear, the worry that we've made a mistake and that nothing we've planned will work, but there's no turning back now. The only way out is through, so we need to be ready to see this to the bitter end. And that bitter end is rounding the corner now, a flash of bloodied hair sending my heartbeat into overdrive. She's found us. Here goes nothing.

HOUSE OF HEARTS

Percy and I ditch screaming in favor of spinning on our heels and running like hell. My chest burns with the effort, and I'm sucking in noisy gulps of air like a fish on dry land. I taste blood on the back of my tongue, the overexertion breaking me out in a white-hot heat.

I can hear Calvin sprinting behind me, his body made unnaturally fast by Anastasia's influence. He's quicker than he should be, and much too close for comfort behind me.

It'd be a mistake to peek back and see his clouded eyes and the screaming maw of the spirit latched to his back. You don't look down when you're teetering precariously on a tightrope, and yet here I am, doing just that. She's hard to look away from. Her humanity has been stolen, and she's made hideous by hate. Her mouth is contorted in a howl, and there's something gangly and unnatural about the way she looms over him, an overall wrongness to the arch of her spine and the wild fury of her hair. Not like the lovesick girl I saw earlier.

We're not far now. We've entered the clearing and the trap is so close, all we have to do is make it into the mausoleum, one of us leaping over the makeshift tarp and trapping her six feet under and—

Percy trips.

I process it in slow motion, the sharp twist of his ankle as he snags it on a loose root. The horror slashed across his face and the fall. He hits the ground hard, and with the cry that slips from his throat, I know he can't run again. The most he can hope for is to crawl, but he's nowhere near as fast as Anastasia. She gains on him in seconds. There's a scream as she uses Calvin's body to pin his brother down, and I feel like I might be sick.

I don't have time to waste here. His fall has him splayed out on the ground, his palms skinned and his fingers grappling helplessly for a necklace that's been thrown out of reach. It lands at my feet, and it's only as I lift it up to my face that I realize it's a near identical match to my own.

These damn necklaces. I feel my own in my pocket; I didn't realize Percy had the other one. *This must be Helen's.* The thought flickers in the forefront of my mind. For the second time today, I wonder why the hell these sisters couldn't have just talked it out.

"Anastasia! Over here! *ANASTASIA!*"

I yell at the top of my lungs, but unfortunately no amount of yelling is enough to distract from Percy's own screams. She'll kill anyone in her way to get to what she really wants: me. I've got to do something else and I've got to do it fast, otherwise I can kiss the plan and Percy's *life* goodbye.

My opportunity arrives with the glint of a blade still lodged in Calvin's leg. I catch a glimpse of it as Percy writhes and thrashes in an attempt to break free, and the sight propels me forward. There's no time to think as I race onto the scene and use Calvin's distraction as an opportunity to unsheathe the dagger from his calf.

With a wounded howl, he breaks away, leaving a limp Percy in the grass. Now it's me he's after, and I stagger back with both the lockets clenched in one hand and the knife in the other. I don't have a second to process what I've done. I run on pure feral instinct, and Anastasia's right behind me the entire time, lunging Calvin's body forward in large strides.

It'll be a cold day in hell before I pause for air. It doesn't matter that all my muscles are actively screaming at me and my lungs have shriveled up in my chest.

I push myself to go faster and repeat my desperate mantra in my head: *This* has *to work.* It has to work because I can't accept the alternative where we die here and the curse continues.

I rush up the steps of the mausoleum, the finish line in sight, and leap over my blazer. Calvin is too busy barreling forward to notice. I turn just in time to see him plummet with a shocked scream, thank God, Anastasia's eyes wide as her hands reach for air, but I can't celebrate for long. Not when nails dig into my ankle and he pulls me down with her. Both of us fall helplessly into the rabbit hole.

If this were a fairy tale, we'd tumble down for an eternity. The grave would portal us to an upside-down world where nothing would be as it seemed. But since it's reality—some strange version of it at least—we crash hopelessly to the ground. The earthen walls surround us, clods of dirt showering me. I was already having a horrible time trying to breathe aboveground, but all the air has since knocked right out of my lungs. I fight the urge to hyperventilate, but my mind's been shaken up and stirred past the point of staying calm. Is this how Em felt when we buried her? Darkness all around, the earth pressing in too tight, wet soil wedged beneath her nails and on her tongue and the fear that this is *it*?

Staring up, I see Ana's spirit swirling above me just like she did in my strange waking dream. The girl from the shower. That was her. I remember lying in bed, the steady drip drip drip of blood trickling from her chest. The knife plunging through her ribs and the thin slanted cursive on the hilt.

Wait a minute.

I let the knife fall to my side. I can't use it. Not only because it will hurt the boy I've come to love, but because Anastasia doesn't deserve that either.

Especially not when she's been murdered once already.

Oleander Lockwell came into Ana's life like all devils did: with the face of an angel and the tongue of a serpent. He'd turn out to be every bit as poisonous as his namesake, but when she first met him, he was just some attractive stranger who looked like he might break her heart before putting it back together. She found that she was fine with that. More than anything, she really just wanted to kiss him, but you don't kiss a man you don't know, so she wanted to go home, stare at her ceiling, and pretend she kissed him instead.

She wanted to pretend she kissed him a lot.

He was Prince Charming in the flesh, the perfect embodiment of the escape she dreamt of. Anastasia was a girl of fairy tales and happily ever afters for those who suffered long enough. She felt she had suffered enough to earn one of her own.

Hers came in the form of her childhood, or rather her lack thereof. She attended "boarding school" in name only, her residence not in the dorms but trapped inside the miserable four walls of her family's house. She and her sister lived and breathed under the militant supervision of their father, and even then, their treatment was considered lax in comparison to that of their mother. Her mother was a modern-day Persephone, withering under her father's rage only to bloom again under the false promise of love. She wore her marriage in two separate rings: the diamond on her finger and the bruised spiral on her upper arm, hidden beneath her sleeve. Her husband's fingertips twisted like a fairy circle and kept her eternally trapped in his domain.

So it only made sense for Ana to dream of salvation, but this boy was far from the knight in shining armor come to whisk her away. He might have been as dashing as one, his corded muscles on clear display as he rowed across the school lake, his face bright and his smile brighter. He might have been as sweet as one, his regard for her dizzying and utterly foreign. But beneath the princely facade, he was anything but.

Unaware of what lay beneath, Ana was smitten. She'd never had an actual suitor before. Her sister was beautiful enough to sway the most courageous men on campus, though their father's temper reached well beyond their family home. As a headmaster, he was strict and short fused, which meant that the men daring enough to talk to Ana were few and far between.

If you asked her father about his distemper (which you would be very unwise to do), he openly blamed his anger on his lack of an heir. Two daughters but no son to carry on the family name and the school alongside it. He'd have to rely on a son-in-law to carry both the bloodline and the role as headmaster, which meant every boy who so much as approached his daughters was scrutinized not as a partner, but as a successor.

So yes, Ana wanted a prince, and her father wanted a capable, trustworthy replacement, but that's not what Oleander was. He was the blighted apple, the gravestone, the cold burial dirt. He was hungry and ambitious and all consuming. When she led him into the maze of her heart, she found he knew the path well, for he had traversed many girls' hearts. He'd learned their patterns so he could come and go as he pleased.

He knew how to set fire to a girl and leave only ash in his wake.

It was late one evening when Anastasia finally thought to ask the question.

The two of them had once again succeeded in sneaking past her father's watchful eye. They lay together in the maze, Oleander's arm hooked over her waist and Ana's back to her own future grave.

He was typically so hasty to get dressed after their dalliances, lurching upright after the act was finished and checking his pocket watch as if the time was more important than her.

Today, however, he'd lingered beside her, brushing the hair behind her ear and peppering kisses along her jaw. "You seem thoughtful as of late."

She was. Her mind was full of her sister's worries, all the horrible, gruesome thoughts she painted her imagination with. She had wanted to ask him about his past for days now, but Oleander didn't like when she pried. She could tell. His lip would curl, and he'd tell her that patience and trust were two traits he found most attractive in a woman.

She wanted to be beautiful for him, right?

Yes, she did, with every fiber of her being. And yet . . .

"There is something I would like to ask you." The words were out too quickly to think better of them, and she could've cursed herself for her loose tongue.

This also wasn't quite true. There were many things she wanted to ask: Did he really, truly love her? Did he ever look at Helen and wonder whether he chose the wrong sister? Would he marry her and take her away from this wretched, horrible place?

None of those questions left her lips. This time she asked what was really on her mind. "How did she die?"

He froze in her arms, his fingertips whitening against her waist. "Pardon?"

"Your . . . former fiancée," she clarified, and he glowered openly at her.

HOUSE OF HEARTS

His response was terse. "It was an accident, as you well know."

"What sort?"

He gripped her chin, and the moment frightened her madly. His eyes were cold, compassionless, and for once she felt she saw through to the heart of him—or where his heart should have been. "You'd ask me to relive it?"

"I want to know," she waged on. "It's silly, but . . . I'd wondered if perhaps . . ."

"Perhaps what?"

She toyed with the hem on her skirt. "If perhaps you might've played a part. It's nothing. Just mere speculation. My sister mentioned it."

"Did she, now?" he growled, and his face was closer. He lorded over her with a cruel twist of his mouth. "I suppose she told you how Eliza died in a rather . . . unfortunate manner, mm? Right in the center of a hunting ground with a blade wedged deep in her chest. But who could possibly confuse poor Eliza with wild game? And if not an accident, then who could enjoy such a thing?"

He twisted her hair around his finger, three careful loops. "Oleander," she mewled, eyes wet and splotchy. "You had nothing to do with it, right?"

The darkness receded from his gaze, and he rewarded her with a beaming smile. "Heavens, no. Your imagination is far too wild for your own good."

If her imagination hadn't been spiraling previously, it most certainly was in the days that followed. For she could not produce a single explanation for finding Oleander down on one knee . . . and not for her.

The campus was alive with the thrum of students at the last bell, but despite the emerging crowd, Ana's vision remained tunneled on the scene in front of her. Oleander held a ring and stared at Helen like she was worth all the stars in the sky and then some. Ana couldn't see the diamond, but she knew it was brilliant and would shine much brighter on Helen's hand than hers. Everything seemed to. She was the sun the world orbited, the center of everything, and Ana was a new moon, overlooked, overshadowed.

And if their world was likened to the cosmos, then their father looked upon Oleander like an incoming meteorite, come to destroy everything it touched. He stormed across the quad with a rising fury, his fists trembling at his sides as he traveled to reach the two of them. "What on earth is the meaning of this?"

"I only thought it proper after the night we spent together that I do the honorable thing and wed you," Oleander said much too loudly, his smile plastered across his face despite the shocked gasps in the crowd. His attention was trained squarely on Helen, but Ana knew he saw her. He saw; he just didn't care.

"Lower your voice, son."

Helen's face blanched, and her mouth hung in clear disbelief, but none of that mattered as Ana stormed from the courtyard.

"How could you?" she asked him when Oleander found her in the center of the maze. He was her opposite in that moment: cool and collected, where she was full of a molten fury that threatened to devour her from the inside out. She shoved him in the chest and gritted her teeth as he failed to budge even an inch. How was it that he could ruin her and she failed to make even the slightest impact on him?

"How could I not?" he replied sweetly, and when she went to push him again, he stopped her fists where they were. "Two sisters can't keep a secret, but one? A disgraced daughter can talk, but after the scandal of her public humiliation and her dead sister, who would believe her?"

"D-dead," she hiccupped, and he responded with a kiss to her forehead.

"Now you're getting it," he whispered, and she felt the blade lodge in her chest then, piercing through her ribs and striking her heart.

She opened her mouth to respond, but her voice was robbed momentarily as the blood seeped from her parted lips.

He hushed her as a lover might and cradled her body as it dropped to the ground. She stared at him in wide-eyed disbelief, but his smile never faltered once. "For what it's worth, my sweet, it was a lie. I never slept with Helen, but I suppose it doesn't matter much in the end, does it? With you dead and her reputation in tatters, I'll be forced to wed her after all."

"Wh-why?" she managed, and the word tasted of iron.

He continued to smile as he freed a forged letter from his coat pocket and placed it gently over her body like a funeral bouquet. "I've wanted your world from the moment I first laid eyes on it. Every girl before you has simply been a rung on a ladder leading me to you. I grew up with nothing, so I feel it's only fair to crave everything. My own happily ever after," he whispered, spitting her fairy tales back at her. "But you should know, Ana, storybooks are often far bloodier than they appear."

He left her behind with the blade and the forged farewell note and the blood, drip-drip-dripping beneath her into the lawn. She lay there, and as she died on the lawn, her disbelief turned to rage and her rage turned to sorrow. She hadn't believed Helen's warning, and now she was dooming her to the same miserable fate her sister had desperately tried to save her from. She'd been too stubborn, too short-sighted to see through to Oleander, and she wouldn't be the only one paying for it now.

She *wouldn't* allow herself to die without taking him down with her. How many days had Ana spent cooped up in her room, pricking her finger and uttering words no churchgoing daughter should know? How long had she practiced in preparation for this moment?

Blood gushed from her chest like a tapped tree. There was a curious ripple in the air, one that only seemed to grow the longer she chanted. She was alone, and yet in that instant, every blade of grass stood upright, the wind stilled, the night sky watched with a thousand starry eyes.

She cursed him with her dying breath.

Lockwell would never get his happy ending; she'd make sure of it.

23

There's no Disney Princess moment. A flock of magical singing birds doesn't fly to my rescue in a musical montage. It's a quiet progression as the thought hits me, a slow understanding striking after I feel the lockets in my left hand burn. The two halves gravitate toward one another like magnets, and I watch, stupefied, as they click into place. There's an otherworldly sheen between them, an almost hypnotic glow as they merge into one. They're a perfect fit, two sides forming to complete a heart.

It's not just a useless hunk of metal. Could it be . . . ?

Her heart?

The tears that spring from my eyes are from a miserable mess of emotions. An insatiable urge for revenge mingled with a confusing cloud of empathy. We're not that different, the two of us. It's funny, really, how similar we are. How grief has skewed us beyond recognition and made us heartless. If love and loss can turn you into the darker version of yourself, is there any chance of redemption?

Staring up at Anastasia, I can't help but think there is. The fall has made her seem briefly human, the hope in her eyes short-lived but enough to tell me that the real her isn't dead. Someone is buried in the beast she's become. I might not be able to kill the queen, but maybe I was never meant to.

Perhaps I was only ever meant to save her.

My palms cup Calvin's cheeks, relishing in the feel of his soft skin in my hands. He stares at me, his eyes unfocused and wavering, but watering the same as mine. Trapped in the prison of his own body as Anastasia takes the lead. I have no clue if this will work, but I'm not using my mind. It's time to follow my heart after I've ignored it for so long. She thrashes and swipes above me, but I don't let any of that deter me from what I'm about to do. Unclasping the locket and stringing it around Calvin's waiting neck, I clear my throat, and the words ripple out of me one by one.

"Blood for blood, I do impart. I invite you, Ana, to take back your heart."

I wait for the horrific inevitability. It could all end so horribly and so quickly, Calvin succumbing forever to the madness and killing me with one final blow. I could join Emoree with all the other dead.

There's a shift in the air like the changing of a tide. Everything softens to an unnatural silence, the world pausing as if with bated breath.

I inhale a breath of my own, and nothing happens. I exhale, and suddenly we're surging upward like a geyser has blown beneath us. Anastasia morphs before my eyes in the air, unmade and remade, a girl who became a monster becoming a girl yet again. I hit the ground hard, and Percy is at my side in an instant, helping me upward and cradling my head as I gather my bearings.

Anastasia erupts from Calvin's body like a cicada brood bursting from the earth. The break is abundantly clear; she's cut the marionette strings and let her puppet collapse onto the earth in a limp heap. He falls, still breathing, but only shallowly.

Anastasia stands by herself, and she's the very same girl I saw in

HOUSE OF HEARTS

the portrait. I recognize the waterfall cascade of her ginger curls and the wide, tear-brimmed gaze of her wide-set eyes. She's not the monster I thought she was. She's a girl who was betrayed and cast aside, her dying breaths transforming her with hate. The necklace I gave her no longer hangs over Calvin's throat, but her own. The pendant has patched together the chasm of her chest, making her whole again.

She doesn't speak. She doesn't need to. The look she gives us three says it all. She'd been buried inside herself for so long, her body a vehicle for her hatred to fester and grow and change her. It's as if she has woken up from a very long nap and is bleary-eyed as the light shines through her window. Sleeping Beauty breaking from her dream and finally seeing the waking world for what it really is.

Her spirit blows away with a ripple of wind, and the hedges change in her absence. They fall inward, graying as they topple to the ground. This otherworldly limbo we've entered is splitting apart at the seams, and reality is seeping through the cracks. The sky above our heads is shining with twilight, the fleeting progression before the sun descends into murky black.

I'm at Calvin's side in an instant, lifting him gingerly from the ground and brushing a soothing thumb against his cheek. "Cal," I whisper, placing a soft kiss on his temple.

He blinks in a daze, his eyes shifting from the sky over to me. Unseeing at first before clearing out. "You need . . ." he pants, swallowing thickly. "To get away from me. Not . . . safe . . ."

"It's over, Cal," I tell him, helping him sit up. He gasps at the brush of my hand against the back of his head and slowly registers the world around him. "It's really over now."

"Violet?" a voice calls from behind me, and I'd know it anywhere.

I'm up in an instant, and I limp my way toward her. I yearn to finally hug my best friend in the whole world, but as I try to wrap myself around her, my arms slip through the air. There's nothing left to hold. Emoree smiles her soft, shadowy smile, and it manages to break my heart all over again.

"Em," I whisper.

"I'm sorry for dragging you into this," she apologizes, her smile frayed at the edges. "It was . . . 'Selfish' is really the only word for it."

How many times have I dreamed of this? One last conversation with Em instead of her lost to the murky realm of the afterworld. And now that she's here, I can't find the words at all. I can only cry. A whole year's worth of bottled grief I've stored up inside me dripping messily down my cheeks.

"Please, Em, can't you stay?" I beg, but I know there's no changing things. What's been done cannot be undone, but that doesn't mean she's *completely* lost. How many times have I kept her alive in my thoughts these past months?

"I've been with you this whole time," she answers, like it really is that simple.

"Yeah, yeah." I snort, wiping the tears away with the back of my hand. "I saw your little stunt in the ballroom and that confusing Ouija-board riddle you left us."

She shakes her head, and when she points at my heart, I know I must have a concussion. For once, I don't feel the urge to tell her how supremely hokey that sounds or how it's impossible for a human being to reside in the thoracic cavity. "I'll always be here," she says, and that has me sobbing even harder.

You don't stop loving someone when they die. Your grief is your love, and they live forever in your hearts. Besides, she's in good hands.

HOUSE OF HEARTS

Percy slowly pushes up from the ground, and every step toward Emoree has him fading further. For a boy who had been teetering between life and death, caught in the gray in between, it would seem he's finally made his choice.

"Percy?" Calvin shakes his head and clutches fistfuls of the grass for support. "What are you doing? You shouldn't be . . ."

"Dead?" Percy asks, and Calvin gulps hard at the word. "I've been gone for a while, Cal."

Calvin frantically shakes his head and swats at his cheeks. "But not gone for good. You were supposed to come back. I . . . I can't lose you! I've been doing everything I could to bring you back and now . . ."

Percy stoops to run a hand over his brother's hair. It washes over him like a gust of summer air.

"What now? You're never coming back?" Wet tears blob down Calvin's cheeks, and in this moment, he looks so heart-achingly young. A little sibling blubbering up at his older brother. "Mom wants me to take your place, but, Percy, I just *can't* be you. You need to come back. The shoes you left behind are too big. They don't fit me and they never will."

"Then wear your own," he tells him, standing back up to full height. "You're Calvin Lockwell, and if that's not good enough for anyone, then you don't need them. Make your own fate." He clasps hands with a smiling Em before turning my way.

I finally get a look at those dimples Emoree used to prattle incessantly about. "I can't believe the curse lived there this whole time." He chuckles bashfully, patting his throat like he might find a locket swinging there still. "Right under our noses. I never would have thought that would be her actual heart."

Calvin leans his weight into my side like a crutch, and I cover his

263

shoulders with my arm. "Why did you have them in the first place?"

Percy scratches his cheek. "It sounds ridiculous in hindsight, but they were family heirlooms I found, and"—he hooks a finger in his collar and shyly casts his eyes to the ground—"I thought they would be *romantic*. God. I know how that sounds now, but it never had any grand meaning until we found Ana's spell book. Even then, I would've never guessed they could be used the way you used them."

Emoree looks up at me, and her smile is strained at the corners. "Despite what Percy told me, I knew there was a decent chance one of us wouldn't make it," she says, toying with a loose curl around her finger. "I sent it to you so that if I died and Percy was still alive, you could show it to him and he'd know I sent you. You're the smartest girl I know, Violet. You always have been. I knew if we weren't successful, then you would be, and I was hoping at the very least, you could get the reward money for your family."

I scoff. "I don't care about the money, Em. I care about you."

She drops her hands to her sides and presses her palms flat against her legs. "I know. I *know*. I'm so sorry again. My whole life has been selfishly expecting you to protect me every step along the way without ever wondering how *you* felt. You were always like a big sister to me, and as soon as I came to this school on my own, I felt the loss of you immensely."

Another sharp sob racks through my body, and Calvin presses a kiss to my shoulder as he leans his weight against me.

"Be good to each other," Percy says. He gazes at Em with so much tender love and care, even beyond death. They share a look that melts me to my core. I don't have to worry about Em anymore, not in this life or the next. She's at peace.

"I love you, Em," I whisper as she disappears.

HOUSE OF HEARTS

"I love you, too."

And just like that, they're gone and the real world is coming back into focus. Illusion lifts from reality like oil separating from water. Calvin and I are back to the present, the moon hanging full above our heads.

I can't say how long Calvin and I sit there in the clearing. The world keeps spinning and the clock keeps turning, but the two of us stay rooted where we are. All we're doing is holding each other, crying, because what else can you do in a situation like this? We cling to each other for dear life, and the emotions that follow are jumbled beyond comprehension. Relief? Despair? Hope? It's impossible to tell. Human hearts are such tricky things, and nothing is as simple as it seems.

One thing is, though.

"I think it's really over now," I murmur into his hair.

I know he can feel it, too. His forehead finds mine, and his breath ghosts across my skin. "I think so, too, Violet."

The Queen of Hart's has finally found her heart. And perhaps she isn't the only one.

EPILOGUE

Not all stories have happily ever afters. Some only have afters. But standing here on stage with Calvin on our graduation day, I'd like to believe ours is happy.

The campus is alive with the swell of visitors—students and families flooding the Greek Theater and an orchestra pit of underclassmen playing our school song over the nervous chatter of onstage seniors.

Despite it being a literal graduation, there are no caps to be thrown in the air or polyester robes to slip on over our shoulders. Graduation gowns are too pedestrian for the academy (of course), so everyone is clad in the *unofficially official* uniform of either a red dress coat and tie or a white dress and floral crown.

The seasons have swept through our school seemingly overnight—autumn stripping the trees, winter lacing the academic halls in collars of ice, spring thawing campus through an onslaught of showers. Now in summer, the Little Garden has come to life and brought with it enough new growth for our daisy chain crowns.

"Introducing your new graduates!" the headmistress bellows into the mic, and Calvin stiffens beside me, his smile momentarily wavering at his mother's voice.

I grip his hand and give it a tight squeeze. He returns it and then, like that, the names are called. Diplomas are handed out in reverse order, so I get to watch Amber grace the stage before the rest of us.

HOUSE OF HEARTS

She's radiant today in her Miu Miu dress, her dark hair contrasting against the bright chain of florals. She'd been the least shocked by the truth and far more observant than any of us knew. "You forget, writing gossip columns is all about reading in between the lines. Which is precisely what I did whenever you three talked."

She accepts her diploma, and there's a chorus of cheers from her extended family on the lawn. Only immediate family are allowed in the theater seats for crowd size, but that doesn't stop everyone else from filling up the grass around us. Her cousins whoop and cheer as she blows them a kiss on stage.

Oliver follows, and there are a million camera flashes from his parents in the front row. They arrived early enough for me to see his mother pinch his cheeks and sob "That's my boy!" into his shoulder.

There's Ash and then, several minutes later, Birdie. She might not have a grad cap to customize with fabric paint and trinkets, but she's made a number of modifications to today's "uniform." Starting with her hair. She cut it last minute into a pixie in the girls' bathroom and then used some of her hair for a braided "flower crown" of her own. I can think of absolutely no one else on the planet who would do this in the last hour before their graduation, but it's got "Birdie" written all over it.

Her mom groaned at the sight of it, but her father let out a deep belly laugh and clapped his knee. Turning to his wife, he soothed her with a "You're lucky it's not a mohawk."

Birdie tapped her chin in contemplation and pretended to type the idea into her Notes app for college.

It wasn't easy picking up all the pieces with her after my last lie. A promise had been broken on my end and a truth told on hers that could have gotten me killed. There were tears and awkward days that followed and finally a hand grab before I left for winter break.

We hadn't spoken right away. There hadn't been an avalanche of *sorrys* and explanations and *never agains*. It had been a quiet minute of understanding, a reflection that transcended the need for words.

"I'll see you in spring," she'd told me, and when the next semester came and the snow piled high on campus, our friendship was reborn.

Just like for Amber and Oliver, I shout out Birdie's name alongside her parents. And also like the two of them, Birdie's handshake with the headmistress is a "cordial for the camera" clasp before a quick smear of her palm afterward.

When it's Sadie's turn, she leans in for a hug and is met with a stiff handshake in its stead. She keeps her smile up for appearances, but it thins at the edges and the transaction is brief.

Still better than Calvin. He avoids her hand entirely and grabs the diploma, exiting stage right with minimal fanfare or theatrics.

One by one they continue until I'm next, and I brace myself for the moment before me. It's as simple as walking across a stage, but it's also so much more. The necklace might've been returned to Anastasia, but my nails are adorned in Emoree's favorite stickers. She never got the opportunity to walk across this stage, so it only felt right to carry her with me in some small way.

It's not the only thing I've decided to do for her today. The Cards were true to their word when it came to the reward money. It was staggering—far more money than I've ever seen in my life or dreamt of in my bank account—but despite it all, I didn't feel good about using it. It was burning a hole in my pocket.

"Cut it in half," I told Headmistress Lockwell in a rare moment of civility between us. Really, how does one interact calmly with a woman who advocated for your murder?

HOUSE OF HEARTS

"You're asking to receive less?" she scoffed, like she couldn't process the concept.

"Half for me and half for Emoree."

She approached the next question with as much tact as she could muster. "What would she use it for in her . . . condition?"

"I want a scholarship in her name."

She stared contemplatively at her desk pen. "That can be arranged, but as for the title of it, I'm not sure if—"

"In her name," I said again. "The Emoree Hale Memorial Scholarship."

"Fine."

I carry Em across the stage with me. Like Calvin, I avoid Headmistress Lockwell's handshake, but she's learned from the twins and strategically angles her back to hide another student slighting her in public. There's no whispered congratulations or pleasantries between us. It's all a cold transaction.

Meanwhile, Mom sits in the crowd with her go-to box of tissues. She blubbers into her boyfriend's side, but for once I'm not worried about her. Ryan is actually good for her, it turns out, and it definitely helps to have another person keeping track of her perpetually lost keys. She mouths "I'm so proud" like it's a chant of her own, and I beam back at her as I exit the stage.

Music flares to life, and most of the girls throw their flower crowns in the air. A handful of them break apart and litter the ground in a colorful shower of loose petals.

"I don't think anyone wants my hair falling on them," Birdie quips.

Sadie inclines her head beside her. "I don't mind."

For most of spring semester, Birdie and Sadie have been engaged in Newton's fourth law of motion: Two people newly in love must be in constant contact with each other at all times. Birdie loops an arm over her girlfriend, and Sadie giggles in her embrace. Even with all the PDA, I'm over the moon for them both.

"What can I say?" Amber asks with a wiggle of her eyebrows. "I'm Cupid. Guess my hit-on list worked."

"Your what?"

Birdie burns bright red. "Amber!"

They're still teasing one another when Calvin comes to my side. He's already been forced into an awkward interaction with my mom and Ryan that resulted in a hundred prom-esque photos, but now that Mom is busy exploring campus with her beau, I have a brief window with mine.

"We'll be right back. I just need to borrow her."

"Going up to the lookout?"

"Haven't you heard? Couples that go up together stay together," Calvin says with a wink.

As I scale the tower steps, instead of the paranoia I first felt here, I'm met with a quiet sense of self-reflection. Em said something really bad had to happen for ghosts to come back, but now I realize the absence of them isn't a denial of their existence. It's a symbol of their peace.

Oleander's knife has scratched a permanent sickle on Calvin's cheek. The scar has scabbed and faded in the months following the incident, but it remains a sheer, glossy white line. I find it makes him twice as beautiful.

This is what survival looks like.

He leads me up to look out the window. A straight shot down still makes me wobbly-kneed, but I'm getting better with Calvin's hand on my back. I stare out at the hedge maze and the bodies buried there, and this time, I know the maze isn't staring back.

Down below, Amber has her arms full of papers. She's handing them out to students, parents, cousins, anyone she can reach.

"Are those more graduation pamphlets?" he asks, squinting down to get a better look.

I don't need to follow his gaze to know precisely what she's passing out. "No, they're the *Hart Herald*'s last article of the year."

"About what?"

I wink. "You'll have to read it to find out."

He leans back and collapses against the wall to situate himself on the floor. I follow suit and take my spot beside him. With my head propped against his shoulder, I ask, "Have you given any thought to what comes next?"

"I know what doesn't," he answers with a sigh. "I didn't apply to Curtis or Julliard or any of the schools my mother wanted. I don't want to attend any school that will let me in solely on the status of my last name, either. I was thinking I might work a gap year and then apply to the same tech school as you."

I bump his shoulder with my own. "Your mother would be angry."

"Let her be. It's better to feel something than nothing at all." Then, in an effort to lighten the mood, he casts a wistful look up at the stairs above.

"Remember the first time we came up here?" he asks, and his pinkie gravitates toward mine on the floor.

I tap my cheek and imitate his flirtatious drawl. "I believe you said, 'I'd never dream of kissing you.'"

He doesn't waste any time as he presses his mouth to mine in a consuming kiss. His thumb brushes circles against my cheek, and when he looks at me, I know he sees the whole of me. Every microscopic part.

"Why dream when the reality is so much better?" he asks like the horrible flirt he is.

I roll my eyes even as a stupid smile spreads across my face. I can't fight the skip of my heart even now. I used to think sappy moments were Em's thing, but lately I'm not so sure. I've always been quick to write off the tender part of me, but behind my careful walls, a heart still beats.

"You're . . ."

"Incorrigible?" he asks.

"Perfect."

It might not be a fairy tale, but I have a feeling we'll be happy after all.

HART HERALD

A MONSTER MISUNDERSTOOD: REEXAMINING LOCAL LEGEND

by AMBER YAMADA, BIRDIE KENNEDY, OLIVER WALTON, and VIOLET HARPER

Withstanding the test of time is no small feat, but for Anastasia Hart, the peculiar circumstances of her death have long cast a shadow on her legacy. For over a century, students have spun her story beyond recognition and created a monster out of a young woman. This macabre urban legend couldn't be any further from the truth.

There once was a girl
whose heart was much too big,
much too broken,
so she dug within the garden of her ribs
and ripped it right out,
but in those heartless moments
strangely
she missed the pain,
missed the splinters of a broken heart
in the empty chasm of her chest;
she learned then that she'd rather feel
something than
nothing at all

ACKNOWLEDGMENTS

This book attempted to murder me on several different occasions, so I'd first like to thank myself for not dying.

I cannot emphasize how every time I sat down to write, *something* borderline catastrophic was happening in the background. All this is strangely fitting because this story began as a super-indulgent secret project of mine that I created to distract myself from the world around me—who knew I'd need to escape to it time and again. I can finally say that after two years, *House of Hearts* and I have weathered the storm and lived to tell the tale.

Now, to the actual acknowledgments! To my husband, Derek, thank you for always encouraging my dreams and listening to book-related vents even when you have absolutely no clue what I'm talking about. I love you! Thank you to my family, friends, and writing groups for all endlessly cheering me on and keeping me afloat the last two years. ♥

Special shout-outs to Kalla Harris and Zeyneb Holdridge. I could write another one hundred pages dedicated to how grateful I am to you both, and I can't wait to have a bookshelf dedicated to all your future books!

To Kalla—you have read EVERY single iteration of this book, and you were there when I didn't even know what this book was *about* yet. You've held my hand through every round of edits and have always been a phone call away for brainstorming help. But more than that, you've been here for me in my lowest points this year and have kept me from breaking down on multiple occasions. I am so endlessly thankful for you! To Zeyneb—you are a brainstorming genius. I can be banging my head against the wall over a plot hole, and it will not only take you two seconds to solve, but you'll come up with SUCH an amazing solution off the top of your head using that magical brain of yours. You have such a big heart and are so creative and I'm so happy I had the chance to meet you.

Lastly, thank you to those who made this book possible in the first place. To my extraordinary, superhuman agent, Claire Friedman—thank you for being my biggest advocate and always going to bat for me. I'd be lost without you. My eternal gratitude to my editor, Maggie Rosenthal, for seeing through all the messy first drafts and immediately understanding the heart of this story; you've completely transformed this book! And to everyone at Viking Children's and Penguin Teen who has personally worked on and helped promote *HoH*—thank you, thank you, thank you.